ARROW OF LIGHTNING

ARROW OF LIGHTNING

Joseph Bruchac

The Third Book of **KILLER OF ENEMIES**

Tu Books

AN IMPRINT OF
LEE & LOW BOOKS, INC.

New York

TU BOOKS, an imprint of LEE & LOW BOOKS Inc.
95 Madison Avenue, New York, NY 10016
leeandlow.com

Manufactured in the United States of America
by Worzalla Publishing Company, May 2017

Cover design by Ben Mautner
Book design by Isaac Stewart
Book production by The Kids at Our House
The text is set in Adobe Garamond Pro

10 9 8 7 6 5 4 3 2 1
First Edition

Cataloging-in-Publication Data is on file with the Library of Congress

*For Carolyn Rose Bruchac
and Ava Rae Bruchac,
my favorite young woman warriors*

CHAPTER ONE

Deep Water

I'm looking down at the quiet water of the long-abandoned reservoir, a three-hour ride from Valley Where First Light Paints the Cliffs. Since returning several months ago, we've built new homes. We didn't touch those destroyed by the Jester's mercenaries, modest lodges where people died and where we buried them. We resettled another part of our valley, leaving that spot to return to grass, earth healing the wounds made by humans.

Like our valley, the water below me is peaceful for now. But if what I've been told is right, what is beneath its calm surface is something that has no interest at all in peace. Unless peace means having one of us for breakfast.

It's a giant gemod, a sort of eel. That's how it's been described by those who've survived to tell about it—those who were far enough from the water to avoid being snapped up like those hapless souls who ventured too close. And by "giant," I mean just that: black as night and the size of the super-snake I disposed of a year ago, but also shy in the way all ambush predators tend to be. It lurks under the surface and waits for its chance to strike. The faint prickling at the back of my neck is a warning that something down under there does not mean us well.

Hussein and I have been scoping things out for the last two days. The water in the lake is clear enough for us to have caught a glimpse of its shadow deep under the surface. Too deep for us to attack it, even with the weaponry put together with our friend Guy's help and placed at strategic intervals along this hilltop.

The dam that holds back the water in this canyon was built more than a century ago—when human beings thought they owned this planet and could do with it whatever they wanted. It never should have been built here. It drowned a beautiful ancient valley, sacred long before Europeans came to this continent.

Before the power plant's turbines stopped spinning forever, its electricity powered the highly charged fences and lasenet enclosures that imprisoned the little pets our former Overlords created for their amusement—gemod beasts that so much of my life has been spent in tracking and eliminating. Like the one lurking in the depths below.

There's no electricity being made here now. The Silver Cloud that blanketed the whole surface of the earth saw to that. But, though electricity has become as defunct as Buffalo Bill (whoever he was—blame my dad for that saying), water still fills this valley where Native people like mine once lived.

Much of the reservoir has silted in upstream. But in the mile of lake nearest the dam, the water is deep. A hundred feet or more. It's as blue as a robin's egg. However, what is inside is nothing like a little chick—with the exception of its hunger.

I lean forward and pat my horse's neck.

Whose horse?

The question doesn't come to me in anything like human speech. But I can understand it quite well.

Excuse me. No need to get sensitive. You are not my horse. You are Striped Horse and much more than a horse.

The thought that comes back to me is amused. Translated into human words, it might come out, "Got you again."

I have to smile. She was part of the ceremony that healed me from enemy sickness. We've been together for months now, but I am still getting used to this sort of partnership. Of course, being able to ride like the wind, to view the world again from the back of a horse—excuse me, a highly sentient gemod being—is worth any of the mental adjustment I've had to do.

It's not the only adjustment I've made in my increasingly shared existence.

Ready?

That thought was in English. It's from the one whose nine fingers draw more magic from the strings of his guitar than I ever dreamed possible. To say nothing of what else those nine fingers can do.

Focus, Lozen. Not the time for anything but the business we are about.

Wait here?

No problem.

I slide off Striped Horse's back. Sure-footed as she is, she can't manage the six-inch-wide trail ahead. I take the narrow path down the slope where I can see Hussein. He's dangling by a thin line down the face of the dam. That line has the tensile strength of a ton or more, but it makes me nervous to see him there like that, even though he's as accomplished a rock climber as he was before the Ones cut off his right little finger as punishment. Just for a moment I wish we still had enough electricity to be able to run wires to the charges he's carefully placed to blow the dam, rather than manually lighting fuses. After lighting them, he will have to get the heck out of Dodge by pulling himself up that line and running across the top of the dam to the safety of this hill before the explosion.

If I raise my right arm and swing it outward, it will mean "light those fuses." I scan downstream again. No people or animals to be seen. Everyone in the nearby community that asked for our help has gone to higher ground. Once the walls of the dam burst, it will release a roaring wall of water. When it's done, the valley will be a valley again, water flowing clean and fresh on both sides. It may take years, but trees will grow again, and in the fertile soil that will be deposited downstream, better crops can be grown.

That torrent will dwarf the flash flood we saw sweep away Tahhr and my enemy Luther Little Wound six months ago.

I close my eyes at that memory. It's not just how tragic it was to see Tahhr killed, a gemod as different from those who love only death and destruction as Luther Four Deaths was from a normal, caring human being. What bothers me more is that Luther Little Wound's body was never found. He might still be alive.

Hey, love! Don't you keep me hanging on.

That last thought from Hussein was sung as much as it was mentally said. His thoughts can be as melodious as his voice.

He's holding the lighter in one hand, the bundled fuses in the other. This will be the first time he's blown up a dam. But he's done demolition before—trained for that long before he passed himself off as a humble gardener to the Ones who ruled our lives at Haven.

I only found out about that part of his past during a conversation with Rose and her partner Phil. They'd been talking about how they'd removed other dams like this one.

It's amazing how many of those concrete monstrosities, built by the old Army Corps of Engineers, drowned places where our Native people used to live, hunt, grow crops.

Uncle Chatto told me a story about a dam—one that he heard from another Indian in their unit, a tough-as-leather Passamaquoddy guy named Ron from the area once called Maine. In Ron's story, a monster built a dam to keep all the water for himself. Downstream from that dam everyone was suffering. The river had gone dry. Fish perished, the crops dried up, and people were almost dying of thirst.

The Creator saw how much the people were suffering and sent a hero to help them. That hero broke open the dam. He squeezed the water monster down into a bullfrog.

"Great story," Uncle Chatto said.

I agreed. "Nobody should try to own everything."

Uncle Chatto had smiled then. He had such a calm smile. Both he and Dad knew so much, had seen so much, survived so much. But neither ever seemed to get angry or to be upset about things. They walked the trail of wisdom with minds that were steady.

"If it was one of our Apache stories, we'd call the place Where Bullfrog's Dam Was Broken. Then we'd just mention its name and people would understand," he said.

My mind returns from my memories of Uncle Chatto. Hussein just slapped his hands together to get my attention.

All set? I think to Hussein.

Two hundred feet away, he nods.

Is that a faint warmth I feel in my palms? Or are they just itchy from the heat and gripping my rifle so hard? I guess it's nothing. Hussein is still dangling there.

I raise my right arm, swing it outward.

Go!

He lights the fuses and begins to pull himself up the hundred feet to the top. I count mentally, knowing that before I get to four hundred, it will all blow.

One and one pony. Two and one pony. Three and one pony.

Hussein is doing fine. His strong hands, stronger than I realized when we first met, are more than equal to the task.

Except my own hands are suddenly burning.

Something is crawling out of the deep water on the other side of the dam from Hussein, up toward the top of the dam and the walkway where Hussein's headed. It's not the giant eellike critter that we're hunting today. It's much smaller, but big enough. Large as a grizzly bear, it has two big, shiny front claws like those of a crayfish. And it's not alone. Two—no, three more are joining it, scuttling up to block off Hussein from his escape route.

Twelve and one pony. Thirteen and one pony.

Hussein can't see them. And he's not looking at me!

I try to reach him with my mind. But my thoughts don't connect. The telepathy I have with him and with others is sporadic. The only one who can always get in touch with me is Hally—when he wants me to.

I push back the hood of the light jacket I chose to shade my eyes from the silvered light. I lift the rifle. But I'm too late. They've gone over the concrete wall on top of the dam and out of my line of sight. The rocket launcher placed next to me might work. But it would send chunks of concrete raining down on Hussein.

I have but one chance, and that is to run!

CHAPTER TWO

Clear Shots

I've always been able to run faster than anyone else.

My father used to say I was like the boy in the old Chiricahua story who lived with his family near three sandstone hills. During the day he could just laze around, eating the food prepared by his mother and napping. And whenever he was given greasy food, he would rub that grease on his legs.

"My friends," he'd say, "I am feeding you, too."

The people began to say things about him.

"That son of yours is good for nothing," they told his mother. "He is lazy."

But that was not so. That boy just rested during the day because he ran every night. He ran when no one could see him, carried by strong legs grateful for the way he fed them.

Finally, a time came when the people had no food. The hunters were not bringing back any game animals. Those animals had grown wary and were staying far beyond the reach of the hunters' bows.

"How will we survive?" his mother asked him.

"Mother," the boy replied, "you have fed me and my legs well. Now it is time for me to help our people."

Then he began to run. He ran so fast that he was able to catch the deer. Ever since then, that place has been called Three Hills Where the Boy Ran.

That boy was even a faster runner than the antelopes. He was able to provide food for all the people. No one ever called him lazy or good for nothing again.

Me, I'm running as fast as I can. I just hope it will be fast enough. I head uphill at a slant to my left to another point where I can see the roadway on top of the dam, over the parapet that was blocking my view. I'm carrying my rifle even though I left another scoped 30.06 at the spot to which I'm heading.

Fifty-one and one pony. Fifty-two and one pony.

Hussein and I had planned this out so carefully. We'd left Star, his horse partner, a mile back along the trail to watch for danger that might approach while we were otherwise occupied. Striped Horse had taken up her post within sight of the dam where we could call for aid if we needed it or ride double on her back for a quick getaway. We'd set up rocket launchers and rifles at two strategic spots. We'd figured how long it would take to set the charges, light the fuses, and get back well out of the way of the blast—with time to spare. The giant eel had never been seen on the downside of the dam or next to it on the upriver side. So we weren't all that worried about it attacking.

But as always, what you plan for in this crazy post-Cloud world can't take into account what you do not expect. As I run, I am cursing under my breath those ingenious bio-engineers who figured out so many ways to concoct nightmare creatures of every conceivable kind, turning dangerous beasts into even more deadly predators and even—as in the case of what I've just seen—making something formerly small and relatively innocuous into a killer with razor-sharp claws.

I reach the vantage point and drop into a firing position even before I center the scope on the creature closest to where Hussein's line is fastened. I can't see Hussein, but the line is trembling from his progress as he hitches himself up, slides up the pulley, steps, and slides it up again.

Eighty-three and one pony. Eighty-four and one pony.

The giant crayfish's glistening back takes up the whole scope. I can't miss, but will my shot just glance off? Gemods tend to have hardened skins—or shells in this case—that bullets can't pierce. An eye shot is my usual choice—a shot that can penetrate the brain. But in this case, that would only half-blind it. There's no way to inflict lethal damage that way on this critter, whose eyes are on stalks, for Pete's sake.

It's at Hussein's line now, reaching out a claw as if to cut it.

There! Where the section of its shell shielding its small head joins to the back section of the creature. There's a space between the two segments that looks soft.

BLAM!

The result is not that dramatic. The gemod crayfish twitches and goes limp, its claws dropping onto the concrete with a clatter that echoes all the way up here. But who needs dramatic? Results are better than theatrical demises.

The next mammoth crustacean tries to climb over the back of Defunct Crayfish Numero Uno.

BLAM!

Two dead crawdads.

But the third one is making its way around the other two, their piled-up bodies blocking my aim.

An arm reaches up over the downstream lip of the parapet. That arm is holding a .44 Magnum. I see the fire spurt twice from its barrel before the sound of the shots reaches me.

And I find myself remembering this old saying of my father's that came from his childhood back when they used to have some sort of club where kids could play Indian.

"A good scout is always prepared."

And that is my partner, Hussein. Having heard my shots, he'd paused before pulling himself up onto the top of the dam long enough to unholster his gun, take a quick peep over the edge, and then blast Crawly-Clawed Critter Numero Tres in the exact spot I'd aimed to dispatch its little buddies.

He doesn't pause after that. He is over the lip of the dam, unclipping himself, taking off at full speed.

Which speed is more than advisable because—double crap on a stick!—those three dispatched monsters were not the last of their clawed clan. More are appearing over the edge. Three, four, a dozen! The damn dam is crawling with them. Hussein leaps high, vaulting over the back of one as it levers itself over to drop in front of him, and—twisting in midair as he does it—shooting it in that same vulnerable place.

"RUN!" I'm yelling. "RUN!"

Although, to be accurate, that is not all I'm doing.

It's more like:

"RUN!" BLAM! "RUN!" BLAM! "RUN!" BLAM!

Hussein is running faster than they can crawl. He's off the roadway now, climbing upslope toward my original vantage point. And further assistance than mine is on the way. Striped Horse, who figured out her help was needed, is galloping toward him. Hussein swings himself up on her back as she wheels on her hind legs to carry him to safety. Yes! They're clear enough for me to take the shot.

I put down my empty gun, pick up the AT-4 rocket launcher. No worries about collateral damage now. I press the button to click up the sights, pull the trigger.

The swoosh of the rocket's flight concludes with a very satisfying KA-BOOM in the midst of the crabby crew that was threatening Hussein—who's now safely away from the rain of fire, chunks of concrete, and chitin.

Nice.

And I have still been counting through all of this.

Two hundred and one pony. Two-oh-one and one pony.

And then the really big explosion happens. It's not a sound like a rifle shot or even the recent blast of the rocket. It's a deep WHOOOOMP that I feel as much as hear. It shakes the stony earth beneath my feet, followed by a brief second of silence and then a crackling rumble and the roar of pent-up water releasing its force as the dam breaks open and crumbles.

I stand up. Fifty yards away, Hussein is sliding off Striped Horse's back. There's a little trickle of blood down his forehead where something—a claw? a chip of concrete?—scraped him.

He must sense my concern, because he reaches up to wipe away that blood as if to say it is nothing. He extends his open palms to me in a graceful gesture.

Habibi, you saved me again. There's a little bit of humor underlying the sincere gratitude in that thought of his.

Not done yet, I think to him.

No, always more to do. Inshallah.

Then, as he pats Striped Horse's neck, he flashes me that sun-bright grin.

CHAPTER THREE

A Slippery Customer

Although the initial burst released a massive wave of water, so much was held behind the breached wall that it's going to take some time for the whole valley to drain back to the original riverbed. Plus, not all of the dam let go. There still a jagged mass of concrete at its base, slowing the flow.

But not stopping it. Hussein's charges were well placed. There is a wide channel right in the center where the waters will flow pretty much unimpeded. It'll be easy enough for people to keep it clear in the future—as long as there's nothing in those waters looking to gobble them up.

Speaking of which, as we scan the diminished reservoir, we see no sign of the major predator we are aiming to eliminate. It was not washed out with that huge torrent of water, and it is not visible there in the remaining shallow lake.

Yoo-hooo. Eeely, where are you?

Don't you hate it when your date keeps you waiting?

That last question was not mine. Nor did it originate from the mind of Hussein, who has now come up to stand beside me. Hussein looks at me, takes note of the irked expression on my face. He's seen that look before and knows what it means.

"Hally?" he asks.

I nod. The deep, mellow voice—if a voice that is unspoken can be that—which just filled the center of my cerebral cortex was that of the large, extremely hirsute being we've come to know as Hally. He's the nonhuman—or more than human—creature who has chosen to be our ally. Or so I hope, since at times I wonder if his whole relationship with us is not just for his own idle amusement. He's saved my life at times and then let me blunder into deadly danger all on my own at others. He's offered an explanation—or two—about why the Silver Cloud drifted in from space and cut off the power that kept our past world in as much darkness as light. Hally seems to be one of those ancient beings that all our original nations knew long before that inept Genoan sea captain stumbled into what he called the West Indies. And not just the people of our hemisphere. On the opposite side of the globe, the people of Tibet called them *yeti*.

There's no doubt that Hally knows a lot more than he's telling us. He also thinks he is funny. A hairy, eight-foot-tall comedian with six-inch fangs.

Where are you?

Somewhere. But not beyond the sea.

15

What?

It's another of those maddening references he makes now and then, usually to some vanished TV show or viddy or song that every sensible human being forgot decades or even centuries ago. I have a good memory myself, but Hally's seems to dwarf mine. I've gotten to know, sort of, my big, shaggy semially over the last year. I have a suspicion that he has the kind of mind that never forgets anything.

Naturally, Hally hears my thought and makes an even more cryptic reply. *Not everything. There are times when I cannot recollect the exact conversations that little Leon and I used to have back in the Italian Renaissance. Poor boy never did quite grasp what I was telling him about the possibilities of aviation.*

What?

Never mind.

Hussein touches my hand. I refocus my eyes, which have started to cross. Hally's thoughts do that to me at times.

"Is he helping us?" Hussein asks.

I shake my head. "Not yet. He hasn't finished messing with my mind."

Little Lozen, be patient. You know my motto is to always play with my food before I eat it.

I nearly smile. Little Food was what Hally used to call me when we first met mentally, when he was a threatening presence suggesting that his entire interest in me was as a potential entrée. I'm more that than to him now, it seems. Rather than terminating my existence in his stewpot, I appear to have become either someone he actually cares about—or is at least a source of amusement.

Don't underestimate yourself.

This time I do smile. That's as close to sincerity as Hally ever seems to come. He's actually being an encouraging ally. I pause, waiting for the next sarcastic message. But none comes. So I venture a question. **Any ideas?**

Remember, Hally thinks back to me, **you are dealing with a slippery customer. The answer is as clear as mud.**

And then, as quickly as the bursting of a bubble, his presence is gone.

I open my eyes, shake my head. Hussein is standing there in front of me, waiting.

He's also been holding one of our remaining rocket launchers at the ready, on watch just in case something with eyes of flame decided to come sliming up the hill toward us while I was in a semicomatose state. Once again I thank my lucky stars that I am no longer on my own, a lone scout sent out inadequately armed to either wipe out some critter or end up on its list of appetizers. Hussein is the best partner a Killer of Enemies could ever hope for.

I reach out to touch his arm. "Thank you for being so patient," I say.

"Those who patiently persevere will surely receive a great reward," he says, patting the pack that hangs under his left arm, closest to his heart. That is where he always keeps the sacred book I gave him from the Dreamer's library. He's both quoting from that book and thanking me again for bestowing so great a gift upon him. "But what did the djinn have to share with us?"

Djinn. That is how Hussein always refers to Hally. It's a word from Hussein's distant desert homeland, a place he was plucked from to serve a succession of masters before we met. Djinns are powerful spirits from the mythology of his people. They can be good or evil, taking the shapes of giant people or animals or even whirlwinds. Though Hussein has never gone into any detail about it, at some point in his past he met some such being. That is why Hally seemed less strange to him than to most people.

"The usual," I say. "Sense and nonsense. But the last thing was meant to be helpful. I hope." I look upstream, where the channel of the river has begun again to appear.

"There," I say. "In the mud."

"Mud?" Hussein looks at himself.

Have I mentioned that no matter what he wears, he always looks nearly immaculate? His brown boots have been shined so often that they almost glow with an inner light. His dark slacks actually have a crease in them. His loose brown shirt is nearly spotless, even after his climb down and up the face of the dam and his mad dash for the safety of the hill. I said "nearly spotless" because there is a streak of blood from the cut on his forehead on one of his sleeves. It's been made more noticeable to me by the fact that Hussein has just noticed it. Moistening the kerchief from around his neck with water from his canteen, he's dabbing at it in an effort to clean it. I don't think he's done that consciously. It's more of a reflex. I have never known another person who makes such an effort—successfully most of the time—to be clean. Being with him is like being with a cat that is always grooming itself.

I think it is kind of cute. And amusing, especially at moments like this.

"Yup," I say, "in the mud. Get ready to start slogging in the muck, habibi."

Striped Horse, who has been quietly listening all this time, cocks her head at me. She looks apologetic.

It's all right, I think to her. *I know you can't make it down that trail. We'll be okay. We'll be back.*

I wish I felt as certain about that as I have tried to make my mental voice seem.

We've been walking along the river that was formerly drowned by the reservoir, trudging long enough for the sun to move the width of one hand across the clear sky. No mud slogging yet, though. The riverside trail that was disclosed by the sinking of the reservoir is all stone and gravel here. The stone is getting hotter as the sun beats down. My forehead is dripping sweat, despite my having pushed back the hood of my jacket, raised my aviator goggles, and taken off my headband to wring it out twice. Hussein's brown brow, on the other hand, looks not only dry but cool. His deserts, he once told me, have a heat greater than anything here in the southwest.

"It was a heat that went into my bones," he said. "It is there in me now, still lending me its strength."

Good for him. As for me, I could use a tree right now lending me the strength of its shade. But there are no trees here on this rocky path, just the occasional stump of some old cottonwood with its roots wedged into the hard earth, a tree cut down before the waters of the reservoir washed over it. The stones and gravel around us glisten, still moist from the receding water below.

It's been long years since any feet followed this trail beside the river. The walls of the canyon rise around us. It's beautiful, even without the trees and bushes and flowers that once lived here and will surely return. A black butterfly has been fluttering around us for the last half mile or so. I stop for a moment, take a little pollen from the pouch hanging at my waist, and place it on the ground, just as a thank-you to that butterfly and this lovely place that once again is feeling the air and the light and coming back to life after being submerged for so long. We've already seen birds fluttering down to explore, including a small flock of ducks that landed in a pool where the river's stone banks curve to make an eddy.

If we humans just leave it alone, the earth can heal itself. That is what Uncle Chatto used to say to me.

"Up there," Hussein says, lifting his chin to the right. He

has learned not to point with a finger, but with his chin or his lips the way we Chiricahuas always do.

I look up, and right away, I see what caught his eye. Petroglyphs. Fifty feet above us on the cliff face.

Those stick figures were scratched into the black stone and were still visible two hundred years ago before the dam flooded the canyon. Maybe they've been here for thousands of years. I always feel something when I see the designs left by ancestors long gone—shapes that served as reminders, as prayers, as a way of communicating with the past and the future, of connecting the vision of those old people with what present-day eyes now see. A message, perhaps.

For long decades, while the dam's deep waters covered these cliffs, those shapes were unseen by any human eyes, which is why looking at them now sends a shiver down my back. Because they seem to tell a story: shapes of two stick-figure humans— a male and a female looking at a huge snake-shaped figure that rears over them.

Just a coincidence? Sure. Aside from the fact that the female figure with the pack on her back is carrying an object that looks an awful lot like an AT-4 rocket launcher.

Hussein is looking at me with one raised eyebrow. I shake my head. No explaining this. Just another part of the inexplicability of so many of the events that await me at every turn these days.

21

I take it as a message for sure, one which, along with the burning sensation in my palms, is an indication of the proximity of our latest enemy. Probably around the next bend.

"Be ready," I say. "Let me take the lead."

Hussein steps aside. It's not chivalry on his part. It's his acknowledgement that in monster hunting, I need to be the one taking the lead. That's partially because he knows that strong as he is, I'm the one who is more experienced and better equipped to deal with whatever we might confront. And it is even more because he knows that there is no way in hell he can prevent me from taking point.

As my dad used to say—rather softly when my mom was out of earshot—"It takes a really strong man to be the partner of a strong woman."

As I take the lead, I do not do it heedlessly. I take a few steps and peer around the bend. Oh, boy!

I turn back toward Hussein.

"You are going to love this," I say. "Check it."

He steps up to take his own look around the bend.

"Arrggh!" he says, reaching automatically to brush a hand along his chest.

"Yup," I say. "My sentiments, too."

Then the two of us stand there for a moment, not quite sure what to do about what we see—a place perhaps a hundred yards wide and half a mile long hemmed in on either side by the cliffs, which come right down to the thick black mud that fills not only the riverbed we've been walking but this entire upstream part of the valley. That mud blocks our path, and probably hides our adversary somewhere below its surface. The only thing visible above the mud is a single huge, shiny black rock perhaps a hundred feet away.

Hussein pries free a straight length of tree branch that was stuck in a crevice in the cliff wall next to us. It's twice as long as his height. He pushes it down into the gooey mud until his hand almost touches the surface.

Wading is clearly not an option.

"Ideas?" I say.

Hussein slaps his palms together softly, then lifts his index finger as he beams me one of his smiles. "One idea," he says. He slips his pack off and pulls out a series of ball-shaped objects, each with a tab fastened to the top. He holds one up so I can see it. It's olive green with a yellow band around it.

"Courtesy of Guy," he explains, tossing it to me. "According to him, each of these shall release several times the energy of the M67s you have used before."

I catch it with one hand. It's a type of grenade I've not seen till now, probably part of the store of weaponry that Rose gave us before she and her band left to head farther west. It was confiscated from a weapons depot that they liberated from an erstwhile warlord who said he was actually glad to see them and accept the democratic regime they were offering to help establish.

"Being a tyrant," he told them, "has been bad for my health. Too much stress."

Perhaps he also realized that attempting to resist those formidable men and women with their gemod horse allies would have been even worse for his health.

The round grenade seems heavier than the fourteen ounces of an M67. The instructions printed on its side look quite simple.

PULL TAB.

THROW.

It also states that the interval between pulling the tab and detonation is twenty seconds. There are seven grenades. If we time it right and space them out, they will have sunk deep enough into the mud before going off to send quite a tremor through the surrounding muck. That should eventually irritate our target—assuming it is here in the mud as Hally indicated—into showing itself and attacking us.

What a great plan, I think. *Convince yet another lethal critter to come and try to devour us.*

"I agree," Hussein says. "Shall I throw?"

I nod as I toss the grenade back to him. Hussein is not quite as good a shot as I am, but he can throw a bit farther. We found that out when we had a little contest, just for the fun of it, to see who was better at rock-throwing. He won, though only by about twenty feet.

I also want to be the one taking the shot at our slippery

adversary with an AT-4. Killer of Enemies is still my main job description, after all.

We still have three of the handy rocket launchers with us. The last three from our armory, in fact. They are not reusable, so once these are gone, we're going to have to do some scavenging to replace them. I put the first two down within reach as Hussein hands me the one he was lugging. I kneel and look down the length of the tube.

"Ready," I say.

Hussein hurls the first grenade in a high arc far out to our right as I count.

One and one pony, two and one pony. It doesn't hit the surface until I hit ten. About fifty yards out. A good solid throw. It sinks out of sight as I keep counting. And when I reach nineteen and one pony, it goes off. Not with a loud boom, but with a muffled thud of an explosion beneath the surface that sends a brown plume thirty feet up and a quiver of ripples in the thick mud, radiating about thirty feet out from the place the grenade landed.

And that's all that happens. Hussein looks at me with a raised eyebrow. I shrug. Six more to go.

The next one, which lands fifty yards out to our left, produces the same unimpressive result. Thud, sploosh, tremble of mud. But I am feeling something beyond the burning in my hands, and suddenly I know where—exactly where.

"There," I say. "Throw it there."

Hussein nods, pulls the tab, sends the third little bomb flying.

One and one pony, two and one pony, three and one pony, four and one pony.

The grenade strikes on top of that huge, shiny boulder, bounces off, and sinks perhaps thirty feet beyond it. The way it bounced—without the cracking sound you'd expect of metal on stone—makes me even surer of what I've just suspected.

"Get ready!"

When I reach the count of twenty, more happens than just the previous spurts of mud and expanding circles on the brown surface. And it happens so fast that my response is more reflexive than conscious.

That big black boulder lifts up and up, getting bigger and bigger until part of it breaks free of the mud, affirming my suspicion that what we'd been seeing was not stone, but flesh.

More and more of the huge body of the eel rises above us, and then its wide tail, almost close enough for us to touch it, flaps up. It cascades a great spray of mud all around us. It almost buries us, and would have blinded me if I hadn't instinctively slapped my goggles down over my eyes and pulled my hood over my face.

Less than a second after the wave of mud hits us, I'm pulling my goggles off with my left hand, mud slicking off them as I do so. Out of the corner of one eye I can see Hussein next to me, down on one knee, both arms over his face.

But that is not what I am focusing on in this split second. Nor am I looking at the monster's tail that has slammed back down into the brown, boiling surface of the mud lake. It's what has risen up fifty feet above us. Reared up like a glistening ebony snake ready to strike is the other end of our latest enormous nightmare beast, its mouth gaping wide to disclose endless rows of teeth and a big red tongue.

Did I mention what I am still holding in my right hand? What I am bringing up to my shoulder and aiming from one knee?

Yup. AT-4 Numero Uno.

Click. SWOOSH.

It leaves a smoke trail behind it that terminates in our slimy buddy's open maw.

BLAM!

A blast that decapitates it. *Cool,* I think. We still have two AT-4s to take back to Guy.

But just because the creature is effectively dead does not mean it is totally ineffective. Hussein is grabbing my arm, pulling me backward as quickly as he can. And just in time, as the monster's immense flat black tail comes swinging our way.

THUD!

It slams down on the very spot from which I'd fired that kill shot.

THUD. This time it lands right on the last two rocket launchers, crushing them.

The two of us stumble back to where the cliffs come together, pull each other around the corner to safety. From that wide mud lake comes the continuing sound of Eely-Weely's convulsing body as it writhes backward and forward, up and down.

WHOMP-WHOMP! WHOMP-WHOMP!

The sound of its body in its death throes echoes down the canyon. If we'd stayed there, we would have ended up as flat as pancakes.

Muddy pancakes.

I look at Hussein. He is covered in shiny brown from his head to his toes. And I look just the same.

He reaches one hand up to his chest, the gesture he always engages in subconsciously to wipe away what is often just an imaginary speck of dust. Nothing imaginary about the handful of gunk that he comes away with this time.

He straightens his back, shakes both hands free of mud, and then grins, his teeth shining even whiter than usual from a face that is caked with muck.

"It appears," he says, his voice filled with distaste, "that I may be in need of a change of clothes."

I wrap my arms around him and squeeze him so hard his ribs almost crack as he embraces me almost as tightly right back. Then we stand there, mud collecting in a brown pool around us, both of us still alive, both of us laughing our asses off.

CHAPTER FOUR

On Our Own

All in all, I'm thinking as we ride back toward our valley, Hussein and I have not done that badly. Especially considering this was our first demolition project on our own.

I replay in my head the last conversation we had with Rose Eagle and her partner Phil before they left.

Phil had just finished recommending an explosive, but Hussein had immediately started shaking his head.

"Semtech isn't bad," Hussein had said. "But it's very twentieth century. I always preferred using that composite the New Delhi group created back in 2040. Ramalite."

Rose's partner looked hard at him when he said that.

"You've used Ramalite?" Phil asked.

Hussein nodded. "Totally inert without a fuse. You can strike it with a hammer. Moldable as plastique, but with ten times the punch. Blows things up quite good. Works either with an electric charge or an old-fashioned fuse."

"You know about demolitions?" I asked.

Hussein shrugged. "Merely at the humble level of a superlative expert."

The broad smile that holds the sun's light came across his face. There was so much mischief in that smile. The way it said, "Ha, you didn't know that about me," made me want to either hug him or punch him in the arm.

"Why didn't you ever tell me that before?"

"You never asked," he said, holding up both hands in a futile attempt to protect his biceps.

Our confab ended with a general agreement that the removal of the dam in question could be handled without Phil's help, aside from providing the necessary Ramalite that Hussein had spoken about. That way Rose and Phil and Aunt Mary and the others in their band of Lakotas and White Mountain people who'd chosen to go with them could move on to the liberation of a community about three hundred miles farther to our west. It used to be called Palm Springs. The exhausted runner who had traveling for days to ask for help made it sound urgent—*our crazy Overlords are torturing and killing us like cats playing with mice.* So our Lakota and White Mountain Apache friends and their Horse People hit the road right after Phil advised us on our plan about the dam.

I worried a bit about their leaving. Not because I thought

their going would make us less secure. We'd made ourselves well enough defended since returning to Valley Where First Light Paints the Cliffs. The training Hussein and Guy and I did resulted in a number of our women and men being almost as competent with firearms as my family members, Guy, Luz, the Dreamer, and Lorelei. Plus the number of people in the stronghold of Valley Where First Light Paints the Cliffs has grown as outliers have come in to join us. Among them is the man who designed our new homes—a lovable Navajo guy named Tom Yazzie who showed up not long after we'd returned here. Also, several of the White Mountain people and some of Rose's and Phil's Lakotas struck up the sort of relationships that made them decide to stay with us indefinitely.

Emily Lewis, the White Mountain woman who helped with my healing ceremony, is one of those who stayed. Her knowledge of medicine (both western and traditional—before the Cloud came, she was an epidemiologist) resulted in her and the Dreamer's companion Lorelei sharing the running of our dispensary. Moreover, Emily Lewis also does weddings. Like the one she did for Rose and Phil two months ago.

"If we'd waited just a little longer," Rose joked, patting her belly, "we'd have had our own homegrown flower girl."

As it was, my little sister Ana played that role, while Hussein was best man and I was maid of honor.

Hally, as might be expected, was not present. Although I am sure he was not far away. Phil and Rose were in the midst

31

of exchanging the objects that were a symbol of their union—not the traditional basket of food plants from the woman indicating that she would cook for him while the man handed her a small bow and arrow indicating he would hunt for and protect their family. Instead, she handed him a .303 with a ten-power scope, while he gave her a sawed-off twelve-gauge shotgun. As they were doing that, I felt the spiderweb touch across my forehead and then heard Hally's deep, breathless voice.

Ah, a true shotgun wedding.

Hally? I looked back over my shoulder. But there was no sign of him and no further unspoken words sent my way.

What Rose joked about—that she was well along in her pregnancy—was the main reason I worried about their heading west to answer the pleas of those Palm Springs people.

Rose teased me as they were leaving when I asked if she was sure it would be all right, now that she was . . . She grinned down at me from the back of White Horse. Though Phil shared the closest bond with the big snow-colored mare, Rose and he often switched mounts, and the day they departed—as it had been when I first saw them—he was on the stallion dark as night that we knew as Black Horse.

One hand wrapped in the long hair of White Horse's mane, Rose had patted her abdomen.

"Baby likes to ride," she said. Then she looked straight into my eyes. "Would it stop you if you were in my condition?"

"No," I said. "It wouldn't. But I'm not."

"Ha!" she said, turning her gaze for a moment to Hussein, standing close behind me. "Just you wait, girl!"

"I am going to . . . miss you," I said.

"Hoka-hey, warrior lady," Rose said. "We'll be back before you know it. And meanwhile you'll do just fine."

Will we? I thought. But I didn't want to sound weak or weepy. So I said nothing more, just raised one hand in farewell.

Then she touched her heels to White Horse's side so she reared up and turned, and just like that, they all galloped off.

"Lozen?"

Hussein's voice brings me back to myself as I drift from one memory into another.

I look over at him, mounted on the back of Star. After cleaning up and scraping off all the eel muck, he's put on the white robes he's taken to wearing, which he'd been carrying in his pack. Bedu robes. He swears they are the best things for our desert climate. He looks like one of the pictures I saw in an old book, of an Arab warrior named Saladin. Or, as Hussein would have it, Salah ad-Din.

Righteousness of the Faith. That's what that name Saladin means.

It fits Hussein as well. There's no one more faithful, more true to his beliefs—as well as to those he cares about—than my partner. I'll sleep well tonight by his side—unless I dream again.

CHAPTER FIVE

Through One Eye

The spiky green hair like the crest of a mad jaybird marks the Jester for who he is as much as the grinning mask that covers his face from chin to forehead.

I'm not sure how it is that I'm seeing him—through only one eye. My conscious mind reminds me that I am still safe in my own wickiup, miles and miles away from his room at Haven where he lounges on his huge overstuffed chair. He cannot see me, even though that one green eye peering out though the hole in his mask does seem to be staring at me, into me.

But it cannot be me he's perusing with the gaze of a hungry predator, like some giant cat. It's someone else who's been left alone with him in his chamber of horrors. Someone I know?

I shudder at that thought, the thought of it being some innocent person escorted up for his amusement. True, there's no way it can be anyone close to me. My family, Hussein, my old friend Guy—they're all safe in our valley with me. Or at least as safe as anyone can be in this crazy world we're struggling to survive. During my time as a prisoner in the former maximum security prison that was turned into a sanctuary guarded against the innumerable threats outside its walls, I was careful not to make friends among the other ordinaries. Friends could have been used against me, just as Mom and Victor and Ana were—leverage to make sure I carried out the bidding of the Ones when I was their Killer of Enemies.

But even if it's not someone I knew or cared about, the thought of anyone being alone with the Jester is enough to put a knot the size of a fist in my stomach. During my time at Haven, more than a few were placed in his presence for the sole purpose of providing him amusement. That amusement always resulted in screams rather than laughter—until those screams were replaced by a terminal silence.

The Jester suddenly rises from his love seat with the easy feline grace that characterizes the way all the Ones move. He poses, balanced on his right foot, performs a perfect spin that ends with his left leg raised high above his head, arms outstretched like the Pueblo Eagle dancers my mom used to love to watch—back before all our Native people's ceremonies were banned by the Freedom from Religion Laws.

The Jester holds his pose, expectant.

"What?" he says. His voice is petulant. "No applause?"

Silence is all he gets at first. Then there's the sound of something like clapping—a hand slapped against an opposite forearm. Just four claps, spaced widely enough to make it clear they're meant as sarcasm, not appreciation.

A chill runs down my back. There's only one person I can think of who would dare to behave that way without expecting a violent and probably lethal response.

The Jester's pursed lips draw back from his teeth to shape his mouth into a wide grimace that might be called a grin. He slowly lowers his arms and drops his long, perfectly muscled leg back down.

"Wellll," he drawls, "modern dance is not everyone's cup of tea, is it?"

"No," a deep, mocking voice replies. A voice that is as cold and impersonal as a block of ice.

It's the one voice I did not want to hear. And as soon as I hear it, my perspective shifts. I'm now looking through the one eye left in the Jester's face after the other organ of sight burned itself out in the last surge of power before the planetary grid went out forever. I'm looking straight at someone as one-eyed as the Jester himself—cyclopean because of the shotgun blast that I'd thought would end his evil life. I am looking at none other than Luther Little Wound, the seemingly unkillable assassin best known by the nickname of Four Deaths.

"So," the Jester says. "You are sufficiently recovered to do business for me and not my . . . colleague? Yesss?"

"Yes."

"She is a bit upset with you, you know. Not that upset, of

course." The Jester giggles, his hands over his mouth, and does another pirouette. "She merely wants to torture you with her own lovely hands and then kill you. Mayhap a slight overreaction on her part—but then again, it might be seen by some as a bit justified. After all, you not only failed your assignment but also did not return her little clockwork toy? Is that not so?"

No response. That does not seem to bother the Jester. He opens both palms, leaps high, and lands on one leg.

"But I have so much more patience than she who thinks that time is on her side. And, after all, if at first one does not succeed, then one must try, try again. Yesss?"

The ghost of a smile flickers across Luther's face.

"Excellent. Now, you know what I want?"

Four Deaths raises his right arm as if to run his hand back through his thick black hair. Then he pauses and looks down at a four-clawed steel hook strapped where a hand used to be—before I cut it off. He takes a deep breath that ends in a chest-deep growl.

"Lozen's head," the Jester says.

Luther lifts the empty canvas sack in his intact left hand.

"In this bag."

CHAPTER SIX

Coming After Me

I sit up in bed. My two eyes are no longer sharing someone else's vision. I'm no longer experiencing that far-seeing ability I seem to have inherited—along with other gifts—from my long-ago namesake and relative, the nineteenth-century Chiricahua warrior woman Lozen. What I just lived was not a dream. Not a vision. It was something going on at the very moment I saw it.

And it is only a few days after our getting back from our well-slimed encounter with that eel. When all I wanted was a little time to just get on with our lives.

What a way to start my day!

"Lozen," a soft voice whispers. Hussein's hand touches my left shoulder. Touches it very gently. He knows enough not to startle me, even after a night spent sleeping together peacefully. No way he wants to wake up those defensive reflexes of mine. Not after what happened halfway through the first night we spent together in this house we built. Luckily I realized whose neck I had in a rear-naked chokehold before I did more than just render him briefly unconscious.

"You are all right?" he asks. "You spoke that name."

I turn and take both of his hands in mine. The dawn making its way into our valley is casting a slant of light through the open door and across my partner's face, making it glow. I want to throw my arms around him, hold him close, protect him from the danger that will soon be coming our way again—even though I know he is more capable than most men of taking care of himself. I sigh, then squeeze his hands tighter.

"He's alive," I say. "I just saw him."

Hussein understands. That is why he responds with a single monosyllabic word.

"Yup," I say. "That's how I feel about it, too."

I get up and walk over to the doorway of our lodge. We left it open for the night breeze, but it's not without an actual door, a stout one constructed from cut timbers that can be shut tight and barred. All of the dwellings we've built to replace those that were burned are much sturdier, with stone foundations, adobe bricks made of clay brought from the nearby river, and heavy beams made from lodgepole pines cut from the slopes several miles away and dragged here with the help of our Horse People allies. Strong enough to act as little fortresses—that's what our new homes are. The only windows in them are slits through which we can fire a gun. That's why leaving the doors open for the breeze is something we all do on hot nights.

Something we may not be able to do much longer. I can feel that.

What was it that the Dreamer said to me the other day? I'm pretty sure it was a quote from one of his books.

"By the pricking of my thumbs, something wicked this way comes."

And it is coming after me.

The best defense is to be offensive. That was one of my father's jokes, if you could call it a joke. One thing that's become increasingly clear to me over this past year is that waiting for something to happen is not the wisest course of action. You can't just huddle back in what you hope is a safe place so that danger, a horseman with cold eyes, will pass you by.

We need to do what Rose and our other Lakota friends have been doing ever since their four-legged allies joined them. We need to be the cold-eyed horsemen, the hunters and not the hunted.

Not that we have exactly been just sitting back on our hands and doing nothing. Hussein and I have not even been back in our valley long enough for our wounds to heal after our bout with that overly clingy overgrown fish. I can still taste its slime in the back of my throat.

But unless my throat is ready to be cut, this is not the time for rest and recuperation. And to be frank, the thought of my head in a bag ticks me off a hell of a lot more than it scares me.

Hussein leans over to look up into my eyes.

"I know that look," he says.

"We need to have a meeting," I say.

It's now late morning. Everyone has been alerted, and the time for the meeting of our council has been set for tomorrow, about this same time of day—when the sun is two hands above the eastern cliff. That will give time for people who've gone out hunting, wood gathering, or reconnoitering to get back from their various tasks.

When I was small, the favorite stories told me by my father were the ones about Coyote. Sometimes he was so foolish that it made me laugh until I almost choked. But other times he was so clever that it made me laugh in a whole different way.

As Hussein and I walk together to the arbor where the community meeting will be, I'm remembering one of those foolish Coyote stories. It's the one about the time when Coyote tried to catch Turkey.

Coyote was out walking around when he heard a sound from overhead. He looked up into a tall pine tree, and there he saw Turkey sitting on the tallest branch. Turkey was big and fat, and all Coyote could think about was how good that turkey would be to eat.

"Don't go anywhere," Coyote shouted up to Turkey. "I'll be right back."

Then Coyote ran home and got his best ax. It was one he had stolen from a white man's camp, and it was sharp and made of steel.

"Now you will help me," Coyote said to that ax. "You will help me get that foolish turkey."

Coyote ran as fast as he could back to that tree. Turkey was still there on that high branch, looking down at Coyote.

"Hah," Coyote said, "I have got you now." Then Coyote began to chop the tree down. It took him a long time because it was a big tree. Coyote kept at it, though, sure that when the tree fell, Turkey would be killed, and Coyote could just take him home and eat him.

However, when that tree started to fall, Turkey just spread his wings and flew to the next tree.

"Oh, no," Coyote said to the ax. "We did not chop fast enough. But this time you and I will do better."

He ran to that next tree and started to cut it down. He worked even harder than before, but as soon as the tree started to fall, Turkey spread his wings again and flew over to the next tall pine.

Coyote kept on like that for a long time, chopping down one tree after another until he was so tired he could not chop any longer.

"This is all your fault," he said to his ax. "You are no good at all. I am not going to take care of you any longer."

Coyote left his ax in those woods, Pine Woods Where

Turkey Flew. Then Coyote went back home, and ever since then, he has never again tried to cut down a tree.

As Hussein and I continue to walk, I wonder for a moment why that story has visited me just now. Stories don't just pop into your head for no reason. Maybe it's telling me that my trying to get rid of our enemies—whether human or gemod— is as futile as Coyote's attempt to catch a flying bird by cutting down a tree. There will always be another tree to which it can fly.

More and more gemod monsters just keep turning up. Or even worse, human enemies such as Luther Little Wound and the two remaining Ones at Haven keep coming after me. Should I just give up? Or is it that I'm like Turkey and can just fly away?

I shake my head. That's not it, not the lesson of that story. If nothing else, it's reminding me that some solutions are just not that easy. I have to keep at it. Anyway, I really have no choice . . . not if I want to protect those I love and also keep living.

My mother says it in another way.

"You need to let go of your worries. Try to keep your mind smooth, daughter. It should be like a wide plain where you can see in all directions with nothing to obstruct your vision. May it soon be usefully so for you."

My mother truly has wisdom. Maybe someday I will, too.

We've reached the arbor where the community meeting

will take place tomorrow. I stop walking to look at it and think about what it means. It's a simple structure that we all helped build. Its twelve upright poles are lodgepole pine logs that were brought in here from the nearby mountain slopes. Fresh pine boughs were woven together in crisscross patterns and placed over the rafters. The roof is low, only about five feet above the ground. Anyone who enters the arbor has to duck down and then take a seat on the floor that is also cushioned with evergreen boughs. There are openings in the walls where our Horse People allies can stick their heads in if they choose to take part. Everyone can be included in this structure, which reminds everyone that we're all equal, all connected together.

It's the old Chiricahua way of looking at things, of making a community, and it's a good way. Much better than the lives all of us were forced to lead until only a few seasons ago.

However, though we're all equal in our new community, each of us has different skills and different jobs to do. Some know medicine like Emily Lewis and Lorelei. Some are good at helping people come to good decisions—like my mother, who is now heading the Women's Council. Some are good hunters, some good at growing things—like Hussein. The corn, beans, and squash our gardeners have planted under his guidance in the fertile soil farther back in the valley are thriving under their care.

Even the Dreamer seems to fit in now, relishing his role as

the keeper of the books. Hardly a day goes by without my seeing him sitting cross-legged with several children, reading to them or helping them read one of his priceless books by themselves.

Then there's me. And you know what job I have. Whether I like it or not. Killer of Enemies.

I can live with that. I just did when Hussein and I terminated that giant eel. I've accepted, however reluctantly, that I'm good at killing monsters. That it's necessary.

But not killing people. Never again. Even if it is someone as evil and dangerous as Luther Little Wound. Which presents me with an interesting problem, seeing as how his motto might be summed up in four words: Kill or be killed.

And where does that leave me?

Whose ironic but unthreatening presence do I sense in front of us, even if he is not visible to my eyes?

The floor of our valley is littered here and there with large stones, some of them marked with petroglyphs like those the release of water from the dam exposed. Markings left by our people centuries ago. The big stone in front of us and to our left, the one with the design that looks like a sun surrounded by its rays of light, is where I sense a certain someone.

Who steps out from behind that stone with one hand raised theatrically in an *I come in peace* gesture but the Dreamer?

He's a dramatic figure, for sure. And that's not just because of his height—well over seven feet—and his athletic grace. There's also his face.

Since coming to live with us in our valley, he's actually stopped wearing the mask that the Ones at Haven wore to hide the deformity of their once-perfect countenances. None of the Four had been in the highest ranks of the planetary elite, those so enhanced by implants and microcircuitry that they were as much digital as organic and also more or less cooked in their own juices when the Cloud came and everything electric either stopped working or spectacularly burned out. However, the upgrades of the Ones who ruled us—primarily to augment sight and hearing—had been sufficient to leave all of them one-eyed and one-eared and spectacularly scarred on half their faces.

What's interesting to me is that doffing that mask has not made the Dreamer look either repulsive or ugly, unlike the face of Diablita Loca when her mask was knocked off her face in my fight with her. The blackened and pitted bones of her face were nothing short of hideous, her visage as distorted and demonic as her bloodthirsty soul.

The Dreamer's scars, though, do not go that deep. Though the skin over half of his face is shiny and tight from the burns, though his eye is an empty socket, it's not that shocking to see, and nothing has rotted like Diablita Loca's wounds did—his burns have healed, if scarred. And when it became clear to us that his true love in life was not for power, but for knowledge, for those books he's guarded as if they were his children, somehow everything about him seemed to change. He'd hidden that part of himself to survive in the presence of the other three who had controlled all our lives at Haven. And unlike them, no ordinary pleb ever actually suffered physical injury from him—though he did his best to portray himself as a monster. Protective camouflage. Plus his devotion to Lorelei, who is actually a sweet soul, has made his humanity more evident. No one is afraid of him now.

That doesn't mean, though, that he is not still maddening at times. Or that I do not groan inwardly when he says words like those he is about to speak.

"Lozen, my dear little efficient assassin, one would like a word with you."

His words are accompanied by that sardonic half-bow and sweep of both hands that make me want to kick him in his teeth. However, aside from a low growl, I control myself admirably. Though Hussein does take a cautious step away from me.

The Dreamer, though, is unperturbed. Which I suppose should not surprise me. I sigh and nod.

The Dreamer cocks his one perfect eyebrow at Hussein.

"Might I borrow your lady for but a brief moment?"

Hussein looks at me. I appreciate that.

"It's okay," I say. "We won't be long."

"Indeed," the Dreamer agrees. "As they say, time and tide wait for no man. Or woman, nicht wahr?"

I have no idea what he is talking about. As usual. But I leave Hussein's side to walk with the Dreamer off to a place some fifty yards away where the blackened trunk of an old tree has begun to return some life to its twisted branches in the form of a few small sprays of leaves. It makes me remember another thing my dad used to say, that life always finds a way to come back.

The two of us sit down on a pair of stones that seem so suited for seats that they may have been used for centuries by other humans before us. He steeples his hands together and places his long index fingers on his lips.

"Might one ask," he says, "of what your long-term plans consist?"

Long term? That is something that's never entered my mind. Just surviving has been enough. Making it back alive from each of my assignments and then making sure my family members were safe has always been as much as I've been able to wrap my mind around. I want to laugh at that question.

But instead it has gotten stuck in my head. More than stuck. It's as if a bee has just crawled in through my ear and started buzzing around in my skull.

Long term.

The Dreamer is waiting, a patient look on his half-face.

Long term.

If I'd been mentally counting, I would be up to fifty and one pony by now.

The Dreamer chuckles. "Nanu nanu? No? Nada? Nyet?"

I shake my head, if only to try to get rid of the buzzing of those meaningless words he's just thrown at me to tick me off.

"Just as one suspected," the Dreamer says in his usual sarcastic tone. Then his voice changes, grows softer. "Lozen," he says, "I have no doubt about the power of your gift—your gifts. But I have dreamt. And that dream was not meant for my edification, but yours. It is time now for you to plan, to set out a course of action that consists of more than just those steps that lead you toward yet another confrontation with an enemy. You have been victorious, but you have also been fortunate. As a great wise man once said, the only thing that does not change about fortune is that fortune may always change. Good luck is better when it is part of a greater plan."

Maybe it's not too late to just kick him in the teeth after all. But even though I am biting my lip, I also know he's right. I can't just keep charging headlong into danger. The words the Dreamer just quoted from that "great wise man"—most likely the Dreamer himself—ring true to me. As my dad said, sometimes you eat the bear, and sometimes the bear eats you.

The Dreamer nods. Is he hearing my unvoiced words as he has now and then done in the past?

"Though a bit inelegant, an excellent metaphor," he says.

Yup, reading my thoughts again.

"Might one offer a humble suggestion insofar as your immediate future goes?" he continues.

As if I could stop him? I raise my hand, swing it out toward him palm up, as a sign of surrender.

"Excellent." He reaches down and picks up a long stick, one that has been stripped of its bark and smoothed. Clearly something he prepared before summoning me to this little chat. He leans to his right, where the sandy earth has been smoothed, and makes a V-shaped mark with the tip of his stick.

"Here," he says. "This is where you are. But where do you go from here?" He hands me the stick.

I look up at the sky, figuring out which direction is east. Then I make a second mark, a large *H* six feet to the east of the *V* that stands for our valley.

"There."

"As one thought. Your wish is to liberate those unfortunates still held in thrall by my former colleagues, in particular the ticking time bomb I oft call La Belle Dame sans Merci. A noble endeavor. Quite chivalric, an appropriate adverb considering the recent addition of your equine allies, eh? But how do you get there? And what do you do when you get there? And what about this?"

He makes a series of marks, *X*s and *O*s, between those two points on our rough map.

"Need one say that those are not hugs and kisses? Especially this one." He makes another mark, a large *L*.

"Formidable foes at every turn both human and non–homo sapiens. Plus well-manned and unbreached walls. And what forces can you marshal aside from your own capable self, our Bedu friend, and your two equine allies now that our recent allies have headed off on yet another mission, leaving us to our own devices until their return?"

I take his stick and draw an *H* to the north, standing for Hally and the last direction from which I'd sensed his presence. Then I draw a question mark after it.

"Ah, yes. The wild card in the deck that is stacked against you. He might indeed play a hand. An ace in the hole? Like one of those tunnels he pops out of every now and then? The joker in the deck—ah, not to be confused with my former tyrannical compatriot."

I slice my hand down through the air to indicate I've had enough of his card game metaphors. "So what is my solution?"

The Dreamer chuckles, stands up, and sends the stick spinning off with one lazy twitch of his hand.

"Solution? One has no such thing. Merely questions to which you must seek the answers."

Then, saving his teeth from their removal with a spinning front kick, he turns and gracefully makes his exit.

CHAPTER SEVEN

A Story Meant to Help

One day, they say, Coyote was out walking around, and he saw a group of white men out prospecting. They had fine horses, strong mules, nice clothing, and lots of provisions.

Coyote had a few silver dollars he had found. He circled around in front of those white men to a place where there was a tree with lots of branches. He took those dollars and put them up into that tree, just balanced on the branches. Then he sat down under the tree and waited.

Pretty soon, along came those white men. They saw Coyote guarding the tree.

"Coyote," they said, "what are you doing? Why are you guarding that tree?"

"I shouldn't tell you," Coyote said. "Then you will want to trade and get this tree from me."

"Why would we want to trade for that tree?" they said.

"Ah," Coyote said, "I should not tell you."

"Tell us, Coyote. Tell us."

Coyote shook his head. "Oh, no," he said. "I really should not tell you."

"Coyote," those white men said, "we are your friends. Please tell us."

"Aoo," Coyote said. "If you are my friends, then I have to tell you. This tree is a money tree. Money grows from it. All you have to do is shake it, and money will fall to the ground."

"Are you sure about that?" the white men said. "We've never seen a money tree before."

"I can prove it to you," Coyote said. "I can shake it just a little, and then a few dollars will fall. But if I do that, then I have to take those dollars because whenever anyone shakes this tree, that money always has to go to that person."

"Go ahead," the white men said. "Shake the tree."

Then Coyote gave that tree a shake. When he did so, the few silver dollars he had balanced on the branches fell to the ground.

"Ah," he said as he picked up those dollars. "Only a few dollars were ripe. I shook this tree too soon. Now I will have to wait at least another day before a good big crop of dollars will be ready."

Those white men were very impressed.

"Coyote," they said, "we want to trade for that tree. What will you take for it?"

"I am not sure I want to trade," Coyote said. "But then again, maybe I should. It is not easy to sit here and guard this tree all day and all night. It would be easier for you to do that because you could take turns with one another."

"Good," the white men said. They were sure they would soon be very rich. "We will trade one horse for the tree."

Coyote shook his head. "Na," he said. "That is not enough."

"Two horses?"

"Na."

"All our horses?"

"Na."

Coyote kept saying no to each offer until finally the white men offered him all their horses and mules, all their clothing, and all their provisions.

"Aoo," Coyote said. "That is not a lot for a tree such as this, but I am getting tired of guarding it."

Those white men were so happy. Even though they had nothing, not even their clothing, they were so happy that they were jumping up and down.

"Now remember," Coyote said, "do not shake the tree until tomorrow, when the money is ripe."

Then he went off with all the possessions of those white men, leaving them under their money tree, waiting in Place Where White Men Sat Naked. Some say they were so greedy that they waited so long that they all starved, and their skeletons are still sitting there waiting.

❖

My mother is smiling when she finishes telling that story. Although I am pretty sure she told it just for me, her audience included my brother Victor, my sister Ana, and Ana's best friend Luz—Guy's daughter.

"Good story," Victor says. His voice has been changing, getting deeper over the last few moons. As a result, it has become so much like my father's that it makes me bite my lip. I miss my father so much it's both painful and wonderful to hear the way his only son is beginning to sound like him. Then Victor stands up, just the way my dad used to stand up so straight and tall from a sitting position with such ease.

"I'm going to go practice my shooting more," Victor says. And then he's out the door in two quick strides on those legs of his that seem to be getting longer every day.

And that is another reason why I've just bitten my lip. The more my stubborn, tough brother grows up, the more he'll want to go out—just like I do—to face any danger that might threaten us. He's stronger than any of the other kids his age or even a few years older than him. He's proven himself already to be capable in a fight—like when we were attacked by those frigging flying monkeys—and he's now almost as good with a gun as Hussein. But he's still my little brother. I'm not ready for him to be grown up yet.

"Us too," Ana says, grabbing Luz's hand. "Come on!" Then the two of them are also out the door as quick as a pair of doves taking flight. Though maybe comparing them to doves is not exactly accurate, unless you are referring to decidedly lethal doves heavily armed with not only holstered .44s, but also three or four hidden knives apiece. Ready for a fight.

And that thought, too, puts a lump in my chest. Because Ana, like Victor, wants to be just like me. And now that she's entering her teens—close to the age when I started being a Killer of Enemies myself—the thought of her being out there on her own has become even more a possibility than just a worry.

How can I protect my family when they want to put themselves into the line of fire to help me?

"You have to let us help, dear."

My mother's voice brings me back out of my cloud of concern. Once again, whether reading my mind or just the expression on my face, she's understood what's in my head. And I know she's right—to a point. So I focus back on what she just shared.

"Was that story meant to help?" I ask.

"What do you think, my daughter?"

I had to smile. Just because an elder tells you a lesson story doesn't mean they are going to spell out the lesson for you after you've heard it. Instead, that story has to sit inside you, remembered because it was so interesting or so funny or whatever. And eventually, if you just let it happen, that story's teaching will become clear to you.

But there is one lesson I think I can draw from that story right now. It's that greedy people may want something so badly that they no longer recognize what is real and what is a trick. Even when getting what they want is made so easy—too easy—that anyone who stopped and really thought about it might not fall for the trick. But greed can blind people. Then they fool themselves.

And maybe, just maybe, our enemies can be led to do just that.

CHAPTER EIGHT

Never Dreamed

uther Little Wound never dreamed. Or so he believed. He just went into what was little more than a half-sleeping state every night. No dreams came, either good or bad. Just a few hours of rest and then back into action.

After all, he was known as the one who was always alert. Who slept, quite literally, with one eye open.

But things were different now that one eye was permanently closed to the light. Now that everything was seen in a single dimension.

He looked about across the desert spread below him, easy to scan in every direction from the high place he'd climbed to gain a vantage point. As well as a slightly safer spot to spend the night. The climb had not been that hard, even considering the little obstacle that had slowed his ascent. Thinking of which . . .

He looked back the way he had come. Perhaps half a mile

below, the turkey buzzards were already spiraling down to the feast he'd provided for them. He smiled, drank from his water bottle, then put it down to pick up the pack from the flat black stone next to him. It was the same color of the indeterminate creature that had lain across his path, waiting for him to step on it so that it could wrap itself around him and drive its sting into him. An interesting strategy. He had to credit the creature for its ingenuity—or perhaps its creators—who seemed to have somehow (he guessed) mixed a sting ray with a chameleon and something like a hedgehog.

But the fact that it had allowed its hairless tail, quivering in anticipation, to give it away negated its ambush predator approach. And though its skin was tough, one of Luther's extremely sharp darts tipped with his own curare-like poison had both pierced its flesh and sent a spasmodic quiver through its twelve-foot-wide body, which thrust its lancelike sting toward the sky. It had rolled itself up like a rug, unrolled itself, changed color from black to green, then to a neutral brown before it finally, decisively, expired.

Luther took out the waterproof—and bloodproof—bag from within his pack, zipped it open, pulled out the creature's heart, and took a satisfying bite. Ahhh. Just what he'd needed—the kill and the nourishment it provided him.

It was further evidence that he'd learned to compensate for the depth perception he'd lost. It had taken some time—in part because he also lacked the hand he'd always favored for throwing. But after ten thousand tries, he had begun to once again bury his throwing knives deep into the center of whatever target he chose—even moving ones.

It seemed quiet in the desert below him. Deceptively so. When the darkness came, things would wake up and hunt. Some of them might even make their way up here to this high place where he would be spending the night without a fire, his back leaned against the sheltering stone. Too bad for them.

However, though Luther knew he was nearly as lethal as he had been before his bodily subtractions, the night would not be easy for him. And it would not be because of any potential or actual attack. It was because of sleep. No matter what, it was happening now every night. Try as he might to keep it open, his one remaining eye would eventually blink, blink again, then no matter how hard he tried to keep it open, that eye would close. And he would find himself first in a darkness that was disconcertingly deep, then floating toward the half-light of a place that held visions he had no wish to see, to feel, to experience either for the first time or . . . again.

They were never satisfying, those nocturnal experiences he refused to classify as dreams. It wasn't because they were frightening. One-eyed or not, awake or asleep, Luther had no place nor patience for fear. Nor was it because they returned him to old battles, including those where he suffered one of his several past deaths. None of those troublesome visions ever were of fights he'd won or lost, adversaries he'd killed.

Instead, insistently, they were usually about the dog. Not one he imagined. A real dog. The dog. His dog.

The first time the visions that he refused to call dreams came to him, he'd denied their reality. After all, he was doped up then, strapped to the cot with restraints that kept him from trying with the stump of his right wrist to pull away the bandages that covered the right half of his face, to run his non-existent hand through his hair.

"Calm," a voice said. "Be calm."

There was no caring in that clinical voice.

But he relaxed, remembering who he was, where he was.

He remembered the long fall, striking the side of the cliff, and then being carried away by the floodwaters. He remembered quieting his breathing, keeping his mouth shut, not gulping in the water that would have drowned him, relaxing and letting it carry him in its rough embrace as stone and tree limbs struck his sides again and again in the churning water. Another man's bones might have been smashed, but he was not another man, and when the flood was finally spent and he was washed up on the sand, he was bruised but unbroken.

And his mind was still working, reminding him that he was vulnerable, weakened and half blinded as he was, with only one hand and no weapons. With that one remaining hand, he picked up a green tree branch and began to walk backward, wiping out his own tracks as he went along, each backward step exactly three feet. Finally, when the hills began to rise about him and he had covered what he counted as a thousand yards, he tossed aside the branch and crawled into a crevice in the lava rocks. Hidden, he'd heard the voices of those who followed the flood, seeking his body. He heard their disappointment as he willed himself to be unseen, using all the powers of his mind to keep his presence clouded, even from the keen mind of the enemy killer.

He'd stayed there two days, licking water from the side of the stone where there was a small seep of moisture. Then he'd risen and begun to walk toward the sunrise. He was halfway to Haven when the armed men with the white armbands of Lady Time saw him staggering their way, their faces blurs as he fell forward into the darkness that had been embracing him.

"Calm," the cold, clinical voice said again as he felt the prick of a needle in his arm and began to return to the long night.

Though before he fell all the way from consciousness, he heard the sound of ticking clocks and then another, sibilant voice hissing a question.

"Will it still be useful, damaged as it is?"

"Of course," the uncaring voice replied. "No need yet to terminate."

Then there was only silence and night. And another visitation.

The next time that vision was stronger. It was not just a fleeting glimpse of a long canine face looking up at him with trust and more than trust in its eyes. And he almost spoke its name before he woke. But he showed no signs of waking to those he sensed standing by his bedside watching. He carefully flexed his arms. The restraints were still there. Not just leather. He'd noted that the first time he woke. Metal threads were woven into the straps. But he felt certain he could break them. Even if they did not break, he could pull hard enough that his handless wrist could slip free. It would hurt, but pain never concerned him—his own or anyone else's. And with one arm free, even an arm lacking a hand, it would be a different story, one that would not end well for those who hoped to confine him spread out on the table like an animal about to be dissected.

"How many times have you failed?"

That was a question no one had ever asked—or *dared* to ask before, especially in such a contemptuous tone.

He knew who was asking it. He could see her head, the clock mask covering her countenance.

Two, he thought. The most recent was the failed attempt that ended with the loss of his eye, his hand—and perhaps, worst of all, his reputation. The other had been when he was only a boy. A failure that occurred before he was assigned to the brutal tutelage of Master Kobiyashi—whose own hissing voice had been silenced forever by the thrust of Luther's blade through the shocked master swordsman's throat.

Two failures, one that was recent, one that he'd kept buried in his memory till now. Two. And that was it.

But he did not say a word. Instead, he showed no sign that he'd returned to a state of consciousness.

"Useless," Lady Time hissed. "It was a waste of effort to do all this. We should have let this creature perish in the desert. My clockwork cycle was worth three of him. It's time to terminate him."

Luther readied himself, breathing in a long breath and counting. When he reached a thirty count, he would explode up, break free, and then . . .

"A moment of your time, my lady?"

A third voice. One that Luther had never heard before. But a voice filled with such authority—and arrogance—that Luther stopped at the mental count of twenty, relaxed. Though he'd been ready to kill and then, most likely, be killed by the bodyguards he sensed waiting outside the room, he still preferred to opt for personal survival if that remained a viable alternative.

"Who let you in?" Lady Time's voice was angry, but also just a tad apprehensive.

Interesting, Luther thought.

"If by 'letting in' you mean 'allowed,' then the answer is no one. N'est-ce pas? Parlez-vous? If, however, you mean 'offered no resistance after I rendered them unconscious,' then the answer would be your three armed but somewhat careless guards. And here are their little white armbands as proof."

Through the slit in his barely opened left eye, Luther saw the green-haired one who'd been speaking toss three mostly white—aside from the smears of blood on them—armbands at Lady Time. She stepped back so they fell by her feet as the one who had tossed them did a series of spins that ended with both of his hands crossed in front of his chest.

"How dare you?" Lady Time said to the Jester. But there was considerably less anger in her voice now.

"My dear comrade, my fellow Overlord, how could you ask such a question of me? Surely you know that my answer will be that I dare because it amuses me. Does it not amuse you?"

The moment of silence that ensued was followed by Lady Time's laughter, a laughter that was close to shrieking, a mirthless laughter that was quickly joined by the Jester's own loud, nearly hysterical giggling. It went on far too long for Luther's liking.

Finally the laughter stopped—quite a while after Luther would have taken matters into his own hands and stopped it himself, had his body not been strapped down.

"Very well," Lady Time said. "He is yours to use or dispose of as you wish. I would choose the latter."

The Jester walked forward and placed his palm—a palm as cold as that of a corpse—on Luther's forehead.

"No," he said. "I choose the former. Shall we make it a contest? I know that you have a scheme of your own, my dear. Your minions have been busy little bees in that workshop. Shall we bet on whose plan comes first to fruition? Your flighty notions against my newly acquired assassin?"

"Yesss," Lady Time hissed. Luther heard a sound that had to be her rubbing her palms together. "A contessst. Lovely. Something to ease the boredom of our existence. But we must have stakes . . . aside from the one we shall plant Lozen's head on."

As before, that prompted a fit of hysterical giggles from the two that ended with Lady Time closer to the other side of the gurney where Luther remained secured—or so they assumed—by the restraints.

She rested one of her hands on Luther's chest, pressing down so hard it would have cracked a rib on a lesser man, and thrust her head forward in a snakelike way. "What do you propossse?"

"Hmmm," the Jester said. "Let's see, now that the game's afoot." The sound of feet striking the floor arose in the rhythm of a mad dance. "I know. The winner gets to cut off the left little toe of the loser."

Lady Time clapped her hands together. "Wonderful," she said.

Crazy, Luther thought to himself as he remembered that scene.

The two remaining Ones were like every other Overlord he'd met, including the former masters, the Primaries (as they styled themselves), who had loaned him out to the Ones of Haven. A thin smile came to his face at the thought of those first Ones who had believed they owned him. Alas that he could not stay around long enough to see the results of his last offering to them. He had poisoned their drinking water before being sent from the mountain-vault shelter against a war that never came. Since the Primaries had their own special water supply, he doubted that any of those held in thrall within Happy Mountain suffered their masters' fate. Not that he cared all that much about ordinary plebs. Caring had been programmed out of him, despite what those recent dreams—no, visions—kept trying to suggest to him.

But no more of that. Perhaps tonight he'd be able to enjoy an untroubled rest.

He leaned back against the sheltering stone, his knife in his left hand, his gun next to it, the claw-fingered device that stood in for a missing hand firmly attached to his right wrist, attached so that the claws would move as he flexed his forearm. He raised his left hand and ran it awkwardly back through his hair.

Then, as he watched the darkness fold in like a dark blanket over the land below, with the silvered sky above him, he renewed his mental promise. He would put an end to all such laughing as he'd heard from his mad employers.

It would be the end of time for Lady Time and the new addition to his list of those in need of termination—the Jester.

But only after he'd taken care of the person who was first on his list: the Apache enemy killer known as Lozen.

CHAPTER NINE

In Council

I look around at the faces of those gathered in our council house. Some of them—my mom, my brother Victor, and my sister Ana, have always been part of my life. Others, such as Guy and Hussein and, yes, the Dreamer, have become my allies and more over the past year. Luz and Lorelei are in that second group as well. Then there are the two beings that have linked themselves to us in the kind of partnership of human and animal that goes beyond even the old bonds my people had with the four-legged ones, Striped Horse and Star.

Although there are now a dozen Horse People who have chosen to ally themselves with us, only my gemod partner and Hussein's have come to this meeting. They are standing quietly side by side, their flanks touching, looking through the wall at the western side of our circle. Since they seem to be always in mental contact with the other ten—and, I believe, with other members of their herd now far to the west with Rose Eagle's band—there's no need for more of them to be right here.

I can sense where the rest of them are. Four of them are in various parts of our valley, grazing on the new grass that has come up with such green freshness this spring, after the burning, new life returning.

The other six Horse People are outside the valley's high cliff walls, keeping watch on the various ways anyone—friend or foe—might approach.

Those six are not alone. Each of them has on its back one of our human people, men and women who've forged the kind of connection with their hooved partners that I felt begin with Striped Horse the first time she touched my mind.

The rest of our council place is filled with the other members of our community. Some, like Emily Lewis, the healer, are White Mountain Apache from the liberated community in the beautiful mountains to our north, land that was once a reservation and before that simply a place that held and nurtured those Native cousins of ours century after century.

If I counted human heads, including the six scouts outside our valley, I would come up with a total of seventy-four human beings plus a dozen Horse People.

Valley Where First Light Paints the Cliffs is comfortable with us. I can feel the way it embraces us, hear it speaking as the land speaks. Never in words, but in waves of feeling, of deep, deep connection, of understanding. It is content to hold us, and it could accommodate twice our number. The corn and other crops we've planted are thriving in the fertile soil; the springs are flowing with clean, clear water. And our hunters easily bring in enough meat without taking too many game animals, and without as much risk to their lives from the dangers that still surround us now that they do their hunting from horseback. With the aid of a gemod steed, they have been able to elude or outrun any of the smaller monsters or such indeterminate beings as the Bloodless ones. Whenever there's been something really big and really dangerous—either here or threatening any of the several freed communities within a hundred miles of us—then my profession as a Killer of Enemies (but no longer solo) has come in to play. Three times over the last four moons—counting the mammoth eel we just terminated.

I just wonder how many more of such creatures there are out there? To say nothing of the very human, seemingly unkillable assassin who is heading my way. My Power has not yet warned me that he's anywhere within range yet—still at least a journey of a few days away. Or so I hope.

"Lozen?"

An elbow gently—very gently—touches my arm.

"Huh?" My mother's voice speaking my name, combined with Hussein's cautious prod, has just wakened me from my reverie. The meeting has already started, may have been going on for a while. The hum of conversation that I'd been ignoring with my conscious mind has stopped. Everyone is looking at me as if I had something to say.

I never hesitate when it comes to a life-threatening situation. I either put my plan into play or just react according to the circumstances. But right now what I feel like doing is vaulting onto Striped Horse's back and getting the heck out of Dodge. I'm not a leader, someone who tells others what to do. That's not my job. I'd like to just find a place to hide right now.

Not that Mom is about to let me do that. The eye contact she's making with me and the amused feel of her mental message—*Just talk!*—makes that all too clear.

"It's all right, habibi," Hussein whispers. "Whatever you say will be good."

Like saying *screw this public speaking crap*?

But he's right. Like it or not, I am who I am and need to accept the responsibility that goes with it. Even when my tongue feels as if it is tied in a big knot.

"Lozen," Mom says again. *Just breathe, sweetheart*, is what she's thinking as she says that, and it helps.

I let out the breath I've been holding.

"My Power," I say. Then I pause, feeling something gather inside me. The one whose name I carry was a leader, one who knew what to do and what to say. I need to honor her legacy. "My Power has spoken to me. It tells me that danger is coming our way. The one called Four Deaths is not dead. The Ones left at Haven still want to destroy me and destroy us."

So what else is new?

That snide mental message could only have come from one person. I glare at the Dreamer, who simply nods with that infuriating smile of his.

Everyone is still listening, though. So I continue.

"I believe that we have some time before such an attack comes. At least two days. So everyone has to be extra vigilant. Meanwhile, the best way to keep that attack away from our valley, or at least delay it, is for me to not be here, to go outside and draw Four Deaths to me."

"And me," Hussein says. I don't disagree with him.

We have to be like Coyote with his money tree. Offer something—in this case, yours truly—wanted by the greedy. But not, I hope, *actually* giving it to them.

Once again, I am about to be the goat tethered to bring in the tiger and the tiger hunter.

Wheeee!

But at least this time, there will be two of us being offered up as tasty morsels.

CHAPTER TEN

A Lot to Digest

It's the day after the meeting and time for me to hit the trail and do what I do best—which is not public speaking. As always, it begins with a visit to Guy; he and his daughter Luz left the meeting before us to get things ready for our next—and I hope not our last—adventure.

Guy has his new armory set up in what is one of the most beautiful parts of our valley. No one is living here now, where the last people who tried to live in peace before us were wiped out by an army of mercs sent by one of the two remaining lords of Haven.

Whether it was the Jester or Lady Time makes no difference. Those two are equally guilty, equally deserving of retribution. But as I think that, think about being the one to bring justice to them, I feel a pang—or maybe a shadow seeking to spread its dark wings again in my mind. Evil as they are, they are also human beings, and I've taken a vow to no longer take human life. I've been cured of the enemy sickness that made me feel as if I was caught in a black night so deep I would never again see the sun. Like for the Hero Twins of our ancient days, the weight of taking lives—even those who would have continued to kill if they had not been stopped—that weight was too much to bear, the imbalance too great.

In the old days, Haven was once a prison, a place where people who had done bad things were kept in confinement. Could we do something like that to Lady Time and the Jester? But who then would guard them? And doesn't being a guard also weigh heavily on any human being's soul?

Too much to think about now. One step at a time, Lozen. Stop driving yourself crazy with what-ifs. Think about now.

We have reached the entrance of the new armory. If you didn't know it was here, you'd never find it. All you would see would be the few sizable trees that escaped the scouring of the valley, tumbled stones, and the steep cliff face rising in front of you. Though I could scale that cliff—and maybe Hussein could do the same—most people would find it impossible to go up or down that sheer two hundred feet without ropes and climbing equipment. Most would just look at this spot and pass by, not knowing what was hidden here, or that inside that hidden place, someone might be looking through one of the several cracks in the wall placed just right to see outside.

I pick up a fist-sized stone and tap it on the wall of the cliff. I could go in without doing that, but it's polite to knock. Almost immediately, a section of the cliff wall pivots inward, a door that is eight feet tall and nearly as wide. Room enough for someone that big to walk in without bumping his hirsute head.

Thank you, Hally, I think as we enter the long stone hallway, eerily lit by luminescence from the stone ceiling. Not electric light, but something else, a biological thing from the flat fungi that cover that roof. They get their energy from dissolving the stone.

I also think something else beyond a thank-you to our troglodyte Sasquatch for showing us this hidden place and giving it over to us for our own use. *How long have you been spying on me and my ancestors from this place? And why show it to us now? Why, in fact, have you chosen to help me half the time and drive me crazy with wondering just what the hell you're doing the other half?*

I pause, waiting for a response. As if I actually expected anything like a straight answer from that massive furry comedian who keeps using me as his straight man.

Nope, no reply.

"He's waiting for you."

I nod to Luz, who'd pressed the lever to open the door and has just closed it behind us. Then Hussein and I follow her down the slanting passageway to emerge in the cozy room that Guy has turned into his workshop. The sweet smells of cordite, gun oil, well-kept steel, and polished wood are everywhere. What's a girl not to like about a place such as this?

Hussein is smiling, too. But his smile is not directed so much at the weaponry as at what is hanging in a finely crafted case with a glass front, three beautiful constructions made of wood, with ivory inlay. Guitars.

One of them is the original, slightly battered guitar with the name *Martin* on its neck that Hussein brought with him from Haven. It's the same guitar Hussein used—and still uses—to accompany his lilting voice back when hearing his music from my cell was one of the few things that could take my mind off my worries and fear for my family.

I used to wonder why anyone would name a guitar "Martin" until Hussein told me, with the gentlest of smiles, that it was the name of a long-ago company that used to manufacture musical instruments.

The other two guitars are ones that Guy found in the ruins of a shop in the deserted town—like most towns—called Bisbee. Guy, it turns out, enjoys playing music, though he's far from being as good as Hussein. That was back before Guy lost his eye and was retired as Haven's enemy killer to become its armorer. He'd been looking for weapons and ammunition, which he found in an unlooted gun store occupied by no one aside from a pair of skeletons with the flesh licked cleanly off their bones.

That made it clear to Guy that whatever ate those people so fastidiously was likely still on the loose, and it was time for him to vamoose. However, when he saw those two guitars hanging in the window of the music store, he couldn't resist taking a look—a look that was interrupted by a pair of gigantic centipede-like creatures that dropped from the ceiling of the building. Dispatching them took a bit of effort, including the use of a grenade—and resulted in even more damage to the already partially demolished music store. But somehow those two guitars survived.

Guy had taken them with him—but not to Haven, where he doubted the Four would have approved of his bringing through the walls anything other than objects intended for lethal use. Instead he had cached them inside hard-shell cases that he placed within the concealed adit of an abandoned mine. He'd gone back to retrieve them a few weeks ago. But that was only after Hussein and he had built the case in which not only Guy's hard-won instruments but also Hussein's beloved music maker could be stored in a place safer and drier than any of our newly constructed homes.

Also cleaner. Dust was always forming on Hussein's guitar, no matter where we put it. In this case his Martin stays as glistening and pristine as if it was new, though he still spends at least half an hour carefully cleaning and tuning it whenever he and Guy bring their instruments out to play them around the campfire.

The bottom of that case also holds some other items that are both precious and indispensable to any guitar player—two whole boxes filled with sets of guitar strings. Boxes which, when Hussein saw them, resulted in his embracing Guy and kissing him on both cheeks.

The memory of that moment has brought a smile to my face. Then I see something else—a new addition leaned against the far wall.

My smile turns into a whistle. What the . . . ? "Are you kidding me?"

I walk over to it, touch it to make sure it's real, run my hands along it from the handlebars, over the levers on its body.

Hussein is standing next to me, and I can feel that he's just as surprised and delighted as I am. "Beautiful," he whispers. "A great-uncle of mine once had one like this. I've seen images of it. A Norton Atlas as black and smooth as oil. Yet this is not like any I have ever seen before."

"Aye," Guy says. " 'Tis a marvel, indeed. A clockwork motorcyle. One that, it seems, you wind up with that lever there. Though I am not sure I'll ever get it to work again. Something corrosive's soaked into its works. And the mainspring came free. Took me the devil of a time to rewind it. Five will get you ten it came from the workshop of Lady Time. See that?" He traces the garish insignia embossed into the machine's side featuring two ornate letters: *L* and *T*.

"Where?" I ask, meaning, *where was it found?* I suppose my question is not really necessary since Guy—unlike Hally— always explains things in clear and direct detail. And sure enough, that is what he does.

" 'Twas in the desert, along old Route 10. Me old Lakota friend Lenard found it before they set out to the west. They loaded it onto a wagon and brought it in here, knowing how I do enjoy tinkering with things."

Guy pats the seat of the bike. "And maybe, just maybe, I'll get you to rolling again, me love."

He turns to us, wipes his hands on the heavy apron he wears when he's working.

"Come," he says, "let's get you two fitted out."

As we leave the armory cave, I sense a presence, someone waiting no more than a stone's throw from the entrance. As the stone door slides smoothly shut behind us, I feel Hussein tense up by my side. He, too, is aware that there's someone down there, hidden among the piles of logs recently dragged down from the mountains to be cut into firewood lengths.

I've learned in the time we've been together that Hussein has always had a more highly developed sixth sense, if you can call it that, than most people. It's the ability, as Uncle Chatto described it, to see without seeing, hear without hearing. Not his words originally, but those of one of the martial arts teachers whose knowledge he then passed on to me in the years—too few—during which he taught me so much of what he knew about the art of fighting. That sort of sixth sense, which is something different from my Power, has been growing in Hussein over the past year, just as my Power has been increasing in me. It seems, as I've noted before, that the coming of the Silver Cloud and the dampening out of electricity has freed other things to develop—both in us and around us.

I put my hand on Hussein's arm. His tension lessens. He understands what I've just said to him without having to say it. *No need to be ready for a fight right now. The person waiting up there means us no harm. Unless you call irritation harm.*

When we are a few feet away from those logs, the person who was sitting behind them—cross-legged, no doubt, in the lotus pose he prefers—unfolds his lanky body to stand and make himself visible.

"One asks but a moment of your time," he says.

I look up at the Dreamer's face. Since he doffed his mask for good, his normally brown skin has grown darker, exposed as it has been to the sun's filtered rays. His hair, too, has changed. It's longer, a lighter brown than before, and he is now keeping it tied up in a sort of topknot which looks a bit like some of the hairstyles I've seen in the photos in some of his old books that he's shown me depicting long-ago Asian sages. Along with the long robes he loves to wear, it makes him look vaguely monkish. Is that accidental?

The Dreamer raises his one perfect eyebrow questioningly.

I hear Hussein chuckle from just behind me. He knows just how crazy the two enigmatic know-it-alls in my life—the Dreamer and Hally—make me. If Hussein were a little closer, I'd elbow him right now—which is why he dropped back a safe space from me as soon as the Dreamer made himself visible.

Hussein makes his way around me, keeping that same cautious distance. "I'll leave you two to have your talk," he says, brushing a bit of nonexistent dirt from his sleeve. "We'll meet by the old juniper tree, Lozen? Yes? I will await you there?"

I just nod. If I said anything right now, it would probably come out as a growl. It's both delightful and a bit disconcerting to have someone know me as well as Hussein does. As I think that, I cannot help but smile.

"Perhaps two moments?" the Dreamer says, motioning for me to take a seat on one of those tree trunks.

Grrr. But I sit down.

The Dreamer sits—or rather spirals—down onto the bare earth into that legs-crossed pose that I'd assumed he was in before I saw him. Even so, his head is still above mine.

"So," he says, "your plan now is to seek trouble before trouble comes seeking you?"

His voice has that superior tone to it that makes me want to strangle him. I clench my fists instead, grit my teeth, and nod a second time.

"Thus," he says, making a flowery gesture that takes me in from head to toe, "your various appurtenances?"

I still don't speak, but the way I knit my brows together makes it obvious that what he's just said is as clear as the mud Hussein and I were inundated by a few days ago.

The Dreamer smiles. "Forgive me, I do tend to wax verbose.

I mean your accessories, armaments, et cetera. Your various weaponry, protective gear, et al."

There is still no need for me to say anything. So I don't.

The Dreamer leans back. "Allow me," he says, "to acquaint you with a bit of history, a tale of old, as it were."

A story, in other words. I have to admit that I'm hooked. Stories always get me. Hearing a tale, even from him, is something I am always ready to do. It's the way I was raised, the way I've come to understand as much of my life and the worlds around me as is possible in these transformed times. A good story knows more than you, more even than the one who tells it. And it always deserves a word or two of welcome.

"Go ahead," I say. And I lean forward to listen.

"Long ago," he says, "long ago and far away, two thousand years and more ago, there was a great empire. It ruled much of what was then the known world. From the Gates of Hercules to the Hellespont and the Holy Land, its armies marched, conquered, brought back tribute to the city on seven hills that believed itself to be the most powerful the world had ever seen. After all, its very founders were legendary heroes, twins who had been suckled as babes by wolves. As the centuries passed, its rulers had come to view themselves as gods."

The Dreamer pauses, his head cocked to one side as if just taken by a thought. "Might there be any parallels to that history, Lozen, my little assassin? But I digress."

He steeples his hands together, then separates them and

lifts a long index finger. "But there was one king, one enemy, who defied them. Time and again when their armies were sent against him, they failed. This rival king's name was Mithridates, and he commanded one weapon so great, yet so subtle, that time and again his adversaries were destroyed. That weapon was poison."

Poison. As soon as the Dreamer spoke that word, a shiver went down my back. In my fight with Luther Little Wound, even after I'd cut off his hand and his eye had been destroyed by my shotgun blasts, he had still been defiant. If Tahhr—the half-human gemod who became my loyal ally—had not attacked, the two of them locked together and falling off that cliff, I'm not sure what the outcome would have been. In that last second before Tahhr leaped in, Four Deaths had raised a tube to his mouth, but dropped it as Tahhr knocked him backward. Guy had picked up that tube—carefully—wrapped it in a cloth, and brought it back to examine it. Inside that tube was a single, incredibly sharp metal dart, its hollow tip blackened with some lethal substance.

The Dreamer keeps on with his story, as if he hasn't noticed my response to that word.

"Perhaps more than any person of his time or even the many centuries that followed, Mithridates knew poisons and used them in battle, and not only by poisoning the tips of arrows and spears. He often used poison in the subtlest of ways. For example, when bees make honey from the flowers of the rhododendrons—which grew in great forests around the Black Sea of Mithridates's homeland—that honey is deadly for human sto consume. As his enemies marched through his homeland, Mithridates arranged for honeycombs to be left in the deserted villages. When the soldiers ate that honey, they collapsed.

"But Mithridates went further than that. Knowing how deadly poison might be and that he himself might be the victim of poison, he gathered together those toxicologists of his time who knew the most about such poisons, whether they came from the venom of serpents, the sap of plants, the exudations of toads. He experimented on prisoners, dosing them or injecting them with his various substances and studying their reactions. Then he embarked upon a campaign to immunize himself against such poisons by consuming tiny portions each day. Each meal, he dined upon various combinations of poisons and antidotes throughout his life.

"I might add that Mithridates was quite right to fear his own demise. In gaining his place, he had, according to the best accounts, murdered his own mother, his four sons, his brother, and various other relatives who might claim the throne. His plan worked, and it is said that, in addition to his immunization, he developed an antidote to all poisons. It became known as mithridatium and was, in those perilous times, quite sought after."

The Dreamer pauses, then raises his palm in one of those dramatic gestures that usually precedes his saying something that, I suspect, is a quotation from one of his precious volumes.

"Mithridates, he died old."

I wait, knowing there's more. With the Dreamer, there is always more.

"But not all that pleasantly. Apparently all of his plotting and planning to remain in power worked quite well in terms of his immunization—though much less successfully in terms of, shall we say, family cohesion? In the end, he was overthrown by his one surviving son. When he attempted to give himself a peaceful death by taking some of the poison he always had with him, he was thwarted by his own body's defenses. No poison could kill him. He had to have his bodyguard run him through with a sword."

The Dreamer folds his hands and crosses his long legs, leaning back against another of the recently cut logs.

"History is so interesting, is it not?"

Again, no need to answer what is clearly a rhetorical question. I've also learned that a silent response is usually the best way to elicit actual useful information from the tall former Overlord whose secret desire has always been to be a purveyor of knowledge, the more esoteric the better. Though I sense that there is a point to his story, especially considering its lethal theme.

And the fact that, though his name was not Mithridates, there's a prominent poisoner in my past and probable future.

The Dreamer reaches into his robes and extracts something shiny.

"Pour vous," he says, handing it to me.

It's a flat packet with shiny foil on one side and pocketed clear plastic on the other. Each of the two dozen pockets holds a single white pill. MITH-ONE is printed across the foil backing.

"Take one per day. Allow it to dissolve under your tongue. Three doses should be sufficient, but take six to be safe," the Dreamer says, his voice surprisingly clinical. "It should be sufficient to immunize you for a lifetime—which should be much longer as a result—against nearly any agent. Enough, as well, for your Bedu paramour."

"How did you get this?"

"Ah," he says, that superior tone back in his voice. "Might one say it is for me to know and you to find out? No, I shall be candid. When one is living among vipers—as one was at Haven—one must take certain measures to insure one's continued carrying on among the living. By my own best estimate, I survived seven attempts to terminate my existence by such subversive techniques—most likely from the lovely lady with the chronographic face."

I'm a little stunned. I know the Dreamer is on our side, but when he does something like this, it always surprises me—though perhaps not as much as when I discovered the cart full of weapons he liberated from Haven contained a library of books hidden under the guns and ammunition.

"You're welcome," he says.

I'm almost too embarrassed to say thank you. But I do manage to bring the belated words out of my mouth.

I slip the precious packet into my pocket and start to stand up.

The Dreamer raises his hand yet again. "One moment more?" he asks.

More? Great. But I settle back down.

"You may," he says, "have noted the change in seasons? Now that we have, as it were, passed the solstice?"

Duh. What kind of question is that? I mean, I have lived here all my life. And if anyone knows anything about the seasons in the desert, it's a Chiricahua. But I hold my tongue. Rhetorical or not, I am not about to answer that question.

"Of course you have. But there is one thing you may not realize in terms of these longer days and the number of sun cycles since our amorphous extraplanetary visitor took up residence in our firmament."

I cannot keep my mouth shut any longer. "What are you talking about? In English."

A coy look creeps over the Dreamer's asymmetrical face. "More elucidation?"

"Yes," I growl. "Explain."

The Dreamer raises an expressive finger as he counters my

question with a query of his own. "How many springs have passed since the Silver Cloud?"

I sigh inwardly. But the only way to find anything out is to play his game. So I answer.

"Seven."

"Precisely. Sufficient time for the maturation to be complete. The full growth cycle, that is."

"Growth of what?"

The Dreamer leans forward, straightens, and then recrosses his legs. "Have you heard of locusts?"

Some sort of insect, I think. So I nod.

"Indeed. Their eggs are deposited beneath the soil, where they spend years in larval form until the passage of a number of years—seventeen, in some cases. Then they emerge to fly, swarm, breed, and lay their own eggs before sloughing off this mortal coil."

The Dreamer pats the soil. "Imagine," he says, "a genetically modified locust, one which—mixed perhaps with various other insectoid and avian deoxyribonucleic acid—is many times greater in size than its harmless ancestor. After existing in a subterranean state, drawing nutrition from the soil, they will emerge to take on new winged shapes that, regrettably, thirst for something other than mineral and microbial fodder. Their new need will be mammalian blood. Rather specific mammalian blood. To be precise, that of human beings."

The Dreamer lifts his hand from the ground. "Quite

flattering to be loved for who we are, is it not? Altogether an interesting concept, not so?"

A horrifying concept. But I have to object. "Are you kidding? I've never heard of a gemod like that before," I say. "Are they real?"

"Ah, there are more things, Horatio," the Dreamer replies. "But I assure you that these vampire locusts are quite real. A first-generation gemod swarm that was planted but a few weeks before all power—including that which created the acres-wide lasenet meant to encase them—ceased for good and all. Their maturation date was set for seven years hence. Hence now being present tense."

Wonderful. Giant flying bloodsuckers. What more do I need to make my day?

"Where?" I ask.

"More or less," the Dreamer replies, "a third of the way between here and Haven. Had I a working screen, I would pinpoint it accurately. However, this"—he reaches into his robes and pulls out a map—"must suffice."

He places his fingertip on a spot perhaps thirty miles away. It's to the left of the major highway halfway between our valley and our former place of captivity. It's a place I remember seeing, a wide field that had once been irrigated, giant rusting harvesting machines scattered here and there beneath long above-ground irrigation pipes that once rotated about the field, spraying the life-giving water. Those fields are now covered, as

I recall, with a thick growth of twisted small trees, dry creosote bushes, and dry grasses. I remember having a bad feeling about it when I passed it. It looked as if the life was being sucked out of it. Something gave me the creeps then. Creeps I now realize were well justified.

"Were crops being grown on top of them?" I ask.

"Indeed. The imagoes—mature beings—were designed to be capable of burrowing up from considerable depths with their formidably clawed front legs—as much as thirty feet. Thus the field might be utilized as farmland until the penultimate year."

Crap!

"So when are these flying horrors going to emerge?"

The Dreamer steeples his fingers, taps them together, looks upward, then shakes his head. "Alas, one cannot be sure, other than to say . . . soon." He smiles. "But be of good cheer. There were not that many of them planted. No more than a hundred or so. Providing the preferred nutrition for more than that relatively few of them might have burdened their creator."

I don't ask what they would have been fed with. Knowing the lack of respect that our departed planetary masters had for ordinaries, I can imagine doomed men and women being introduced into those fields as fodder. Thinking of doomed people . . .

"How far can they travel?" I ask. "Could they reach us?"

The Dreamer's face takes on a sorrowful look. "Alas. They

will be quite capable of flying great distances. And since they were designed to be good at finding . . . their prey . . . through both sight and scent, locating us should be quite easy for them. Further, though their feeding cycle before breeding and dying was designed to be no more than a few weeks, they will be quite, ah, voracious and will quickly consume their nearby food sources."

Food sources, right.

"So," the Dreamer says, "I believe that you have a rather urgent task to complete prior to seeking out your possible demise."

I'm shaking my head at the thought of immense winged horrors descending on our valley—or any other group of human victims. But I have to agree with him. If we can get to that place before they emerge—and on our way there figure out some plan to deal with them—then it takes priority over a confrontation with Luther Little Wound. A hundred flying deaths outweighs Four Deaths.

I stand up, start to walk away. Then I stop. There's a question I have been itching to ask ever since he started his little scientific discourse.

"How do you know so much about monsters?"

"Elementary, my dear Lozen," the Dreamer says. "The explanation is, I believe, obvious. As you know, quite regrettably, printed matter became after mid-century not merely outmoded but, to those at the top of our Terran food chain, unnecessary. Yet when it comes to whims, need ceases to be a factor. And those who ruled were nothing if not whimsical. To my delight, one must admit, those whims included the writing and printing of actual books. None of those books, alas, were literary. But they were books and, to my mind, worthy of salvation. What were their subjects? More often than not, they were written about the hobbies of their authors, such hobbies as the creation of new, interesting, deadly species. R. Mawaba, par exemple, was engrossed by the possibilities of creatures with six or more legs. But wait!"

The Dreamer reaches into the folds of his robe and extracts, like one of the cowboys in the old viddies drawing a gun, a shiny red-covered book that he hands to me with a flourish.

Guide To Pets: Their Making, Care, and Feeding is the title.

"Why didn't you show this to me before?"

"It only came to me this past week. A present from our Lakota friends prior to their departure."

I open the book. It's arranged alphabetically, which makes it no less horrific. Especially when I read the headings of the first two chapters: *Arachnids* and *Arthropods*. I look at the shiny, three-dimensional images that seem ready to leap off the page. Like those death-dealing seven-year locusts we have to eliminate before their swarm emerges and opts for us as their favorite dining spot.

I tuck the book under my arm and walk farther downhill to the place where Hussein is waiting for me.

"What?" he asks, his voice soft. He can already tell from the look on my face that whatever the Dreamer had to share with me was troubling news.

"Let's walk," I say, reaching out to take his hand. "We have a lot to digest—before something shows up to digest us."

CHAPTER ELEVEN

A Place to Sit

Hussein and I sit looking out over the wide plain that stretches to our east. The sun, which rose an hour ago, has painted the land with more shades of red and yellow and brown than I have names for. From here we can see for miles and miles. Aside from the lengthening shadows, nothing seems to be moving out there in the distance.

We have just walked together through our valley, taking the trail that curves up above our homes, where people were starting their day.

Smoke from small campfires and the good smells of food cooking drifted up to us as we turned a narrowing part of the trail, just wide enough for agile people to climb single file. Two or three small stones dislodged by our steps rattled down during our otherwise silent ascent. They didn't make much noise, but when we reached the top of the trail, the person sitting there was looking our way, ready.

It was my brother Victor, his favorite Remington rifle, equipped with a variable scope, held up to his shoulder as he crouched behind a boulder. Seeing it was us, he lowered the long gun and relaxed. Behind him, a leather sandbag was placed on the cliff rim to use as a rest if a long shot across the plain was needed.

Early morning has always been one of Victor's favorite times of day. He's usually up before dawn. That is only one of the ways he's like his namesake, the first Victorio, who was the older brother of Lozen. That Victorio often referred to Lozen as his right arm because of the way she could use her Power and because she was an even better strategist than he was.

Like the Victorio of almost two centuries ago, my growing little brother is a great runner. He started training to be a runner when he was four years old. Our dad had him do a certain exercise every morning, pick up one stone in each hand and run with them up to the peak near our valley. He had to leave those stones in a pile that he built on top of the peak. And the next day he had to add two more stones to that cairn. When the pile of stones was as tall as he was, he then had to start bringing four stones down each time he brought two stones up. By the time he was six, he had built and rebuilt that stone pile more than a dozen times. And by the time he was eight, the one person who could beat him in a footrace was guess who? Yup, me. I'd been building my own stone piles, too.

Running was one of the most important things that any

Chiricahua could do back in the time of the first Lozen and Victorio. Unlike many of the other tribal nations, we didn't raise our own horses, but just relied on whatever ones we could get by raiding the Mexicans—which was only fair, since they raided our camps all the time to take our people to work as slaves in their mines. Often we had no horses at all. But because everyone, old and young, could run fast and run far, we traveled greater distances than our enemies expected. And a Chiricahua runner could keep going without stopping from sunrise to sunset—or all through the night, if need be, going much farther than a man on horseback. Of course those horses were not like the Horse People who've become our allies, but still you have got to admit that is pretty dang impressive.

Getting back to my brother—after running my mouth about as far as one of our old long-distance joggers—Victor is also, as I've mentioned before, an almost supernaturally good shot. That's why, despite his youth, he's never had anyone challenge him when he requests morning sentry duty.

Victor didn't say anything. Like me, he doesn't believe in wasting words. He simply nodded and gave a thumbs-up sign as we made our way past him. All clear. Nothing threatening in sight.

Yet, I think.

The place we've chosen to sit is one where generations have rested before us. I've heard it said—by my mom and others— that wherever Holy People used to sit, the stone shaped itself to fit their bodies. Maybe it's just that the passage of time, of wind and rain chanced to sculpt this spot so that the red sandstone seems to embrace us. But I prefer my mom's explanation.

"Good place," Hussein finally says.

I nod. Then I point with a turn of my head to our right two hundred feet below.

There's a dip in the nearby plain, and a seep of water has made it greener there than elsewhere immediately below us. That is where our two four-legged allies, Star and Striped Horse, are. They're not just waiting for us, ready to carry us on our mission—a mission that has changed from its original immediate purpose. Instead, with a joy and an abandon that lift my spirits, they are playing.

As we watch, Striped Horse rears up on her hind legs, paws at the air in front of her, spins, and then runs with a sudden speed that takes my breath away. I've ridden her when she's been running that way, and it is the closest I've ever felt to being part of the wind, even when I was gliding through the air on that parachute during my encounter with the monster birds. A part of one of the old horse songs that my Navajo ancestors used to sing comes to me as I watch her.

My horse is the wind
Lightning flashes
from the eyes of my horse

she stands on the curve of the rainbow
She circles about the people
My horse is on my side
and surely I shall win

Star rears up and dashes after her. The two of them run together, muscles rippling under their sleek coats. They leap—almost taking flight—over a fallen log, turn and rear, kick up their heels as they engage in mock combat. Then they suddenly stop, settle side by side, and stand head to tail, leaning against each other as they crop the sweet spring grass around their feet.

"Such beauty," Hussein says. "A gift of Allah, truly."

Allah, I've learned, is the name his Bedu people have for the Creator. I cannot disagree. We used to say that horses were a gift given our people by the gods. And even though the actual creation of our new friends was by means of genetic manipulation done by augmented humans who believed themselves—a delusional belief—to be as far above normal humans as sky-dwelling deities, I think that those now-defunct Overlords may themselves have been acting unwittingly as a tool for some greater power when they "made" these gemod horses.

"No human can truly understand Usen, our Creator," my dad used to say. "But we can give Usen thanks for the things we enjoy."

As I think that, Striped Horse lifts her head, looks up at

me. Her eyesight and all her other senses are much better than that of a normal horse. Her vision is as keen as an eagle's. So she sees me clearly, even at this distance.

I nod to her, and she lowers her head again. I've pretty much gotten used to the fact that she can get into my head just about anytime she wants. She and Star already know everything that the Dreamer shared with me, and they are fully prepared to assist us on our new mission. The bags holding our extra gear are hung from the branches of a cottonwood tree near them. Everything is ready.

Thinking of which . . .

I take out the anti-poison pill packet and pop two of them out. Unslinging my canteen, I hand one to Hussein and put the other into my mouth, followed by a swig of water. Without asking, Hussein does the same. He trusts me as much as I am trusting the Dreamer. Actually, to be candid, more than I trust our overly literate confederate.

Then I tell Hussein, with considerably fewer words, the story of Mithridates and the purpose of the MITH-ONE pills we'll both be taking over the next few days.

Hussein nods. "Excellent," he says. "But what of our noble friends?" He looks down at Star and Striped Horse. "What will protect our valiant steeds?"

Why didn't I think of that? What if one of those poison darts that Four Death uses were to hit them? *Lozen, you are so stupid!*

Hussein chuckles, interrupting my typical session of self-condemnation.

"Not to worry," he says, looking down into the green meadow. "Observe."

I follow his gaze. A tall, brown-robed figure has just entered the meadow, two hands held out. As we watch, Star and Striped Horse amble over to delicately take the pills from his out-stretched palms, bump their heads against his shoulder, and then go back to their peaceful grazing.

The Dreamer looks up at us, does a highly mannered genuflection—which, if bows can be ironic, has just taken the prize for bowish sarcasm. Then, with a broad gesture, he places a shiny packet into one of the saddlebags hung from the tree, spins on one foot like a dancer, and exits our field of sight.

Hussein grins. "It seems as if we are well prepared."

I shake my head. "Ever hear of locusts?"

CHAPTER TWELVE
The Choosing

Luther sat quietly as the sun rose. But not quiet within. After waking from another . . . vision . . . he'd tried the techniques taught him by Kobiyashi.

Quiet body.
Quiet breath.
Quiet mind.
See Nothing.
Think Nothing.
Be Nothing.

But each time he came close to that state of being and not being, the image came again into his mind. And not just an image. The sound of feet pattering up to him, the feel of paws touching his knees.

Perhaps if he had not killed his sword master when he did,

driven his blade through his cruel sensei's throat, Kobiyashi would have taught him more. Or perhaps Kobiyashi would just have killed him as he had killed the prior four students picked to train with him. All of them, like Luther, had been viewed as promising . . . and difficult. Pass the test of carrying burning embers bare-handed, and a student might be ready to assume a role like that masked man who'd moved like a shadow and killed Luther's parents. A true servant of death, a master killer.

That was all Luther had aspired to. To be one like that one. To meet that one who murdered his parents, express his admiration, thank him for the career at which Luther planned to excel—and then kill him. It was all he had cared for. Until the dog.

Was it his last near death that brought memory of it back to him? Had striking his head as he fell from that cliff affected his mind?

And why was he asking these questions of himself?

Enough. It was time to get on with his mission. And this time he would not fail, as he had failed many decades ago at the age of thirteen.

By then, he had already been in training at the Force Academy for more than four years. The top of what might loosely be called his class. No one loved him. But every other student respected him. No, not respected—something better. A boy who was first in every exam and test, who made no friends, who never smiled, who bit off the finger of an older trainee who tried to push him, a boy reputed to never sleep, up all night sharpening his knives, oiling his weapons, humming quietly to himself as he did so—that kind of boy was not respected, but feared.

The only part of his training left was Final Stage. No one was ever seen again after being sent off to the Final Stage barracks miles away from the Force Academy's main campus. Final Stage was deep in the Black Hills that had once, if Luther remembered right, been sacred to the Lakota people. A fact that meant nothing to the young man, just a dim memory from a childhood left far, far behind.

So, when he was told—along with six other advanced trainees, all of them older than Luther—to pack his duffel, he almost smiled.

"No one's ever been called up so young," someone whispered.

Whoever it was shut up as Luther made his way slowly out the door, pausing to cast a baleful eye at first one student and then the next, none of them looking up, some visibly shaken by his gaze.

He and the other six were loaded into a mag-lev all-carrier. "The Magnificent Seven," the oldest of the boys said, a redhead with heavy shoulders and unusually large hands.

The laughter stopped when Luther said in a flat tone, "Cut the crap!"

And for the rest of the hour-long glide to the special section camp, no one said another word, especially the boy named Red who kept his hands clutched together—hands whose knuckles bulged because Luther had methodically broken each of his fingers one by one in no-holds-barred sparring.

The Final Stage barrack where they were housed was not like those at the Force Academy. There were individual rooms— seven of them. Sparse—bed, washstand, toilet, footlocker, a single door, and no window. Also one other thing seemed strange: a thin pillow in the corner with two bowls next to it. They were also given new shoes to wear, with metallic soles.

Behind their quarters was another building, barn-sized with fencing behind it. Ordinary fencing. Not the mega-mesh super-steel, electrified, and laser-threaded security fencing favored by the Overlords for the pens and paddocks of whatever DNA-spliced horrors they fancied like the sample creatures displayed at Force Academy. Monsters that always attracted Luther. Rather than shrinking back in fear from whatever bat-winged or saber-clawed creature rushed such a fence before being stung back by a jolt of current, Luther liked to stand as close as possible where he could feel the heat of the fierce being's breath during that split second of near contact.

He'd studied each of those monsters that longed to devour him, observing its weak points, imagining what weapon would be most useful to kill before being killed.

Those gemod creations each had their own peculiar odors, most of them strong, sharp, musty, some nearly sickening.

But that day, Luther's much-better-than-average olfactory sense picked up another, subtler scent, one that was almost pleasant to his nose—warm, milky, almost sweet. Strange.

The sergeant who lined them up in front of the barnlike building had a softer voice than any Force officer Luther had encountered before. The tall, narrow-shouldered man's face was pleasant, round, and unlined under his close-cut black hair. But his black eyes held a coldness that Luther recognized, a killer's coldness that made Luther feel reassured that this phase of his training might be worthwhile after all.

"The important work you'll be doing in the future for our Primaries, assuming you passed through this stage of your training, will require unusual skill. All of you have shown promise, even if you are worthless pieces of crap. But you can be trained to be useful pieces of crap. That's why you are here. Here you are going to be taught one skill you have not yet shown—the skill required to work as a team."

Sergeant Barker paused, looking at each of the seven in turn. Each of them looked back, straight into his eyes, though only Luther's eyes were half closed.

"Skill," the sergeant continued, "skill that you can only develop through experience."

Blah blah blah. Luther listened without really listening. Not that he wasn't taking it in. If asked, he could parrot back every word that Sergeant Barker had spoken. Luther's memory was accurate as a digital transcripter.

But what was being said seemed unworthy of full attention, devoid of real meaning. He'd heard such speeches before, usually barked at the trainees rather than delivered in a soft monotone. To amuse himself, he was counting the number of times the man spoke the word "skill." An even dozen thus far.

"So," the sergeant concluded, "it is now time for each of you to meet your new partners."

He raised his right hand and touched his thumb twice to his middle finger to activate the subcutaneous device implanted there. The large door behind him folded upward.

Seven people stood there. Each of them was holding a chain, and at the end of each of those chains was an animal.

Luther had never seen one in the flesh before. Before he was born, the edict had come out demanding the surrender of all nonessential pets owned by ordinaries. Only the Primaries—and those few families that had found shelter in remote areas—were allowed to have house animals.

But it had not always been so. He'd heard whispers back at the reservation—only whispers, for it was not allowed for them to speak out loud about the old days and old ways—about animals like the ones he saw before him. They'd once been an important part of the lives of his Lakota people, as important in their way as the horses that a few still owned—horses that would soon vanish when a laboratory-created equine plague swept across the planet. Luther's half-closed eyes widened.

Dogs. They were gemod dogs.

But large as they were, each of them well over two feet tall at the shoulder, there was something about them that made Luther think they were not fully grown. Their feet were too large. Puppies. He peered at them more closely. The look in their eyes held something Luther never recalled seeing before in an animal's eyes. Keen intelligence? Was that it? No, it was that plus something else.

"Walk forward to the line and stand on it," the sergeant commanded, his tone stronger now.

Luther and the other six did so. The line, a long foot-wide bloodred mark drawn on the black paved surface, was about fifty feet from the open door where the dogs and their handlers stood.

"Each of you scum will be assigned one animal. A special animal, one that, if it is treated right, just might outlive your useless ass. So you had better take care of it. For the next ninety days, it will be your responsibility. It will live with you, walk with you, share food with you, sleep by your cot. You will be given specific instructions on training. You will follow them to the letter. Do you understand?"

"YES, SIR," seven voices replied at once, Luther wondering if the uncertainty—a most unfamiliar feeling—in his own voice was evident.

One of the seven, Red, started to step forward.

"TRAINEE!"

Red froze, his foot still in the air.

"Were you told to move?"

"No, sir."

Red pulled his foot back and placed it on the pavement.

Sergeant Barker raised his left hand, pressed his thumb to the first joint of his index finger, pointed at Red's feet, and made an abrupt downward movement. Immediately Red's body began to convulse. Smoke rose from the metal soles of his shoes.

Sergeant Barker snapped his fingers, and Red face-planted on the ground.

Everyone stood in silence until Red groaned, dragged himself first to his knees and then to his feet.

"On the line," Barker said.

Red stood on the line. A trickle of blood ran down from his nose, but he did not lift a hand to wipe it away.

"Good," Barker said. "Now, to continue, you will not name your animals other than to call them 'Dog.' Is that clear?"

"CLEAR, SIR."

But as he spoke that word in unison with the others, Luther noted that Barker had now said the word "you" fifteen times.

Barker looked at them with a satisfied smile. "Excellent. Now comes the choosing. But you will not choose. Number One, release your animal."

The man standing directly in front of Luther unclipped the leash. The young animal took one step forward, then another. It paused, looking at all seven trainees, then ran directly to the person who stood to the left of Luther, and put its head against the boy's hand.

That trainee, a blond, broad-shouldered boy with a crooked nose—broken by one of Luther's elbow strikes—looked at Sergeant Barker, moving only his eyes.

"Go ahead, Maxton," Barker said. "Get to know him."

Maxton dropped to one knee and put one arm around the dog's neck as the handler who'd released the dog walked up and handed him the leash.

"Good dog," Maxton said. Then he looked quickly up toward Barker, who nodded approval.

"Check your palm," Barker said to Maxton. "Instructions there."

Maxton looked at the subcute screen in his palm, nodded, touched it with his index finger, then stood at attention with the dog by his side.

One by one the dogs were released, each choosing a different boy. The fourth, the most wolfish-looking of the seven with a white mark on its chest, went directly to Luther. As the others had done, Luther dropped to one knee, placing his left arm around the animal's neck. He swept back his thick black hair from his forehead with his right hand.

Easy to break, Luther thought, tightening his grip. *Just fall to one side, wrap my legs around it, and twist.*

The dog looked up into his eyes as he thought that. Strange

thing for an animal to do when death was so close. Was that what changed what he was thinking? Or was it the way Barker looked at him so intently as if reading his thoughts?

Luther stood up, accepted the chain from the handler, clipped it onto the animal's collar. Then he checked his palm screen. The message there in all caps was simple:

IF YOUR DOG DIES
BEFORE TRAINING ENDS
YOU DIE
NOW STAND AT ATTENTION

Something was approaching from behind him. Fifty feet or so away now. Most would not have heard the slight scrape of a stalking foot, no, feet across the stone. But most were not Luther.

It was no longer twenty years ago. It was now. Luther realized he'd been sitting too long in one place in an exposed spot.

Another soft scrape. Closer now. But no other sound. None of the sort of breathing he'd expect from anything reptilian or avian or mammalian. *Interesting.*

He let his left hand drop to the hilt of the huge, heavy knife on his belt, used his thumb to flick off the strap that held it in place.

Close enough to jump at my back. Now!

Luther rolled to his right, a single fluid motion. He pulled out the big blade as he did so, coming to his feet, turning, slashing down at what he saw striking the spot where he'd been. As his knife cleaved through the hairy, segmented leg that had tried to pierce his neck with its single, glistening claw, blue ichor sprayed from the severed limb.

A second black leg that struck down at him met the same fate as he sidestepped and cut through it with a backhand strike.

Alas, almost too easy.

He smiled as he looked up into the compound eyes of the enormous spider that now seemed hesitant as it towered over him.

Two legs gone. Six to go, Luther thought.

A sudden spray of white silk jetted toward him, enveloped his left leg. The spider lurched forward, aiming at the throat of its prey with venom-dripping fangs—that Luther smashed with one blow of his steel-clawed right fist.

Silent till then, a sound almost like a cry of despair burst from the spider's mouth. Perhaps it was only a result of Luther's left elbow striking into its thorax before his blade—sharper than any razor—cleaved off a third and then a fourth limb. The creature toppled onto its side, Luther riding it down, his blade weaving its own net of destruction.

Five, six, seven, eight. And done.

Luther stepped back off the limbless creature that writhed on the ground. Its abdomen and thorax scraped against the stone as the stubs of its legs left blue streaks on the red sandstone.

He felt something on his right wrist. His steel hand had been pulled off, straps separated by the force of his blow. One of the spider's fangs was stuck in the flesh of his forearm, black venom dripping from it. Luther had been injected with more poison than it would take to kill any ordinary man.

The crippled arachnid's compound eyes seemed to be staring at his arm. Then he heard in the back of his mind its triumphant thoughts.

Killedyoukilledyoukilledyou.

Luther pried the fang from his forearm, watched as the venom-burned flesh began to change color. The black veins emanating from where his skin had been pierced faded as his antibodies did their work. The long, agonizing process of immunizing him against every known poison had included toxins employed by innumerable creatures, from snakes to stonefish. Including spiders.

"Sorry," Luther said, thrusting his blade between the creature's head and thorax. "Only one of us was killed today."

CHAPTER THIRTEEN

Take the Enemy Unprepared

As the four of us, Striped Horse and me, Star and Hussein, are crossing the first range of hills between us and the abandoned field where monsters are waiting to wake beneath the soil, I'm hoping our plan will work.

Guy had taken his time thinking it over as I told him the problem and offered what I thought might be a solution.

"Ah, lass," he said. "Dragon's tooth soldiers, it seems. You ken that old tale?"

I actually did, more or less. It was a story of how an ancient hero in Greece had to raise an army to fight for him. So he buried the teeth of a dragon, and every one of those teeth turned into a full-grown soldier that rose up out of the ground. Except those soldiers were there to fight *for* that hero—not suck his blood and then fly off through the air to kill everyone he loved.

"So," Guy said, "when is a warrior at his weakest? There

was an old Chinese general who wrote about that, you know."

"Sun Tzu," I said. "*The Art of War*. My dad had a commanding officer who was always quoting from that book. Like, 'Avoid what is strong and attack what is weak.'"

"Ah, lass. Good one. *The Art of War* is a lovely book, and I had me a copy of it once. But I prefer another quote from that very volume: 'He will win who, prepared himself, takes the enemy unprepared.'"

Ah.

"The enemy is weakest when they're either asleep or just waking up," I said.

I could hear Hussein's thought agreeing with me as he placed one hand on my shoulder and squeezed it gently.

"Aye," Guy said. "Full marks."

"So you think our plan might work?"

"I dinna say that," Guy replied. "But I think it sounds better than any other plan I can think of at such short notice." He turned and lifted two ten-gallon cans onto the tabletop, bent, and brought up two more. "These should be enough," he said. "I hope."

I hoped so, too. This was, it seemed, the best we could do if we didn't have an Arrow of Lightning.

The Arrow of Lightning? Why had that thought come into my mind just then? Almost as if someone had sent it there. I looked around the armory cave, half-expecting to see a grinning hairy giant step out from some hidden doorway in the rock wall. But, despite my suspicions, Hally did not appear.

Which maybe meant that he didn't feel it was necessary for him to step in and assist us as he'd done in the past because we could take care of it without him. Which was good, I suppose. Unless maybe our Bigfoot buddy had finally become bored with us and was simply about to let us sink or swim all on our own.

Quit it, Lozen. You are just making yourself crazy.

I sighed and picked up two of the heavy cans.

The Arrow of Lightning. I'm thinking of that again as we continue to ride. It is part of one of the oldest stories told by my ancestors on both the Chiricahua and the Dine sides. Maybe the oldest. I heard that story—or parts of it, because it is really, really long—so many times from my mom and my dad. I still sometimes hear my mom telling some part of the story to Ana and her best buddy Luz as they help her with such household chores as cleaning our rifles and handguns and sharpening our knives.

Long, long ago, White Painted Woman had two sons. Those were dangerous times for those boys, whose names were Killer of Enemies and Child of Water. Dangerous for all the human beings who were yet to come because the land was filled with monsters. So White Painted Woman kept her boys hidden from the monsters that would come looking for them. Those monsters could not eat White Painted Woman. She was too powerful. But they would have eaten those boys, especially the big cannibal giant.

Luckily, Big Giant was really stupid. He would come to White Painted Woman's lodge and say, "I know there are boys here for me to eat. I saw their footprints in the soft earth."

But White Painted Woman would fool him every time by pressing her knuckles into the earth to make shapes like children's footprints, saying, "I made those marks myself because I am lonely and wish I had children."

Then Big Giant would go away.

Finally those boys were grown. They told their mother they wanted to get rid of the monsters so the world would be safe for the human beings to come. They asked her what they could do.

"Your father is the Sun," White Painted Woman said. "If you can get to his lodge, he could give you weapons to use. He could give you the Thunder Bow and the Arrow of Lightning. But the way to his lodge is long and guarded by terrible beings that might destroy you."

The sun has been moving lazily across the sky as we continue to travel. Ahead of us is the glistening thread of a stream that has risen from the foothills. It's a good place to pause and dismount. The rippling water is beautiful, singing as it makes its way. It is so clear that I can see small fish darting about in its waters, and downstream where it flows through some stones, two small brown birds are playing. They flutter their wings on top of one of the stones, then leap off to disappear beneath the surface. A moment later they pop up again, water insects in their beaks.

Our two horses are not just drinking the water. They are also observing the birds' purposeful play, seeming to get as much pleasure out of it as Hussein and I are getting as we sit with our feet in the cool, running flow.

"It would be a good thing to be able to just sit here and watch all day, would it not, habibi?"

"Someday," I say, "I hope." Meaning it, but also not entirely sure that such a someday will ever come for us.

We mount and start off again. We can't afford to pause long. If what the Dreamer told us is true, based on his best guesses, we have no more than two or three days before the swarm will emerge. Best to get there as early as possible.

Our four-legged allies move with such power, such grace and speed, that at times it seems as if we are not moving but the land itself is flowing past us. We're crossing distances in half a day that would have taken me three or four days to cover—even at that consistent loping run that Uncle Chatto taught me.

It's early evening, the sun still two hands above the horizon and we've arrived on the hill whose height allow us to look down across the entire abandoned field. Below us loom the shapes of rusting metal that once were giant harvesting machines and the long pipes that once sprayed artificial rain down onto the earth. Those machines are surrounded on all sides by the thick tangles of dry brush. Everything is quiet—outwardly.

But not inside my head, where I am receiving an urgent wordless message from Striped Horse.

She can smell them. Beneath the earth, beginning to move.

How long? I think back to her.

Again, I sense her message. Though not in human words, it's "felt" to me in a way that I can understand.

Soon. One more dawn.

"Tomorrow," I say to Hussein. "Striped Horse can sense that."

He nods to me. "Star tells me the same. A busy night ahead, yes?"

Yes, I think, as I reach out to take his hand and squeeze it hard. We have a lot of work to do, but at least we'll be doing it together.

CHAPTER FOURTEEN
A Burning Question

I f you are stable and strong, it will be the same whether your eyes are open or closed.

That's something Uncle Chatto taught me. He learned it from another of the men in their Special Assignments company back when he and Dad were serving as soldiers, being dropped at night into the middle of conflict zones, each man gliding down on black parawings carrying enough weaponry to wipe out a hundred times their number.

Chan, the man who taught him that ancient Taoist saying, was from the North Asia Fed, what used to be a bunch of different countries back in the twenties. I can still list some of their names—Korea, Mongolia, China, Siberia—though maybe that last one wasn't a country but part of something else.

Not that any of that matters. It's just typical of the random thoughts running like crazy squirrels through a tree in my head as we sit here waiting, me outwardly calm but actually a bundle of nerves, Hussein breathing easy, his back leaning against mine. I can't see him because he's behind me, but I know there's a peaceful expression on his face.

"When I am with you," he said, "my spirit is calm."

Wish I could say the same. His being with me is reassuring on one level. Having a real partner is an amazing thing. But it also means that I am that much more worried about his well-being. I can't let anything happen to him.

I turn around toward him. He does the same, smiling back over his shoulder. He looks as if he just put on a freshly pressed uniform. I think he could crawl on his belly for a mile and still end up with a crease in his pants and not a speck of dirt on his sleeves—even though he would still be brushing them off. I think his being caked in mud by that giant eel was almost a worse experience for him than when his little finger was cut off at Haven as punishment for singing a song that was interpreted as subversive—a song that was meant for me.

We're back on the hilltop where we first looked down on the field. We're dressed in black from head to foot, partly by choice and partly because that's the only color available of the thin, flexible body armor we're wearing. It's light and soft as silk, but will immediately harden like steel against any impact.

Striped Horse and Star are standing close by, one on either side of us. They're as awake as we are—maybe more. Their senses are incredible. Seeing, hearing, smelling . . . the world is one huge tapestry of experiences for them, their big brains taking it all in, never being overwhelmed.

The sun has already appeared over the wide desert land, risen to the height of one hand as Hussein knelt and offered the prayers he makes at the start and end of each day in that sunrise direction, his musical voice offering praise and thanks to the Creator of all.

The scent of waking has been rising from sage and rabbit-brush, the first birds have already made their twittering greeting of the dawn, and . . .

The message our horses send reaches us. I start to stand up and feel Hussein doing the same behind me. One of the cans we brought with us, empty now, clanks as I accidentally kick it to one side, the faint scent of the accelerant we carefully poured from it reaching my nose.

"It's time," Hussein and I both say at the same moment.

Star nudges his head against Hussein's back. Hussein kisses me on the forehead as he squeezes my hand one more time.

"Allah be with you," he says. He vaults onto Star's back. The two of them head for the eastern side of the field, where he'll start his half of the fire at the same time I light mine.

As I climb onto Striped Horse and we gallop toward the western edge of the field, I think about the work we did last night to get ready, hoping that what we've done will succeed.

It was not an easy job, chopping brush with the machetes

we'd brought, forcing our way through the dry tangle throughout the night. We couldn't have done it, had Star and Striped Horse not gone ahead of us, smelling out the imagoes under the soil, making sure we were directly over the top of each of the buried members of the swarm as we poured the accelerant, a special chemical many times more volatile than gasoline, able to burn and keep burning even longer than napalm. We would not have had enough to soak each spot and then make a trail of flammable liquid from one to the next, were it not for the gasoline already there in the fields in the airtight tanks of those abandoned harvest machines. The wrenches we'd brought with us proved adequate to open the drain valves under the tanks.

When we were done and had climbed again to the hilltop, the moon had been bright enough for us to see the pattern made by our efforts at cutting and matting down. It reminded me once again just how whimsical and insane our Overlords had been. Visible from our hilltop are the shapes of two letters, a gigantic *R* and an equally large *M*. The letters were large enough to be seen from space, if we still had contact with a landsat from our electrified past.

After seeing the Dreamer's book of monsters, I had no doubt about the meaning of those letters. R. Mawaba, self-published author and insane Overlord, had sown his last generation of gemods in the pattern of his own initials.

I'm counting as I ride, my usual one and one pony. When

I get to sixty, I'll touch a match to the well-soaked pile of brush at the edge of the field and watch the trail of flames shoot forward, making Mawaba's self-aggrandizing signature a funeral pyre from which no phoenixes will rise. Or so I hope. Will it work? That's the burning question.

We reach the western edge at fifty and one pony. I slide off Striped Horse's back, kneel, take out the box of matches, and strike the first one. It breaks in half, doesn't ignite. I try another, with the same result. The matches are all wet. The lid of my canteen wasn't tight. The box of matches was at the bottom of my pack, where that water dribbled down.

Lozen, why didn't you tighten that canteen? Why didn't you put the matchbox into a plastic bag?

But wait, I have flint and steel. I can strike a spark with them. Except, as I search my pack, I can only find the steel striker, not the flint. And there are no stones around me that might serve as a substitute. Only sand.

Hussein has no such problems. He has a lighter, the one he used to light the fuse when we blew up the dam. I don't see flames rising yet from the far side of the field where he is. Maybe it's because he senses I'm having a problem. But he can't help me. He has to light his side and retreat from the inferno that will erupt when the brush catches.

I feel something. A soundless call echoes inside my mind and sends a shiver down my back. A cold, hungry cry, answered by another and another and another. The voices of the vampire locusts calling one another, ready to emerge and feed, clawing their way up through the soil to emerge into the silver-hazed sunlight of the new day. Soon their talons and their heads will emerge. They'll spread their wings and fly.

I've got to light this fire. But how? How? Why am I so stupid? How did I get us into this mess?

Speaking of fire, my hands are feeling hotter than they've ever felt before. They tremble as I hold them up, feel the threads of power coursing through my fingers, feel the presence of so many enemies, such terrible hunger. And then suddenly there's a pain in the center of my forehead, and I hear a voice.

Strike!

Without thinking, I strike my hands together. A spark leaps from between my palms onto the oil-soaked pile of brush, setting it afire.

I don't have time to think about what just happened or how it happened. There's only time to leap on the back of Striped Horse and ride. A small wind has come up and is blowing right into the roaring flames, making them move faster, hotter. And even though the fire is moving away from me, I feel its growing heat at my back as I ride.

Striped Horse and I reach the hilltop just as Hussein is arriving from the opposite direction on Star, a look of concern on his face. Just as I had suspected, my anxiety over the soaked matches had been transmitted to him.

"What was wrong?" he asks, sliding off Star's back and

reaching up to grasp my hand—which is cool now, no longer feeling as if it is about to burst into flame. "What happened?"

No time to explain that now—as if I could explain what just happened. Lozen, the human torch?

"It's all right," I say. "We did it."

The field is fully ablaze now. The crackling roar of the fire is filling the air. Half a mile away, we can feel its heat.

"There!" Hussein says.

Something is rising up from the burning field, a winged creature. It's larger than we'd expected, the size of Striped Horse. And now I hear its voice as it hovers, its wings scattering embers and bits of burning brush.

SCREEE! SCREE! SCREE!

I pick up one of the several loaded rifles, a scoped 30.06. We'd placed them at intervals along the hilltop, just in case. Next to me Hussein is doing the same. But when I find the vampire locust in my scope, some of the anxiety leaves me. It's blackened and still burning, its gauzy wings are starting to wither, and then it falls back to thud down into the inferno.

The same thing is happening all over the field. More and more of the creatures are giving off that earsplitting scree as they try to take flight and fail. Only a few rise up—no more than a few yards—before the heat and flame take their toll. The accelerant we poured soaked far enough through the soil to reach them and make them highly flammable as soon as they reached the air and were touched by the super-hot blaze.

Our plan has worked.

Suddenly, out of the corner of my eye, I see Striped Horse rearing up to my left at the same time as a message from her mind reaches me.

Danger here!

I turn just in time to see a flying nightmare diving down at us like a missile. A missile with clawed front legs like scythes, a black, gaping mouth, and angry red eyes.

SCREEK!

BLAM! BLAM! BLAM!

Two of Hussein's shots missed. But the third one hit the monster locust between its eyes. Convulsing in death, its wings fold, and it crashes down beside us.

It wasn't on fire, I'm thinking as I sweep my eyes across the sky to see if more are coming.

Yup. More are coming.

CHAPTER FIFTEEN

A Hand Out

Luther sucked the last of the spider's toxin from the poison sac he'd cut out of the creature's head. Its odiferous meat was not attractive. Ah, but its venom was quite another thing. He licked his lips, savoring the burning taste of it on his tongue.

He felt rather grateful to the deceased web spinner. He'd been in need of a distraction. Something to distance him from the troubling memories coming with such intense insistence.

Thinking of distractions, where had his metal hand gone? Torn free during the brief combat. Yes, he remembered seeing it bouncing off down the slope to his left.

He began to search as the morning sun moved across the sky. Another man might have given up, but Luther was never one to leave a task half done. He only paused briefly to observe that a pillar of black smoke was rising far off to his west beyond the plain and the several ranges of hills that rose in that direction. More than fifty, less than a hundred miles away. Curious. But not his immediate concern.

The smoke had vanished and the sun was in the zenith of the silvery sky when he located his missing artificial addition wedged at the bottom of a deep crevice . . . well beyond his reach. Not that it would have mattered if he could have retrieved it. Though it was some sixty feet below, the sunlight penetrated well enough that he could see that the steel hand had been damaged past the point of usefulness.

Luther sat back. Alas. But the fight with the big spider, brief as it was, had been a satisfying experience. Unconsciously, forgetting that there was no hand at the end of his right arm, he reached up to stroke his chin—to no effect.

Which led to his looking down at his terminated limb, where he noticed a tingling feeling. A result of the spider's venom? Or just his body's uncanny ability to heal almost any wound? In the past, he'd recovered from injuries that would have terminated the existence of any other human. But not him. That was why he was known as Four Deaths.

Or should it now be Five Deaths? No, Four had a better ring to it. But it did make him wonder about the substances that had been pumped into his body during those previous resurrections. Were they merely human stem cells? Or had they come from some other nonmammalian source? No matter. The result was what counted. And now the result of that infusion of nonhuman genetic material was becoming evident and moving at an accelerated rate. Until now, the regeneration had been hidden within the cup of that lost steel hand.

But no longer. Small as yet, only partly formed, unfolding itself from the site of severance was a new right hand.

As he studied that pleasing sight of regenerating digits, palm, and wrist, it came to him that he was intensely hungry. Was it from the recent struggle and ensuing search or his body's increased efforts at regeneration? In any event, he was in need of nourishment. Though it would take him in the wrong direction and delay his mission a bit more, one or two animals from that small herd of mule deer he had glimpsed back to the east would certainly provide an adequate repast.

The wind had been in Luther's favor as he stalked up on the herd in the box canyon. It was strong enough to carry his scent away from the deer, but not so strong that it affected the flight of his lethal darts. No need to use his rifle since he had been able to approach so closely. Plus, a bullet's tearing passage through the body could spoil some of the meat—especially the heart, Luther's favorite part of any being he killed. As always, his poison was quickly effective. The two that were struck, a yearling buck and a fat doe, bounded only a few times before collapsing, froth coming from their mouths.

Luther loosened his knife from its sheath as he came upon them. He touched the larger deer on its chest, feeling the heartbeat slow and then stop.

It was the time when his ancestors would have thanked the animal's spirit for giving its body. Offered a gift of tobacco.

Not something that Luther did. Instead, he opened the deer from chest to rectum, being careful not to puncture its stomach and intestines before pulling them out. He located the liver and then the heart. Placed them next to each other on the deer's warm side.

"Good," he said, flicking the blood from his blade. Then he picked up the liver and began to eat.

He'd finished the liver and was about to start on the heart when he heard the old man's voice.

"Hey! Hey, heyyy? Lookee here!"

Blood dripping down his chin, his hands red with the deer's blood, Luther turned to look.

An elderly man, his skin brown, his limbs emaciated, his long hair matted, and his black eyes as bright as dark flames, was squatting a stone's throw away, motioning to him.

How did this old fogey manage to creep up without me hearing him? And why does he look so familiar?

Luther felt confused. Then he wondered why he simply felt confused and did not take any logical action, such as killing the old bastard.

But before Luther could explore that thought further, the old man spoke again, his voice an insistent whine.

"Hey, got some for me? Just a little for me. Gimme a hand out. Me hungry."

Luther picked up the heart. He almost threw it to the old man before stopping himself.

Why did I almost do that? he thought.

"Share, right? You want share?" The old man had somehow moved closer, so close that Luther could smell him, a rank scent like musky fur. It made Luther's head spin.

Luther shook his head.

"No," he said. Then wondered why he said even that. Why didn't he just get rid of the old beggar?

"We talk before. You remember?"

Luther shook his head again.

"Okeydokey. No problem. Jes gimme heart, and I leave you 'lone." The old man was close, too close. His two hands were resting on the deer. His breath was in Luther's face.

Luther opened his eyes and closed them. A memory was coming to him and with it a rising anger. He knew and did not know who this was, this old man. He lifted his knife.

"I give you this!" Luther said, thrusting hard at the old man's chest. But his knife met no resistance. In fact, it was suddenly gone from his hand.

"Good gift."

Luther looked up. The old man was back where he'd been when Luther first saw him. In his left hand was the deer's heart. In his right was Luther's beautiful knife.

"Bye-bye now," the old man said. He no longer looked so skinny and raggedy. His hair shone now. He turned, dropped to all fours, and was gone. Along with Luther's favorite blade.

Luther shook his head, trying to clear it from what felt like cobwebs inside his mind. What had just happened? Was it real, or was he just imagining it?

"Heyyyy!"

The old man's voice came from somewhere farther off, almost a howl. Luther raised his head and his rifle at the same time. But he could see nothing to aim at, even though the coyote voice that came reverberating down the canyon was as clear and ringing as a bell.

"Don't forget your suuuunkaaa."

And then, except for what kept echoing inside Luther's mind, all was silent.

CHAPTER SIXTEEN

Seven to Go

Seven. That's how many big bugs are dropping out of the sky with earsplitting cries.

SCREEK! SCREEK! SCREEK!

POW!

Well, actually six, now that I have ventilated the head of the one heading for me.

None are trying to fly away even though retreat might be prudent on their parts, considering the fact that . . .

BLAMBLAM!

. . . thanks to Hussein's next two shots, another vampire locust has tumbled to the ground.

Five left.

The lure of our warm bodies is attracting them. As Mawaba's book said—they're unable to resist the heat signature of a human.

However, the humans meant to have been gemod fodder would not have been armed with high-powered rifles.

KA-CHUNK! KA-THUD KA-THUD-KA-THUD!

Or accompanied by a large, hooved ally adept at delivering lethal kicks followed by thorough trampling of said battered buggie.

Four to go.

Unable to resist the prospect of having us for breakfast, they continue screeking and coming—and falling as we keep firing.

POW!

Three.

BLAM!

Two.

The last is knocked from the air by Star as he leaps, spins in midair, and hits the final flying horror's brain box with his hind hooves. Yellow ichor flies from the crunching impact.

The four of us stand there. Well, actually only Hussein and I are standing there. Star and Striped Horse are busy trampling the broken bodies of those deceased immense insects into locust pancakes. Our equine allies are not taking a chance on any of those critters rising up to attack or escape.

It may be that they are just being thorough. But from what I caught from my reading of Striped Horse's mental emotions, it's also that they were quite irritated by those screeking cries—which hurt their ears and pissed them off. Poor sensitive horsies.

I look across the field. The smoke rising from the burning brush and barbecued behemoth bugs is starting to diminish. The wind brings us the unpleasant scent left by the accelerant and charred locust flesh. I'm glad we're half a mile away. Any closer and I'd be choking from the stench.

There's nothing living left on that field except for ashes swirling in the heat. Our plan was effective. But not totally so. How did these eight escape to attack us?

Hussein has heard my thought. "There," he says, nodding as he brushes a glob of yellow locust ichor from his forehead.

The place he's indicating is to the right of the immense initials, still visible since the gasoline and accelerant made their shapes burn longer and deeper than the brush around them. It is a vertical line that we missed, a place where we did not pour either accelerant or gasoline just outside the burned area.

I see that line because of the way the earth was churned up there by the eight ravenous arthropods maddened by our scent. It's not just a line. It is an example of how insane and self-centered the Mawabas of our world were in the pre-Cloud days.

Meant to be visible after those initials *R* and *W*, the shape made by their emergence is that of a large exclamation point.

CHAPTER SEVENTEEN
Watching Us

We are halfway back to our valley when I sense it. Something or someone is watching us. But the hair on the back of my neck isn't standing up as it does when such perusal has my terminated existence as its eventual goal.

I can see him out of the corner of my left eye. Funny how I expected just that, expected him.

I look over at Hussein, who's busy trying to scrape yellow locust blood off his shirtsleeve—to little avail. The stuff dried on and into the fabric not covered by our protective vests, from which the ichor quickly flaked off.

"This was my favorite shirt," Hussein says, a rueful smile on his lips. "It was not meant to be polka-dotted."

"Better their guck than our blood corpuscles," I reply. "And you have other shirts."

"True," he says. "As always, you are right."

Five of the most romantic words any girl would want to hear from her guy.

I lean close, but the kiss I plant on his cheek is not my sole motive for this moment of intimacy.

"We're being watched," I whisper.

Hussein nods. "Also true. I first saw him a mile or so back. Not the big djinn, but the smaller hairy one, I believe. Are you going to try to talk with him?"

As if I had a choice.

"I suppose."

I pat Striped Horse on her left shoulder. She stops so I can dismount. Hussein rides on a bit farther. Then he and Star pause next to an ocotillo, its tall, slender, upright branches bursting with red blossoms. Bees are buzzing around those flowers, and he leans forward to watch them as I walk off the trail to what looks like a convenient fallen log and sit.

Waiting. But not for long.

I feel his breath on the back of my neck, and my nose catches the scent of the raw meat he's been eating. I am pretty sure that anyone else would have jumped. Probably what he wanted. But I don't give him the satisfaction of thinking he's crept up on me without my even noticing till he was inches away—which is true.

"Ba'cho," I say.

"Hey, hey, heyy, you know my name, Little Girl!"

I turn slowly to look at him. He's not as close as when I first felt him breathing on me—he's at the far end of this twenty-foot log. He looks the same as when he took on human form to trick me out of that wild pig I'd killed to feed my family. His appearance is that of a scrawny old man wearing a dirty fur cap with ears on it and a torn leather loincloth. He's barefoot, though, not wearing the boots he made from the skin of that giant Gila monster I dispatched.

I look down at his feet, whose toes have brown, broken nails resembling those of other members of the dog family, and raise one eyebrow quizzically.

"Me got hungry," he says. "Ate them boots."

I believe it. One thing to count on about Old Man Coyote: His appetite drives him to consume just about anything.

"Got food?" he says.

I have to smile. I slip the pack off my back, reach into it, and pull out a large piece of deer jerky.

Just like that, without my seeing him move, he is right next to me with his hand held out palm up. I quickly drop the dried deer flesh into his hand. Polite as he's being at the moment, the way his eyes widened when that meat came into view tells me he is only a split second away from snapping it out of my hand—and maybe taking a few fingers with it.

The jerky vanishes down his gullet in one gulp. He licks his lips with a tongue much too long for a human mouth.

Old Man Coyote nods, then belches loudly. "Good," he

says. "Little Girl, you got good manners. Me like you. Here. Present for you."

I haven't seen him pick it up or pull it out from behind his back, but a knife is in his left hand, and he's holding it out to me handle first. I know that big blade.

"Four Deaths's knife," I say.

"Was," Old Man Coyote said, chuckling softly. "Then he give it me, fair and square. Now me give it you."

I take the knife. It's not wise to accept things offered by the Trickster. But then again, it's more unwise to refuse.

"Can I ask where you saw him?"

"Sure. Ask."

"Where did you see him?"

"Somewhere."

Right. I try, with only limited success, not to growl under my breath.

Calm, Lozen. Just try again from another direction.

"When did you see him?"

"Before now."

He is enjoying this far too much. I find myself wondering again if, despite their being obviously different species, he and Hally are cousins.

I take a breath and start to count to ten. I get up to seven and one pony when he takes pity on me.

"Me just tease you, Little Girl. Him that way, off sunrise way. Three days' travel—if you travel human being way."

Three days, I think. *Too close.*

Coyote grins, a grin that shows far more teeth than should fit into any anthropoid mouth. "No worry so much, Little Girl. Him come slow. Me give him something to think about."

"Thank you," I say.

"No problema. Got more that deer meat?"

Holding Little Wound's oversize knife in my right hand, I dig into my pack with my left and extricate a second piece of the cured venison that was stuck deeper down. I've taken so long that Coyote's long-nosed snout is right next to my hand as I pull out the dried piece of meat. Fully in his animal shape, he snaps the jerky from my fingers, spins, and disappears into the brush—a shadow scattered by the sunlight.

As always, I am left feeling just a little disoriented. But I guess that is normal when dealing with the paranormal that has become part of my everyday life lately. Uncle Chatto used to warn me that whenever you shake hands with Coyote— whatever shape he might take—you should always make sure to count your fingers afterward. So I look at both my hands.

Yup, the usual ten fingers are still in place.

I reach into my pouch and take out a pinch of pollen.

"Thank you," I say. "I guess."

And even though I'm semiprepared for it, I still jump when a loud answering howl comes out of the nearby brush, followed by a very human chuckle.

CHAPTER EIGHTEEN

You and Your Dog

L uther had not moved. The darkness had come again. The moon had risen. Full now.

Luther was sitting the way he'd been taught by Kobiyashi, cross-legged in what he'd learned was called the lotus pose. He rested his wrists on his knees, breathed in slowly through his nose, his eyes closed. It was supposed to bring him to a state of consciousness where everything that was troubling or confusing would not vanish—it would just not be.

Then he could be without being. Without thinking. Move with spontaneity and no mind, like the poem Kobiyashi recited to all his students, usually accompanied by a blow with the flat of his sword to their backs or shoulders if he thought they were not listening properly.

The moon reflects itself in the water.
Without thought.

The ten thousand ponds and streams
each contain their own reflection of the moon.
But the moon is unaffected
neither added to
nor subtracted from . . .

WHACK!

The memory of that blow from the sword was as much a part of that poem as the words of it, which were lodged in Luther's mind.

Along with that other memory, which had grown even stronger since the old man had taken his knife.

Luther's fists clenched at the thought of the scruffy old man. From here on in he would not talk, not listen. He would simply kill every old man he met. That was a pleasing thought, but only briefly so as another unbidden image came into his mind—dark eyes looking up at him, trusting him.

The allotted time with the dog had passed quickly.

He'd been reluctant to do as the instructions required in terms of feeding, training, and disciplining the animal. But it had turned out to be so easy. Provide food, provide water, be consistent with words, signals, and rewards, and the creature would become a useful tool for you.

His only deviation, his only rebellion—Luther being Luther, such rebellion was natural—was in his naming of the animal that grew larger, more agile, stronger as the days turned into weeks. His dog that he did not call "Dog" as he had been told to do. He called him "Sunka," one of the few old words he knew from the language his ancestors spoke. That was the name he used, though he spoke it quietly under his breath, quickly followed by a louder "Dog" for the benefit of anyone else who might walk in and overhear.

Luther attempted to be dispassionate about how well the training went, tried not to take an inordinate amount of pleasure from it.

There was, after all, no need to like having this companion that was, though living and breathing, no more than a tool—like a well-made weapon such as a sharp, perfectly balanced knife or a well-oiled gun. No need to feel gratified at the way it readily does your bidding. No need to enjoy tossing a stick and having it eagerly returned to you. No need to feel pleased at the way it answers to you and no other, growls when other humans come too close, but sits quietly at a simple hand signal. No need to allow it to crawl onto your narrow cot and place its head on your chest. No need to appreciate the feel of its soft fur beneath your palm, its warm body pressed against you. No need to love it.

The eight trainees stood once again on the red line, backs straight, eyes forward, their dogs sitting at each trainee's side.

Sergeant Barker had walked down the line, nodding as he passed each young man and his animal.

"Good," Barker had said. "So far."

He turned and walked up the line, stopping now and then to snap his fingers or clap his hands. None of the dogs moved from their positions, perfectly following the commands each had been given to SIT, STAY, FREEZE.

"Very good." A wide smile crossed Barker's round, pleasant face.

"Your dogs have passed. Now it is your turn."

He walked over to the lanky ginger-haired boy named Red, leaned close, and whispered in Red's ear. Out of the corner of his eye, Luther saw Red's upper lip tremble as Barker continued to whisper words that Luther could not quite make out.

Barker stepped back. "Now!" he said.

Red made the hand signal for his animal to stand up. "Dog," he said, "heel." Then, his obedient animal trotting by his side, Red walked toward the barn, passed through a partly open door, and disappeared from sight.

Barker nodded, a pleased look on his face.

Too pleased, Luther had thought, realizing at that moment just how repellent he found the sergeant's smooth, even features, his small, round head. He realized for the first time how much he disliked Barker and also realized, though he was not sure how he knew it, that the loathing was mutual.

Barker stepped to the next trainee in line and whispered a second time. This trainee, a stocky boy with East Asian features named Low, showed no emotion as he called his dog to heel and went through that same open door.

A third trainee, a fourth, a fifth. Each followed whatever those instructions were. None of them came back out of the barn.

A sixth.

Am I being saved for last? Luther had thought. A seventh, and he was certain.

Barker stood in front of him.

"Now," Barker said, "it is your turn, trainee."

Luther noticed that Barker was holding his right hand slightly away from his side, his fingers slightly curled. One touch in the right place and he could send a paralyzing jolt of current that would drop Luther to the ground.

"You and your dog. Your Sunka." Barker spoke in a contemptuous tone the name that Luther had secretly given his dog.

Luther realized then how foolish he'd been not to think of the fact that their seemingly private rooms would, of course, have been equipped with sur-tech to pick up every move, every whisper of each of the eight trainees.

I will not make that mistake again, Luther thought, waiting for whatever command the odious man was about to give him.

But Barker was taking his time. Clearly his plan was to enjoy the moment, make Luther squirm.

Luther, however, stood impassively, waiting, willing himself not to twitch a single muscle, not to blink.

A frown came to Barker's face. "You think rules do not apply to you?" he said, his voice louder. "Just because you can make the others cower, you think you are in control. You're a fool, boy."

Barker was close now, so close that as he spoke, spit hit Luther's cheek.

"So here's your command. No need to whisper it since you're the last—the same command I gave every other trainee to test their obedience, to teach them the final rule in this training, the rule that no matter what, they have to follow orders. You will take your dog into the barn. You will sit down behind it, wrap your arm around its neck, and strangle it to death. Your precious Sunka is going to die, and you are going to kill it."

"No," Luther said. "I am going to kill you."

His words were so calm and yet so cold that they made Barker hesitate for a split second before trying to touch his finger to the implant control in his palm.

More than time enough.

Faster than a viper's strike, Luther's right hand had already shot forward, index and middle finger extended and pressed tightly together to penetrate the flesh in the hollow of Barker's throat, curl, and—as Luther pulled back with equal speed—rip out the sergeant's windpipe.

Blood gushing from his neck, an inarticulate gargling coming from his mouth, Barker collapsed to the ground, his feet kicking in the final throes.

Luther knelt and unclipped the lead from Sunka's collar, then unstrapped the collar and tossed it to the side.

"Run," he said, his voice calmly commanding. "Go!"

The big, young dog took off, his long legs carrying him with increasing speed toward the facility fence, which he cleared with one great leap. The guard on the far tower fired twice, but the shots missed, and Sunka vanished among the rocks and trees of the Black Hills.

Luther stood up. He knew that he had not saved the dog's life, merely delayed his death. He would surely eventually come back to the compound looking for Luther. Then he would be shot on sight. But at least he would have enjoyed a brief time of freedom by then.

Luther smiled as he looked down at the body of Sergeant Barker.

It was worth it, he thought.

Then, standing at ease, hands behind his back, he waited for the sound of the gunshots that would kill him. To his surprise, no shots were fired. Instead, four men—all cautious and well-armed—eventually came out of the barn, gesturing for him to hold out his hands to be cuffed.

It turned out that there was not just one way to pass that stage of Force Academy Training. The obedient ones were sent to the Oakland Facility to continue their indoctrination as useful drones. But those rare few, like Luther, who displayed the ability and initiative to kill their instructors (who were, themselves, unaware of this secondary means of passing) were set on another course entirely. It was a training regimen that very few survived, but a course that produced the most lethal of assassins.

And so it was that Luther had found himself in Kobiyashi's gentle hands.

CHAPTER NINETEEN

Questions

'**ve been sitting and looking at my hands for a long time now. I'm up on the point of land we call Place Where Moon Puts Down Her Pack. It's the highest spot in our valley, where the full moon seems to pause as it crosses the sky. From most spots below it looks as if Moon is resting atop this upright slab of rock.

The story that goes with it, because like with all our place names there's always a story, reminds people to focus on what they are supposed to do. A girl bringing back water in a clay jug was distracted by Moon sitting up there. Without looking, she put her jug down on an uneven spot of ground. It fell over and spilled out all the water.

Anytime my mom said the name of this place, it was usually when I was not paying close enough attention to something I was supposed to be doing.

The four of us arrived back at our valley not long after

sunset, our way lit by the full moon—which seems to shine even brighter from the skies since the coming of the Cloud. The Dreamer said it has something to do with the refraction and dispersion of the light—whatever that means.

In real-life terms it means that you can see your way almost as well when the grandmother face of the moon is fully smiling down as by the light of day.

Long ago, Mom says, Sun and Moon were always in the sky at the same time. They moved from north to south. But half the world was always without light. The Holy People changed that. Sun would shine in the day, Moon in the night. Sometimes both can be seen in the sky, greeting each other, but they no longer travel together.

That story makes more sense to me than all the scientific things about Moon that the Dreamer has in his books. Of course, I do know that the moon is another world, a satellite that circles the earth. Back in those not-long-ago days of rocket ships, humans lived up there in four colonies founded by the world corporations. I don't know what happened to them when the Cloud cut off all communication. I am pretty sure they would not have survived if their electricity was blocked as it was here. That makes me a little sad, even if they had no business living up there. So I usually don't think about them.

The moonlight made our travel back here faster than it would have been in the dark. It meant nothing was able to sneak up on us and delay our journey by trying to repurpose us as midnight snacks. Our trip was so uneventful that it seemed a little unreal. Hard to remember any time we've forayed out of our valley without having some sort of beastie introduce itself into our narrative.

It meant that as Striped Horse galloped along, I had time to think. Probably too much time. And all of it was about one thing in particular. One thing that, despite all the weirdness I have more or less gotten used to, was really peculiar.

I think you know what it was: clapping my hands and making a spark shoot out of them. I mean, how did that happen? Sure, I'm glad it happened when it did. But how?

I've tried it a dozen times since then, but no luck. All I've done is make the palms of my hands sore—and break a fingernail. I'm chewing on it now as I ponder the question. Did I get something on my hands that generated the spark?

I've gone over that moment again and again in my mind, replaying the moment like people used to be able to move back the arrow and replay parts of viddys. My memory is really good, and I am sure I am remembering it right.

It was a simple sequence. My matches were wet. I was upset about that and not sure what to do. Then my hands got hot, hotter than they've ever felt before. So hot it was as if I had just laid my palms against a burning log. Then a voice in my head said, *Strike!* And then, as if I knew what I was doing, I struck them together, and this giant spark shot out and lit the trail of gasoline to set my side of the field ablaze.

That's it.

Wet matches.

Upset Lozen saying, *Stupid me.*

Hot palms.

Voice.

Slap.

Spark.

Done.

My confusion made it impossible for me to sleep. I sat up in bed. I must have been tossing and turning, maybe even striking out in my sleep as I do sometimes, because Hussein was awake, too. He had already gotten out of bed and was sitting in our one chair near the fire, rocking quietly and carefully looking nowhere. He didn't look like he had any new bruises on his face or his bare chest, so maybe I hadn't been punching or elbowing him again as I slept.

Our little house is simple. Like the other homes in our valley, it was made from whatever we had available here or from the nearby hills where ponderosa pines grow. It's built like the old-style hogans that Uncle Chatto told me the Navajo ancestors who make up an eighth of my ancestry used to construct.

In fact, as I mentioned earlier, our Navajo friend Tom Yazzie is the one who helped us build our hogan and the others. Tom came with his whole family—a wife, two sisters, and their daughter—and like Uncle Chatto and Dad, Tom had been a soldier. Not only that, he'd been a friend of my dad and Uncle

Chatto. They hadn't heard from him at all after the coming of the Cloud and had assumed he was dead. So when he showed up, my mom greeted him and his family with great warmth as soon as our sentries escorted them in.

"Heard from some Lakotas on special horses you was having a private party here," he said. "No gemods allowed?"

They'd all looked trail-worn, but every one of them was heavily armed—even their seven-year-old daughter. Tom had a field dressing wrapped around his left thigh and limped some as he walked along. As I was taking him to the infirmary, I glanced down at that bandage, which was heavily soaked with blood.

"Had a little argument"—he chuckled—"with something that looked like it was half lizard and half barbed wire fence. Seemed it wanted to borrow my leg for lunch, so I had to resort to a .44-caliber explanation of why I wasn't done using it yet."

Tom Yazzie has been such a great addition to our community. He never seems to stop cracking jokes, but also never seems to stop working—even while he is making everyone around him laugh. And as soon as people do that, he starts laughing, too, which makes his big stomach shake.

"Man," he says, putting both hands on his abdomen, "this is what you call a real belly laugh."

And that makes people laugh even more.

Our home is what Tom calls a female hogan, not the simple "male" one, which is conical and made with three heavy forked poles leaned together and covered with logs, brush, and mud.

"Maybe we call 'em male because they stick up that way, eh?" Tom said after some of those first simple ones were built as temporary shelters.

Our female hogan, being much bigger and stronger built, took a lot longer to make.

"I don't make no jokes about female hogans," he said as we put the final layer of earth on it. "Not when I got a wife and two sisters who might just toss me out of the one they let me live in with them." Then he patted his big stomach. "No way I could survive without them cooking for me, innit? A man has got to know his limitations, eh?"

As far as building fine hogans goes, it seems Tom Yazzie has no limitations. Ours is perfect. Six strong walls of piled stones and logs and a dome-shaped roof also made of logs cribbed together and covered with dirt. A smoke hole in the center of the roof with a fire pit on the floor of hard-packed earth beneath it. Plenty of room inside for our bed, a couple of trunks for us to store our weapons and our clothing (can you guess whose trunk is bigger?), and four shelves to hold books and things for cooking.

We also covered the floor with a beautiful old handwoven Navajo rug that my brother Victor gave us the day after our hogan was completed. He showed up with it rolled up across the back of Spotted Horse—a broad-chested mare that had chosen him as her rider not long after we came back to the valley. He had found it during a foray with some of the other scouts that took them through the ruins of a place called Glendale—close to where my dad told me the city of Phoenix used to be before the war between the Overlords that took place prior to the coming of the Cloud. That rug was the only useful thing to survive inside the crumbled building that had been some sort of store. It had not been burned because it was inside a sort of metal safe used to protect valuable items.

When I asked Victor how he knew that rug was in there—and for that matter how he figured out to open the safe—he simply shrugged.

"I just knew, Big Sister," he replied with a big grin. "I guess you're not the only one in our family who can do things."

The rug showed the bent rainbow image of two of the ones we call the Holy People. Having it on the floor of our hogan has been a double blessing for the way it feels beneath my bare feet and the peace that its image brings me whenever I sit on it and feel the embrace of its healing, gentle, powerful shapes.

It's so comfortable in our lodge. It's cool in the heat of the day and warm at night, and though it took quite a bit of work to make it properly, we were able to complete it in a few days since so many people helped. Because it is covered with dirt and made of stone and thick logs, it is bullet resistant and not easy to burn—unlike the shelters that the people who previously lived here in the valley made—and died in—before we came back here. Our new shelters, and the weapon stashes we have placed at strategic spots around the valley, will make us more secure than those previous unfortunate folks.

But secure and comfortable as the place we share is, tonight when I woke up, I felt as if I had to get outside. Right away.

"Walk?" I said to Hussein.

He nodded, and the two of us set out in the moonlight. I had nowhere in particular in mind. I just needed to move. We passed several sentries as we walked—including my sister Ana, who sleeps even less than I do.

When we came to the base of Place Where Moon Puts Down Her Pack, I knew where I wanted to go. I looked at Hussein, pointed up with my chin. He nodded. Then I started to climb, and he climbed with me.

I'm alone now as I sit here. For a while Hussein stayed up here with me. At first that was what I wanted. I felt comfortable with his arm around me, the two of us watching the moon and feeling grateful to be alive after surviving yet another adventure that could just as well have ended up with both of us dead.

"It is good," he said.

Three words that said so much. And I just replied "Yup," with my usual eloquence. Which was enough for him to understand how much more I meant.

But then the question I had begun pondering as I rode—about what happened and how—started building up in me again, and I felt myself stiffening up between my shoulder blades. That was when Hussein carefully drew his arm back, got up, and climbed back down from the point, so quietly that after his first two steps I didn't hear a thing. He can move quieter than a cat, quiet as a shadow, even when scaling a vertical rock face with only a few handholds at night.

I appreciate so much that he could sense I wanted to be alone. That's another thing about him that makes me wonder why he is so loyal to me. It seems as if I have these moments when I just want to push him away. And instead of getting resentful or asking me why, he just knows what I need, gets up, and quietly walks away. I don't deserve him.

But I will also kick the crap out of anybody or anything that tries to take him away from me. Gemod, human, giant ape-man, or whatever.

"As if I would try," a deep voice says from behind me.

I manage not to jump. Which is good because it would have ended up with me in midair a hundred feet over the extremely rocky slope below Moon's resting place.

"Hally," I growl.

"Pleased to see you, too, Little Food."

Hally's voice has an especially self-satisfied tone tonight. Is it just because, like always, he was able to sneak up on me without my sensing his presence? Or is it something else?

"I thought you weren't going to call me that anymore."

"You did think that," Hally says as he sits down next to me. He is so broad that there is barely enough room for me to stay on the natural seat formed by the stone.

"Yes," Hally says, "it is a bit narrow. Rather hard to believe Moon was able to fit her big butt up here, isn't it?"

No point in asking why he's here. That never gets me anywhere. Nor does it make sense for me to comment on whatever cryptic remark he makes. He'll just come up with something even more obscure.

"I see the moon," he says, "the moon sees me." He pauses. "Does it shine on the one I love?"

Even if I don't say anything, I think. Then I wonder something else. Is that a random song or poem he just quoted? Or is there actually someone else he's thinking of? Some other Bigfoot far away? Except he told me he was the last of his kind. Or did he? And even if he did, can I believe him? Did he ever have a girlfriend or whatever?

"Let us not go there," Hally rumbles. "For now, at least."

Reading my mind, of course. What else is new? Can I just put my fingers in my ears and go, "Lalalalalala!" and both drown him out and keep him out of my head?

You could try.

Never mind.

I could try emptying my mind. Uncle Chatto told me that back in their training days, they had a Japanese martial arts teacher who tried to teach them how to do that, to think of nothing, be nothing, and then become totally at one and thus be more effective as a warrior. To get into that state, they were told to chant a single word again and again, a mantra that would help them find that way of being.

I also remember what else Uncle Chatto told me about that. The trainees were told to choose their own word for that mantra. After he and my father were praised by their teacher for doing better than anyone else at their meditation, they compared notes.

"What word did you choose?" Dad asked.

"Cheeseburger," Uncle Chatto said.

"Me too," Dad replied.

"Wise men, your uncle and father," Hally said.

Okay, so he is totally in my head. And I cannot keep from asking him something.

"Why are you here?"

"Ah, that is a question pondered by all the greatest philosophers of the ages, young Padawan."

I don't ask who or what a Padewan is. But I don't leave it at that. It's like that hangnail of mine I was just chewing on. I can't leave it alone. Maybe if I make the question more specific?

"Why are you here sitting next to me right now?"

"Because I have to be somewhere."

Arrrggggghhhhh!

Hall chuckles, a sound from deep in his chest that sounds like a volcano deciding whether to erupt.

"I do enjoy my conversations with you, Lozen."

He sounds almost sincere. So I reply with just two words. "Thank you."

"Most welcome."

We sit together, both of us looking at the moon. I am starting to actually feel peaceful. Crazy as Hally makes me, his presence makes me feel safe. I can't believe that there's anything in this world that could shake his composure.

"Not exactly," he says. His voice is strangely serious for a moment. "There are things even we, even I worry about."

"Like what?"

"Oh, like how to get blackberry stains out of my fur."

We are back on the road to silly town. So I shut up. If he has something to say, he can say it. Otherwise he can just melt back into the stone or whatever he does and leave me alone.

"It was no accident," he says. "The fire that leaped from your hands. I came to tell you that. It is part of your path to the arrow. Be patient. It will all come to you in its own time."

Not exactly an explanation, but it does make me feel better, even if I have no idea what frigging arrow he is talking about.

I don't intend to say anything else. Apparently neither does he. I sit there enjoying his company. Then I sense him starting to withdraw. Turn my head, he won't be there.

So I do say something after all.

"Hally, is there anything you came to warn me about?"

His voice is no longer close to me when he replies, which is strange considering how narrow this point of stone is up here.

"I might caution you to beware the Ides of March," he rumbles, "but it didn't do any good for the last person I told that to. Poor Caesar. So I will leave you with this wee bit of advice—keep your eyes on the skies."

What?

He laughs. It's a deep, growling laugh filled with something more than just amusement, the sort of laugh a father might make while watching his children try to do something they are not quite prepared for yet. That laugh fades away into the distance, and I am left sitting there all alone with everything except my thoughts. Which are much more company than I want right now.

Keep your eyes on the skies?

CHAPTER TWENTY
Look Up

Morning. That's how some of our stories begin. Just the one word that means "dawn." And that is what comes through the open door of our lodge as I look up. Sun is beginning to show his face above the cliffs that circle our valley like sheltering arms.

Long ago, my mother said, there was no such thing as morning. There was no light and no earth. There was nothing but Darkness, Water, and Great Wind. There were no fishes, no animals, no plants. There were only the Hactin, who were the powers of all the natural forces. They were here from the beginning of the beginning.

Those Hactin, they made Earth, made Earth in the shape of a living woman facing upward. They made Sky, made Sky in the shape of a man facing downward. Sky, he is our father. Earth, she is our mother.

Our people were there then, dwelling under the Earth

where all was dark. We were not yet flesh and blood. We lived in a dream in that place where everything was holy.

The first ones to be shaped and walk on the earth were the animals and the birds. They were shaped by the one some of our people call Black Hactcin. When that was done, those creatures had a meeting.

They told Black Hactcin that they were lonely. They needed companionship. They gathered together all sorts of pollen, clay, abalone shell, white stone, turquoise, jet, red stone, and other stones. They asked Black Hactcin to use those items to make a human being in the shape of Black Hactcin's own body.

I'm thinking about that story of the time before light as I look out the door of our hogan at dawn. Was it all in balance back then in that world? That world when the animals asked that we humans be made? That world where they wanted us for companionship and there were no gemod creatures?

But even as I ask myself that question I know the answer, that it was not perfect then. For things went wrong in that First World. The animals and people had to leave there and emerge into the world of light where there was a sun. And just like us today, human beings suddenly found themselves in a world where there were monsters that wanted to destroy us. And as I've mentioned before, if it were not for the Hero Twins, Killer of Enemies and Child of Water, those awful giant creatures might have succeeded.

I suppose it has always been that way. We cannot expect

the world to be perfect. Things will always change, and there will always be challenges. I have to face that simple fact.

It's another day on this earth, a day into which Hussein and I are going to head out once again. We'll be looking for the one who is after us—well, me in particular. Except we, too, will be hunting—just doing so while pretending to be the prey.

How, you might ask, do I intend to do that? To which I reply, have you forgotten about my Power—or that the assassin who wants my head has a similar ability to touch another's thoughts, to hunt not just with his eyes and ears, but with his mind? I think I can turn that ability of his against him.

When I fought him the first time, I never had time to use my mind against his. I relied on my physical skills and my weapons. He attacked, and I dodged that big knife of his—which now hangs at my side.

Though Hussein and I are leaving our hogan at dawn on what appears to be a peaceful day, we both throw on the various belts and harnesses for our sidearms, ammo, and assorted cutlery. My .357. His favorite .44. My bowie knife and new big blade. Hussein's half dozen throwing knives and favorite eighteen-inch-long scimitar. Nothing extravagant, mind you. Just a few of the necessities to match a modern couple's casual wear. After all, in these PC times you never know when you might have to entertain company.

I've had plenty of time to think back on my encounter with

Four Deaths. Though he did not succeed in killing me, I might have done better. Even when I half-blinded him and cut off his hand, he never lost his composure, his certainty that I could not stop him.

Maybe he was right. If it had not been for the gemod creature Tahhr, that strange being that was a mix of human and ape and cat, Luther Little Wound might have won. Even after being hit center mass with a .357 slug, losing an eye and his right hand, the last thing he did was raise one of his blowgun tubes to his mouth, about to shoot a poison dart at me. Only Tahhr's sudden attack that took both of them over the cliff edge ended our encounter.

Thinking back, I see there was something at the back of my mind as we fought, as Luther answered every move I made with ironic comments.

In retrospect, I now realize that I wasn't just hearing the words of Four Deaths out loud—voiced in that deep, surprisingly pleasant voice of his—I was also listening to his thoughts. And those thoughts were not as sure as his spoken words. I've been thinking about it even more since my vision told me that he was still alive and placed me briefly in his head as he was being sent out on his mission by the Jester.

There's a seed of something deep in the mind of Luther Little Wound. Beneath that deadly surface of competence, of cold focus and self-confidence, there's a flaw. It may seem that nothing can shake him. But I felt something. I can't quite describe what it is, not yet. But I know it's there, and perhaps can be used against him. Not just with physical weapons, but with my Power. I'll be probing for that hidden weakness when next we meet.

When, not if.

An hour has passed. I'm sitting alone in one of my favorite lookout spots high on a tower of stone near the southern cliff face. My hands are tingling. I look down from my perch—I can see half our valley from up here. Nothing seems unusual. Just people starting their morning. Some bringing food and wood to their cooking fires. There's always a lot to eat. Not just our corn and beans and sunflowers and squash and melons and the game animals we hunt. There's all sort of plants to gather. Although the Sonoran desert might look bleak to people who've never relied on it, there's food to be found at different times of the year. In spring and summer there are all sorts of edible roots, wild potatoes, and wild onions, and lots of different berries. The hearts of the spiky agave plants can be roasted in earth pits. When it gets to be fall, we'll be able to gather the nuts of the piñon pine.

Right now, what's drifting up to me is the scent of a stew that has been sweetened with the dried leaves and flowers of the yucca that Mom and Ana and I gathered in the spring.

I look farther along the valley to a group of people working together with Tom Yazzie on the construction of a new hogan.

Peaceful, everywhere peaceful. It's hard to believe that anything could break the peace and calm of this place I love.

However, I also see Hussein. He's sitting cross-legged at the foot of my tower, cradling a rifle he must have brought from our lodge while I was up here buried in thought.

The fact that he has that weapon with him—and that leaning next to him is my own favorite scoped 30.06 rifle—makes me feel concerned. I've observed lately that Hussein seems to also have some Power of his own that alerts him to incipient danger. He raises a hand to signal that he's seen me looking. With a second open-palmed gesture, he signals that he hasn't actually seen any problem yet. At least not with his eyes.

Lozen!

The urgent voice that has just touched my mind is not Hussein's. It's my brother Victor. Like Ana, he's gotten better lately at sending and receiving mental messages.

Look up!

I do that—just in time.

CHAPTER TWENTY-ONE
Kill Something

badly need, Luther thought, *to kill something.*

Perhaps that would get him out of this state of mind. His meeting with that scrawny old man had made him feel uncharacteristically confused. So confused that, after a long day of steady travel alternating between a fast walk and a loping run, he realized as the next day's sun rose that he had been heading not toward the west but east.

He would have to backtrack at double time. Quite disgruntled, he sat down cross-legged. He needed to think. What did he need to help him out of this frustrated state of mind?

Killing? Yes. That will help me feel better. It has been too long since I've taken a life. How long? Who or what was the last one?

Sergeant Barker, that was it.

"NO!"

Luther shouted the word out loud. Then he shook his head. The vision had come again during the night and ended at the moment his curved fingers ripped the windpipe from the odious officer's throat, Luther's eyes focused on the heavily muscled body of Shunka as he leaped the fence.

But that was long years ago. Lives and deaths ago—his own and those of so many others.

Luther grasped his head with both hands—the normal one on his left, the still-growing six-fingered one on his right that was now as large as that of a child.

What was the last life he had taken? He looked at his new hand with its additional digit, and a small smile curved across his lips.

The spider. I drank its venom. Yes. That was it.

And as the image of the dying, legless arachnid blossomed in his mind, so did the memory of the bodies of the others he'd terminated during his lethal career. One after another, a long cascade of mental images.

Ahhh.

It was almost as satisfying as killing Barker had been in his most recent dre—no, vision of that ultimate day of his team training. He lifted his right hand, drew it back through his hair, enjoying the feeling of those small, new fingers against his scalp.

Chikak-chikak-chikak-chikak

The faint clatter of clawed legs scuttling across the rocks

brought Luther out of his pleasant reverie. He dropped his hands from his forehead and looked up.

Scorpions. There were four of them. They were outsized creatures—but not all that gigantic. The biggest one's body was no larger than that of a wild pig.

They'd paused a few yards away when he lifted his head. Now they spread out to form a circle around him, their claws raised, pincers open, their fang-tipped tails coiled over their backs and dripping venom onto the limestone that hissed and smoked each time a drop fell.

Luther felt the touch of their self-satisfied thoughts—rather like spiderwebs—across the inside of his forehead.

Ha, they were thinking. *We have you, kill you, eat you.*

Luther remained in his cross-legged position. He opened his arms wide.

"Welcome, friends," he said. "So nice to see you."

The white muscle flesh inside their tails turned out to be rather tasty, especially when seasoned with a few drops of the poison from the glands at the end.

The rest of their poison, however, went unharvested. He was sated and had nothing in which to collect it.

So sad to waste such good venom, Luther thought.

First the spider, then these fine fellows. This was turning out to be somewhat of an arthropod adventure. Each with its own unique mix of lethality.

Alas, nothing to be done about that now.

Next time, he'd remember to bring some empty containers to harvest from whatever poisonous creature he might encounter. Though rather than berating himself for negligence, he knew that the actual blame for his embarking poorly equipped rested on the shoulders of his employer. That did indeed irk the durable assassin.

The Jester had allowed him but brief access to the materials he had left stored at Haven. Yet another reason to make the Jester's final painful moments of breath stretch out when Luther had completed his task. A life for the taking of a life.

Then, perhaps, he would set up two sharpened stakes—no, three. So that the craniums of Lozen and the Jester and Lady Time might quietly contemplate one another until the flesh rotted from their skulls.

A sound from overhead drew Luther's attention. He looked up, and what he saw made him purse his lips in displeasure. They were quite a distance above, but the sight from his single remaining orb of vision was keen enough for him to discern what it was.

Clearly one of the innovations from the desperate scientists in Lady Time's workshop. Moving along quite rapidly, keeping the wind at its back as the legs of the men on the attached bicycles churned away to spin the propeller.

Luther thought of taking a shot or two at them with his handgun. But they were probably too far above. Rifles with high-powered scopes had never been Luther's favorite. He so much preferred killing at close range. But for just a moment he rather wished he had one of those long guns.

He had no doubt where they were heading. This was Lady Time's flighty notion to beat the Jester—and his assassin—to the punch. Flighty indeed.

How unfair, Luther thought.

Then he smiled as he considered the possibility that had certainly not been in the mind of that elegant madwoman with her chronometric mask.

Taking into account who they were going up against, their victory was far from certain.

CHAPTER TWENTY-TWO

Sneak Attack

What is swooping down toward me from a hundred or so yards away seems at first to be a bug-eyed, bat-winged creature. It takes me less than a split second to realize that it's a man in goggles a little like my own, strapped into some sort of winged contraption designed purely for gliding.

My mind is working so fast that in another microsecond I'm also able to ponder just where he's glided down from—since I'm at the highest point for miles around—before my eyes catch sight of the huge black shape hundreds of feet above him and recognize it as a blimp.

I also, in that same split, split second, know just whose blimp that is. I mean who else would have an ornate *L.T.* emblazoned in silver on its ebony side with a clockface painted next to it?

Lest you think I have been paralyzed by this ominous set

of sights, let me assure you that none of that instantaneous recognition slowed down my reactions to my imminent attacker, who has just banked his glider to set a course straight at me. And has just taken one hand off the cords he's been using to direct his parasail to pull out a handgun from a holster strapped across his chest.

But his actions were much slower than it took yours truly to draw her own .357, point it, pull the trigger, and shoot her winged assailant in his right shoulder.

The gun falls out of his hand, and his glider turns sharply to the left and begins to spiral down into our valley as two closely spaced gunshots are fired from the area near the armory, where I am pretty sure my brother stationed himself. They are followed by two more from near where my sister and mom should be. The sounds of those shots echo through the whole valley. And though they seem not to have hit the man and his glider, the sound of them brings me a small feeling of relief.

Two shots are a warning. Two more an acknowledgement. Those answering rifle shots show that our people know we're under attack. It's time for them to do the things we've rehearsed: arm themselves and hurry to the secure places we've chosen in the rocks and edges and caves of our valley.

Looking up at the blimp, I can make out every detail of that machine and its passengers now. It's easy to see things in our clear desert air, combined with my own acuity of sight, which has been getting even better over this last year.

The blimp is perhaps a hundred feet long and half that high, shaped more or less like a fat cigar. Its sides are not totally rigid, because I can see it billowing in and out slightly as it travels. There's a much smaller, low-sided platform hung by cables beneath it with a few people on it. Just four of them, two of whom stand at the front.

One of them holds something that I am pretty sure is a pair of binoculars trained on me. He must have been the one who located me and directed the glider guy to attack. As I watch, he puts down those binoculars and joins the second man. And now they seem to be moving something.

The other two in back are busy with a single task. They are on bicycles attached to a big spinning propeller at the back of the platform, which is being used to make the blimp move forward. A wide, flat rudder like a fish's tail behind the propeller is keeping the machine on course.

I'm expecting more gliders, but I don't see any. Maybe one was all they could manufacture or scavenge from someplace. Or maybe one was all they could manage to fit on their aircraft. But that doesn't means their assault is over.

The two men in front are now lifting a round object the size of a big backpack. They drop it, and it plummets straight down—toward our hogan. It misses, striking just a stone's throw away. When it hits, it explodes and a cascade of flames flows out from it, burning out just before reaching the door.

The people in the blimp are having a hard time directing the aircraft, keeping it over our valley. They've dropped another incendiary bomb, and it's falling not in the valley but on the side of the southern cliff, blowing up and harmlessly spilling fire down the painted stones.

If there'd been much of a wind, I doubt they could have managed to steer their lighter-than-air craft our way. It might have blown them off course. But, as everyone who lives in the desert knows, there's usually little or no wind in the early hours before and after dawn.

Ineffective as their attack has been thus far, there's no doubt that those bombs they are dropping could injure or even kill some of our people. The next one that falls, a bomb bigger than the others, is more effective than the first two, falling in the midst of three male hogans that were constructed close together. The blast shatters all three structures and sets the exposed wood frames ablaze. Luckily, it seems that no one was inside them.

Below me, people are shouting. A group of four armed people, my sister Ana among them, have captured my winged attacker.

She looks up at me.

We got him.

Good for you, Sis.

The man from the glider is clutching his shoulder. But he

is still able to stumble on his own feet as Ana drags him away. I'm glad of that. I could have aimed to kill him, but took a chance that a wounding shot would be enough.

That's good, but what is happening right now above me is not. The blimp is hovering right over the top of our valley now, the men churning their feet on the pedals to maintain its position and prevent it from drifting away toward the east. They're working hard to keep the wind, which has begun to rise, in front of them, where the breeze flows around it rather than pushing against its broad side.

I hear rifle shots from below me. It must be Hussein shooting at the blimp. His bullets are not hitting the men, who are hidden from his view by their metal platform.

I am the only one at the right angle to see the two men who've been dropping bombs. Now they are wrestling an even larger one toward the low wall of their platform. It's so big they can barely move it. If it is proportionately as powerful as the others, it could do some real damage. And it looks to me as if they are directly over our meeting arbor—where a number of people have gathered now. Why are they there? All our people have been told again and again to get out of the open and under cover if we were attacked. To go to one of our safe areas among the rocks next to the cliffs. But people don't always do the right thing or the safest thing when they are being attacked.

Tom Yazzie is there. He's trying to pull people out of the arbor, move them toward the safer places among the rocks. But people are foolishly resisting him, wrongly thinking the arbor will provide enough shelter.

I look to the west, toward the dispensary, just in time to see the Dreamer, his arms spread wide, herding a group of children into its rock-roofed place of safety where Mom and Lorelei are waiting for them.

I turn back toward the east, pick out my brother Victor. He and Luz have taken up a position near the entrance to the armory. Like Hussein, they are also firing at the blimp with their rifles. But their angle is wrong, too. The platform that the four men are on is hiding and protecting them. It must be made of some kind of very sturdy metal because the bullets that strike it are pinging off.

I can't hit them, Lozen. What should I do?

Victor's thought comes to me as clearly as if he spoke it out loud from a few feet away.

Just keep trying, I think back to him. He looks my way and nods.

I do not see Guy, but I am pretty sure I know where he is. Guy is inside the armory looking for an RPG of some sort to launch at the craft. But I doubt he's going to find one. The two AT-4s that were crushed by the giant eel's dying throes were our last. And we haven't had the time to find any new abandoned weapons depots to scavenge replacements for them yet.

Only a few seconds have passed, but it seems like an eternity.

There's no longer any firing from below me. I'm not sure where Hussein has gone. I have to do something. But what? I can try shooting at them with my rifle, but will bullets be enough?

You know.

And as soon as that voice touches my mind, I do know. I know it with a certainty that is scary. I can feel it through the heat building in my hands. Like Killer of Enemies, the hero twin in our ancient story, I've been given an Arrow of Lightning like the one he earned from his father the Sun.

I put down my rifle. Power is coming into me, pulsing into me. I'm not sure where it is coming from. Is it from the air around me? From the morning Sun whose silver-filtered light seems even stronger than usual, a light that is not just all around me but suffusing every part of my being? I feel like the world's biggest battery, ready to discharge that energy.

I'm lifting my hands, starting to point them at the blimp. I feel as if all I have to do is strike my hands together and let it go, send a bolt of pure fire streaming that way to knock it out of the sky, perhaps explode it into an even bigger ball of flame if it is filled with hydrogen or some other explosive gas.

But if I do that it, will surely kill those four people.

Yes, what they are doing is intended to kill us. I have good reason to blow them out of the air. Otherwise that big bomb is probably going to kill and injure people I know. But I've promised I will not intentionally take another human life.

Even to save your own?

Yes!

I strike my hands together, pointing my index fingers as I do so. And what I'd hoped for happens. The release of the powerful energy built up in me pushes me back half a step as a bolt of energy, not forked like lightning but a golden ball of fire like a second tiny sun, shoots from my hands. It hits exactly where my mind and my pointing fingers intended, striking and destroying the propeller and rudder at the back of the craft.

And though the body of the blimp and the men in the platform below it are unharmed, the lighter-than-air craft is spun halfway around by the force of that strike. It's turned sideways to the wind, which is beginning to grow stronger. The men on the bikes are no longer pedaling. Along with the two bombardiers, they are holding onto the cables to keep from falling off their platform.

That huge incendiary device has been released, though. It's tumbling down, spinning end over end—and dropping out of sight beyond the cliffs of our valley. A second later, we hear the heavy thud of a distant explosion. My Arrow of Lightning and the gift of that helpful morning wind pushed the blimp out of range. The men on it are helpless now to guide its flight. Their blimp is being carried farther and farther off to the west.

I raise both of my hands toward the east.

"Thank you. Morning Wind, I thank you."

But as soon as I make that simple gesture, speak those few words, I realize how much has been taken out of me by what I've just done. I feel like a streambed drained of all its water. I try to keep standing. I know that a fall will take me right over the edge of the stone, down to my death on the valley floor far below.

But my knees can no longer hold me up.

Darkness washes down over my eyes as my limp body pitches forward.

CHAPTER TWENTY-THREE
Our Plucked Chicken

I open my eyes, wondering if I am going to see the Happy Place where hunting is always good or the luminous faces of the angels who welcome the righteous into the Garden of Paradise.

The face smiling down on me is more welcome than that of any angel.

"Habibi," Hussein says, "are you all right?"

He's holding tightly to my right wrist. The grip, I realize, that saved me at the last second as I was about to fall from Place Where Moon Puts Down Her Pack. That is why I hadn't seen him in the valley below. He was climbing back up here, his rifle slung over his shoulder, to help me.

"What you did," he said, "it was truly amazing. Many lives might have been lost, if not for you."

I sit up, and he looks down, realizing he's still holding my wrist. He releases his grasp, on the verge of apologizing for keeping hold of me. I don't give him a chance to do that, immediately wrapping my arms around him and squeezing him hard—just short of breaking ribs.

"And if not for you," I say, "my life would have been lost."

He doesn't say anything, which is the perfect thing to say. He just stays there on his knees, his right arm around my neck, his left hand holding the sling of his rifle. Finally, reluctantly, I let go of him. My strength has come back.

"All right," I say, "let's climb down and see how things are."

Not bad at all, is what we quickly discover as people come running up to us. Ana, Luz, and Victor lead the crowd, all of them talking at once.

"How did you do that?"

"Thank you so much."

"Are you all right? I saw you start to fall before Hussein grabbed you."

That last from my serious little brother, who I can sense is quite disturbed that none of the shots he and Luz fired had any visible effect.

I open my arms to embrace all three of them.

"We all did it," I say. "We did good. And I'm fine. We can talk more later. But tell me, what happened to that guy with the wings?"

Ana takes my hand.

"Come on," she says.

She leads me to the dispensary. We arrive there just as the Dreamer is walking out the entrance, surrounded by a dozen or so children who seem to have accepted him as a surrogate uncle. In fact, one little girl is riding on his shoulders while he cradles a smaller child in his arms.

The change he has gone through while living with us is nothing short of miraculous. Or maybe totally unbelievable. That he has gone from being a distant, threatening figure of fear to someone who reads stories to little kids from his beloved books is mind-boggling.

He smiles down at the children swarming around him like a flock of quail with their mother.

"Forgive my entourage," he says. "They are a bit demanding, I know. But one tends to forgive almost anything when one's audience is so appreciative of classic literature. We were quite enmeshed in *Charlotte's Web* when the alarm was sounded. And now I must return to acquaint them with the fate of its porcine secondary protagonist."

Huh? Even when he is being benevolent, I can't understand half of what he's talking about.

The Dreamer grins, enjoying my bemusement. That is one thing that has not changed in our relationship.

"I suspect," he says, "you have arrived to inquire about the fate of your alar assailant, the one whose Icarus-like flight you terminated so effectively."

My brow is furrowed as I stare up at him.

He chuckles. "The man you shot is in there. He'll live. And now, my little literati, shall we repair to my reading room to hear more of E.B. White's minor masterwork?"

The Dreamer and his gaggle of children flow past me, leaving me and Ana looking at their backs.

Ana giggles. "He's funny, isn't he, Lozen? Even if he does get you so angry?"

No need to answer that question. I just turn around and walk into our makeshift hospital, where half of the dozen cots are now occupied.

The man I shot is not the only patient being tended to by Lorelei and the several men and women she's trained as paramedics. It looks as if all the others' injuries are nothing serious. A woman with an ankle she either badly sprained or broke as she ran to shelter. A man with a burned arm where some of that jellied gasoline splashed. A few others with cuts or bruises.

Tom Yazzie and another younger man are standing guard by the bed occupied by the birdman. I can't quite recall the other man's name, though I recognized him as someone who was also a prisoner at Haven when he arrived to seek shelter with us a few weeks ago. He's a short, brown-haired man with a Spanish name and a soft voice, the kind of self-effacing person you easily take a liking to. He's been a hard worker and helpful to everyone. His one aim is to find some way to rescue the rest of those held inside the former penitentiary's thick walls—especially his sister and his two nephews.

Rogelio. That's his name. I remember it as he smiles shyly up at me through his thatch of hair.

"Buenos días, señorita Lozen," Rogelio says.

I love it that he greets me in Spanish, that he has remembered his language.

"Ya-ah-tahey," Tom says, a serious look on his face as he speaks his own greeting in Navajo.

I do my best to repeat it back to him. "Ya-ta-hey, Tom." That one word is about all the Navajo I know, and I'm not sure I pronounce it right. Unless you get the right inflection, you might be saying something entirely different.

Tom nods. "Good job, Lozen," he says. "You are doing much better at saying hello, even if what you just said means 'suck my socks' in Dine."

"Oh," I say.

The serious look vanishes from his face. "Got ya," he guffaws. Then he points his lips at the guy in the bed behind him. "But you got him even better. Didn't know you was such a good wing shot."

"Ho," I say. "Ho, ho." But as usual, Tom's put a smile on my face, not just with his corny remarks but with the way he said them. Some people seem to be natural comedians, and he, for sure, is one.

Tom looks toward the door. "Here comes my relief. Gotta go check on the kids. Have fun with our plucked chicken."

As Tom goes, I turn my attention the person who came

flying out of the sky at me. He's been bandaged and cleaned up and propped up with a pillow behind him. He no longer seems all that threatening. I am shocked at just how small he looks, stripped of his wings, his black leather coat, his leather hat, and goggles. He can't weigh more than a hundred and ten pounds, if that. In fact, he looks like a kid, a kid whose drawn face shows the pain he must be feeling from that shoulder wound.

I step forward, and I can see the apprehension grow in his face. Before I can speak, he lifts his one good hand.

"I didn't want to do it," he says in a high voice that cracks as he speaks. "That's why I didn't shoot you."

"Aside from the fact that I shot you first," I say.

That shuts him up. He drops his hand and looks even more miserable than he did before. Probably expects, if we are anything at all like his sadistic Overlord back at Haven, that we are now going to torture him. But I have to admit that he might have a point. Thinking back on our encounter, there did seem to be hesitancy in his attack on me.

"Explain," I say.

He looks up at me again, a little hope in his eyes now. I can see even more clearly how young he actually is—younger than me.

"My father," he says, "and my brother."

He pauses. He really doesn't have to say more, even though he's going to. It's the same old story as it was with me when the Ones made me their Killer of Enemies, forcing me to go out and risk my life for them by holding Mom and Ana and Victor as hostages.

Do what we tell you, and we will not kill them. Maybe.

"The wing suit they scavenged wouldn't work for anyone bigger than me. I'm skinny, but I'm strong. So they knew I could wear it. If I didn't, they would have—"

"Okay." I put my hand on his shoulder—the unwounded one. "Enough said about that."

"What about that dirigible?" someone asks from behind me. It's Guy. He's the one who came in to relieve Tom Yazzie just when I started to question our captive.

Captive. I don't like that word. I'd been one for too long, and there are far too many innocent people still being held in bondage back at Haven and, from what Rose and her Lakotas have told me, at other enclaves all over the country where powerful nut jobs like Lady Time have managed to still hold sway.

Hostage? That is way, way worse.

No, until he proves otherwise, I am just going to think of his as our guest. A guest who might provide some useful intel.

He opens his mouth to answer Guy's question.

"You mean the—"

"First," I say, cutting the boy off before he can say anything further, "you got a name?"

"Mohindas," he says. Then, proving just how adolescent

he is, he eagerly adds, "but my friends all call me Mo. So you can call me that, too."

With my peripheral vision I can see Guy rolling his eyes at how innocent this kid seems to be. Almost too innocent is what Guy is thinking. Is this just an act?

But I know that's not the case because right now my Power has kicked in, and I'm not just hearing his voice. I'm also hearing the inner dialogue going on inside little Mohindas's skull.

He is scared to death right now. But his fears are more for his family back at Haven than they are for his own well-being.

"Okay, Mo," I say. "First of all, before you say anything else, you should know that I'm sorry I shot you. But that was in self-defense."

"I know that," he says, a little deflated. "I don't blame you at all."

Poor kid. Looking at him closely, I think I may have seen him back when I was at Haven. He was smaller then because that was more than a year ago, but the shape of his face, those big eyes of his haven't changed. I'm pretty sure now that I did see him and his father and brother a few times. Like in the crowd when they were passing sentence on Hussein. Small people, doing what they were told to do by our Overlords and trying not to be noticed. People who never wanted to hurt anyone—just survive.

I feel as if I should hug him. But that wouldn't get the

answers any faster, and it would probably hurt that shoulder of his. So I do the next best thing. I try to reassure him.

"Thank you," I say. "You should also know that we are not going to hurt you. We are not like Lady Time."

A visible shiver goes through his body at the mention of her name, and he shakes his head.

"Nobody is like her," he whispers. "She's so very, very bad."

I nod my agreement. "And what we plan to do is put an end to what she and the Jester have been doing. We are going to set free everyone held hostage in Haven."

Or so I hope.

Mohindas gives me a weak smile. "That would be great," he says. "You don't know what it is like there since you left. It's worse than it was before. I mean, every day they, they . . ." His voice chokes, and he starts coughing.

I wait till the coughing stops and then pat his shoulder softly. It's not the sort of thing I usually do, me not being the type to try to comfort little kids. I almost say, "It's okay." But I don't, because it is not okay. Instead I choose another word.

"There, there," I whisper, leaning close to him, "there, there."

He finally looks up. "Sorry about that," he says.

By now, Guy is as convinced of the boy's actual innocence as I am. When he speaks, his voice is soft and has more of his Scottish accent.

"Mo, my lad," Guy says, "kin ye tell us now about that

flying machine ye and the others were on? And do they have others of its ilk?"

"The blimp?" Mohindas asks, looking at me.

"The blimp," I agree. "Tell us all about it."

Mohindas nods. He speaks hesitantly at first, but then with more certainty. It seems that, young as he is, he has a good understanding about building and designing things, probably because his father was once an engineer of some sort. His father worked as a minor supervisor in a factory back before things all changed.

"My father's a very intelligent man," Mohindas says with pride. "It's unfortunate that he was not able to hide his abilities from those bad people. He made the mistake of fixing something small and came to the notice of Lady Time, who forced him into her workshop."

The blimp, it seems, had been his father's design. Several parties were sent out to find whatever might be of use to build it, and one happened to locate a facility where canisters of helium gas had been stored. It took some effort—and perhaps a dozen lives, since that storage facility was inhabited by some very hungry large creatures—but they managed to drag back a large wagon filled with helium canisters. That, combined with the weather balloons that had been found at another location, was enough to fabricate that one ship.

Just that one. There had only been enough helium to fill a

single craft for a single flight. And it had been constructed with only one purpose.

"She hates you so much," Mohindas said. "She'll do anything to kill you. She dreamed you were here. Then, when the scouts she sent out came back to Haven and told her you had indeed returned to this valley, all she could think of was sending men to destroy you and all your people. We're only the first wave."

Theirs had been a one-way mission. The objective had been to float over our valley and drop enough bombs to either kill us all or drive us out of our well-defended sanctuary. The lifting power of the blimp was such that only the five people, plus their payload of lethal explosive devices, could be carried. The other four men on the craft, unlike Mohindas, had been loyal henchmen of Lady Time. If large enough gliding suits could have been made, then they would have joined in that attack on me.

Sending him down on a suicide mission to try to take me by surprise had been a part of the plan that was only to be carried out if the opportunity presented itself. My being on top of the tower of stone had been just such an opportunity.

It takes perhaps half an hour for Mohindas to tell us all he knows about that. He's holding his right hand with his left as he talks, rubbing his palm with his finger in a sort of nervous tic. His forehead is covered with sweat when he finishes, and he's clearly exhausted.

I'm feeling tired, too. But it's not just physical exhaustion. I am tired of being hunted, tired of seeing other people hurt by those evil bastards at Haven.

"Mo," I say, "from now on, you are our guest. Not our prisoner, okay? Get some rest now. And thank you."

"No," he says, rubbing his hands together. "It's you who should be thanked, Lozen. You know, I used to watch you. You looked so strong and sure when everyone else was just afraid. You were greatly admired by so many of us. You gave us hope, especially when you escaped. Most of those kept prisoner in that awful place still think of you. They pray for you to return and set us free."

"Oh," I say.

"Oh, yes, yes, indeed." A shy smile comes to his lips. "I never could have pulled the trigger on that gun," he says. " I was just going to throw it away as soon as I got it out of the holster, but then it got stuck there." He nods. "You know," he continues, "I'm not so worried about my family now that I've met you. You have been so kind to me. I know that you will find some way to save them. You are my hero."

A hero who feels about as low as a worm's belly after hearing him say that.

CHAPTER TWENTY-FOUR
One Way or Another

There's no two ways around it. There's only one thing we can do now. It's what I decided after my battle with Luther Four Deaths. We've have all been so busy getting resettled here in this valley that I've been putting it off.

But I can do that no longer. I have to take the fight to them.

That is easy to say. But it's the doing of it that's the hard part. My first idea, to head out with Hussein to try to lure in Luther Little Wound and trust that my Power will warn us in time, now seems a little naive after that aerial assault.

Whatever we do now, plan Numero Uno will not be enough. The four of us—Hussein and me, Striped Horse and Star—might be enough to take Four Deaths. But from what Mohindas told us a few hours later after he'd rested, we are about to be under constant attack. The blimp was just Lady Time's first foray.

Hussein and Guy and I are back in the dispensary listening to Mohindas. We've now learned that, just as my Power told me, Luther Little Wound was, indeed, sent out to terminate me. Sent by the Jester.

"So," I say to Mohindas, "what else are the Jester and Lady Time putting their heads together to do?"

Mohindas strikes his forehead with his palm. "Ah, that's right. I didn't tell you."

"Tell us what, laddie?" Guy asks.

"They're not putting their heads together at all. They're fighting each other," Mohindas says.

Then he proceeds to fill us in. The two remaining overlords in Haven—the Jester and Lady Time—are engaged in a contest with each other to be the first to cause my demise.

That contest, Mohindas explains, involves winning the right to cut off one of each other's fingers or toes every time one of their attempts misfires. He is not sure which of them has won or lost thus far. The gossip that always flows throughout Haven about the Ones is still a mix of real information and partly informed speculation. The thought of Lady Time walking with a limp after word gets back that her airship failed brings me a little pleasure. But only momentarily.

Four Deaths and the blimp are merely the first two prongs of an assault that is going to continue until one of those two insane megalomaniacs either succeeds or runs out of digits to wager.

Mohindas's dad is one of several teams of engineers and scientists at Haven who are working on weapons of destruction—with their families being held over their heads.

"I don't know all the details of the projects others were charged with," Mohindas says, "but I know the next one due for completion for that frightening woman involves a steam engine mounted in a heavy vehicle. One with armor plating." He pauses. "Actually, several such vehicles, I believe."

Great, I think, *tanks a lot.*

(Forgive me for that one. I've been spending too much time listening to Tom Yazzie's puns.)

"So what does the Jester plan to counter with? A nuclear weapon?" I ask.

My attempt at ironic humor falls way short. Mo stops talking, presses his lips tightly together, and stares down at his hands wrestling with each other.

No, I think. *No.* Then I say it, even though I've already read the truth of it in Mo's troubled mind. "No, you're kidding."

He shakes his head, an action that clearly brings a stab of agony to his wounded shoulder despite the drugs that Lorelei gave him to deaden the pain. My bullet tore through muscles and ligaments.

In the old viddys, people were always shooting each other. And those heroes and villains would just carry on after they were shot like it was no big deal. But in real life, getting struck by a slug anywhere on your person is far from a minor thing.

A .357 bullet is 35.7 percent of an inch across. Imagine something of that size traveling at greater than the speed of sound entering your body. It takes a lot to make that bullet come to a stop, transferring the energy of its flight to the flesh and bone it's impacting. A well-placed bullet sends shock waves through your system as its kinetic energy is transferred to you, into you, through you.

Even a flesh wound is serious. You can bleed to death from something like that. Plus the pain lasts, sometimes even after the flesh and bone have healed.

Once again, I am feeling real regret at what I did to this poor kid, even if I thought it was necessary to save my life. But there's no time for that now. I have to make sure I heard what I think I heard—both from his lips and in his thoughts.

"The Jester has a nuclear weapon?"

"Yes," Mo says in a voice so small and high I can barely hear it. Then he coughs.

"Bloody hell," Guy says.

"Bismillah, indeed," Hussein adds.

I hold up my hand. Enough swearing, more information.

"Where did he get it?"

"From a place to the west. It was an old secure facility. Yuma, I think my father called it. There was some fierce fighting over the bomb with another mercenary group from someplace farther west that has its own Overlords. But the Jester's army won."

"Does he know how to use it?"

Mo's face brightens a little, and he looks up at me.

"That, my father said, was the good news. Apparently there would be a problem of detonation if the bomb works on an electric circuit. Without electricity, there might be no explosion."

"Good," I say.

But Mohindas has gone back to rubbing his fingers in his palm and staring into his lap. He coughs again, several times, before speaking.

"One man, though, is saying that is not so. He's saying that the bomb is one that need only fall to explode when it hits the ground."

Oh, joy.

I feel as if my head is about to explode. Steam-powered tanks, nuclear bombs? It makes me long for the good old days when the only thing I had to worry about was being the main course for some giant gemod.

"Ah, sadly, that is not the only thing one worries about."

I don't bother to turn around. The Dreamer's lugubrious voice doesn't startle me. I both heard his nearly silent entrance and felt the presence of his mind halfway through our questioning.

"What"—I sigh—"does one worry about?"

"The nearly obvious—obvious at least to one as well versed in the subtle stratagems of the past as this humble bibliophile."

"Meaning?"

The Dreamer takes a few steps forward so that he is looming over the comparatively miniscule figure of Mohindas in his cot. He looks at me, holds his left hand palm up just below his heart, and gestures down at the wounded boy.

"That our young drop-in is more dangerous than you or he realizes."

I do not understand, nor does Mohindas. The confusion on his face is matched by the absolute innocence of his thoughts. Plus, it seems he is not feeling well. He's sweating heavily, his hands are shaking, and he's coughing again.

"I shall elucidate," the Dreamer says, raising his voice slightly to be heard over the boy's coughing, "but first I have a small request. Might we gather"—his voice changes to take on a note of real urgency—"with as much expedience as possible, everyone and anyone who has been in contact with our little Icarus?"

I am not sure what is going on, but I can sense that for whatever reason, we need to do as he says. Hussein has sensed it, too.

"I will take care of it," he says. And within a few minutes he has done just as the Dreamer requested. There are now a dozen people in the room, including my sister Ana and Tom Yazzie, who is scratching his chin with one hand and holding his rifle with the other. Every person who laid hands on Mohindas is here.

The Dreamer looks around the little group.

"This is all?" he says. "No one else touched this child?"

The directness of his statements and the grave tone of his voice—not a bit of his usual superciliousness—worry me. What is up?

"Excellent. Now," he says, steepling his hands together and looking over the arch of his fingers at Lorelei, "the door."

Lorelei shuts the dispensary door, latches it, and stands with her back against it.

The Dreamer nods. "Forgive my theatricality, a compensatory mechanism that has become engrained in one's personality. And now I shall explain. But first a question or two. Has anyone in our little assemblage heard of the poison maidens described in Sanskrit lore? Most notably in the *Kathasaritsagara* writ by the poet Somadeva? One of whom was sent by the king of India to none other than Alexander the Great? Nyet? Admittedly, it was awhile back, a tad more than a millennium. Non? Then perhaps the name of that more recent vector of mortality, Typhoid Mary, might ring a bell? Nicht wahr?"

The Dreamer shakes his head. "Ah, education these days."

I am clenching my fists together—rather than wrapping them around the Dreamer's throat and throttling him. "In English," I growl.

He looks at me and smiles. "Of course, my little assassin. But did you not think it a bit piscatorial that yon lad should be dropped down into our valley so ill-prepared for actual combat? Was it not a bit too obvious that whatever weapon he carried was superfluous to his purpose? That rather than bearing a weapon, he *was* the weapon—or at the least, its unwitting carrier."

All of a sudden I get it. And I feel like kicking myself for not having seen it sooner. It's one of the oldest weapons in the book—one used by Europeans against Native people for centuries.

"Like smallpox blankets," I say.

The Dreamer nods sadly. "Full points," he says.

CHAPTER TWENTY-FIVE
Death Walking

Coyote, they say, was going along. He had seen no one for a long time and wondered where everyone was.

Then he saw someone coming toward him. That person was strange looking. As he got closer, Coyote saw just how very strange that being was. He was all black, as if burned by fire, and covered with pustules. His eyes were red as fire, and his lips were dry and cracked.

"Hello, my friend," Coyote said. "Who are you?"

"I am the one everyone fears," that being said, his voice a dry rasp. "When they see me coming, they pack up their lodges and run. But I follow them wherever they go. After I touch them, they will soon look like me. I am Death Walking. My name is Smallpox. Now, who are you?"

Coyote saw that what that frightening-looking being said was true. He had heard about this one before. So he hopped up on top of a big boulder to keep his distance. He had seen the villages empty of all but corpses where the one who called himself Death Walking had visited.

"Ey-hey," Coyote said from atop that boulder, "Smallpox, I am pleased to meet you. My name is No One."

"No One," Smallpox said, "come down here and take my hand."

"Ah," Coyote said, "I am feeling tired. This is the place I go to rest. So I will not come down right now. Is there anything else I can do for you?"

"You can tell me where the camps of your Chiricahua people are. I want to visit them."

Coyote looked out over the desert in the opposite direction of where he knew the Chiricahuas were camping. There was nothing but desert that way and then the ocean.

"You can go that way," he said. "It will be a long walk. When you come to the big salt water, you can wade in and keep going. And when you find any people, you can tell them that No One sent you."

"Good," the blackened being said. "I will do that. Then I will come back for you, No One. Will you promise me that you will be here when I come back?"

"I promise you that no one will be here if you come back."

"Good," Smallpox said. He turned in the direction of the far-off ocean and began to walk.

Coyote watched until that terrible creature was out of sight.

Then he hopped down off the big rock and ran to warn the Chiricahua camps.

That is the story my mom told me when I was little. And it was true that although that terrible contagious disease caused the deaths of countless Native people all over the continent, most of our Chiricahua people were able to avoid it by being so hard to find.

But what has found us now here in Haven?

"He's carrying smallpox, right?" I ask the Dreamer. "How did you figure this out? Are you sure?"

"Are you sure yourself?"

"Yes. Now answer my questions. How do you know it? Why are you sure?"

The Dreamer sits down on one of the chairs near Mo's cot. He does it with such grace and elegance that, as usual, he makes it look like some sort of dance move. Though he has proven to be much more benevolent than any of his three former peers, he still has their flair for the dramatic, a theatrical propensity that emerges whenever he has an audience. One that, with the dispensary door closed and locked, is truly captive.

"While yet at Haven, one was made aware of the desire of my chronometrically countenanced compeer to engage in microbial combat. Germ warfare, that is. It was rumored that she—or rather her team of biochemists—had managed to either concoct or salvage something from some storage facility. A genetically modified form of smallpox that could be spread by contact. One so lethal that it would, within a matter of hours, prove fatal to both host and those further infected. I suspect it was within the suit donned by our little Rocky the Flying Squirrel."

The Dreamer pauses again. He seems to be seeking some sort of reaction. "No?" he says. "Bullwinkle the Moose? Never mind."

I look around at the faces of the others in the room. Guy, Hussein, Ana, Tom Yazzie, Rogelio, Lorelei, the Dreamer, and five others. Half of them are people I've grown to love. These are probably the last faces I'll ever see if what the Dreamer says is true. And there is absolutely nothing I can do to stop it.

Unless—hope against hope—our towering former Overlord is mistaken in his analysis. Then a sound comes from the cot behind me.

"Ahhhrrrrhhhhhh-ahhhh." It's the rattling of laboring breath.

Mohindas's brown face is covered with sweat. His eyes are closed in agony, and there are red blotches forming on his cheeks.

It's true.

We are all so screwed.

CHAPTER TWENTY-SIX

A Minor Interruption

Luther looked at the sun. Two hands high. He'd already covered a good ten miles. He was making decent time, regaining ground lost when he strayed off course the day before.

He'd spent another relatively peaceful night in a small shed empty but for a small stack of rebar—six-foot-long reinforcing rods used in construction. Two had come in handy when his privacy was interrupted by a pack of gemod creatures. Absent on his arrival, their scent inside the shed had forewarned Luther he'd not be without company for the entirety of the hours of darkness.

The first one appeared in the doorway soon after the cloak of dusk descended. Of course Luther was not sleeping. He'd positioned himself in such a way that he had a clear view of the entrance. Anything that arrived would be silhouetted against the night sky. He heard it before he saw it, the scratch of clawed feet accompanied by a snuffling sound as it picked up his scent. A long snout appeared around the edge of the frame, followed by the rest of the animal's large-eared head and bulbous body. It stood there for a moment, first on all fours, then rearing up on its hind legs.

Even with one eye, Luther's night vision was superb to the point of being catlike. He'd been able to make out the beast in some detail: short, matted fur, red little eyes, the impressive array of teeth displayed as it gaped its drooling mouth wide. He noted a number of similar shapes behind just before it sprang.

Each medium-sized predator—none larger than an average leopard—attacked in the same way: a loud, toothy snarl and a leap for Luther's throat as he sat there cross-legged.

His hands, however, had not remained idle. Each—even the one still slightly smaller than the other—held a length of steel rod. Luther's training had included the mastery of arnis, a form of stick fighting from certain islands of the western Pacific.

Those techniques proved quite effective, spraying blood and brain matter from cracked craniums as one after another of the creatures came squealing and shrieking in.

Thwack! One down. Next. Thwack! Two.

The narrowness of the door prevented the entrance of more than one at a time. The stubbornness of the beasts—which resembled giant rats crossed with wolverines—ensured the eventual demise of the entire pack. He dispatched all fourteen, the final one strangled after one of his steel rods lodged in the eye socket of his next to last attacker.

A satisfying exercise, made more so by the tasty haunch of the largest wolverat cooked over the fire he kindled in the doorway. Placing it there provided not just heat and light, but also security against other would-be intruders.

That delicious repast but a memory, he was now well fueled for another eight hours of loping toward his goal.

When on a mission, Luther's thoughts were usually focused on his goal. Other concerns would be nonexistent—his only thoughts of the immediate task. However, since his last re-vivication, that had not been so. He was never without at least two or three extraneous concerns buzzing about in his brain like bees. Even sleep provided no solace. The only time when that was not so was when he was engaged in violent physical activity—such as that satisfying run-in with the wolverats, whose numbers had been all too few.

As he ran, he was not merely considering the most efficient way to terminate that little female assassin. He was deviled by those dogged visions that returned to him each night. He'd attempted to erase them, mentally chanting a mantra, then doing so out loud. But the image of two brown eyes looking up at him refused to take its leave. He tried counting, a tactic that had always given him a feeling of security. The steps he took. The number of large rocks he passed. His own breaths. He even tried enumerating the number of human lives he'd taken during his long and successful career as an ambassador of the Grim Reaper. All to no avail.

He was now passing an area of red sandstone cliffs and tall rock outcroppings carved into phantasmagorical shapes by eons of wind and water. Natural bridges, looming megaliths, spires and arches lifted above him. He paid no attention to their strange beauty—aside from keeping a watchful eye for any predacious creature that might be lurking behind them.

As he turned a corner in the canyon, though, something did gain his full attention. A human voice. An exasperated one, to be precise, engaged in suggesting a number of anatomical impossibilities regarding a disabled craft and its pilot.

Might it be?

A slight smile that would have sent a chill down the back of any onlooker crossed Luther's lips. He crept forward, peered through a convenient natural spyhole in a stone sparkling with red and green crystals. His smile briefly grew broader, exposing his perfect teeth. There before him was the flying device that had passed overhead the day before. No longer the shape of a cigar, the deflated blimp was draped over the broken stone spire on which it had lodged. Prior to its final landing, it must have been drifting too low to clear that obstacle. Its cables slack, the platform on which the aviators had ridden rested on a slant of bedrock, bent into a V by the impact. Three of the five men who'd been on board stood on the level sand below the spire, apparently unharmed.

The same could not be said for the final member of that original quintet, now reduced to a foursome. Curled into a ball, he was on the ground being kicked by one of the upright aviators, an angry man whose voice Luther had heard.

"You stupid bastard," the burly kicker was screaming. "Running us into this frigging canyon."

Between the thuds of the man's steel-reinforced shoe against his ribs the kickee was protesting his innocence.

"No rudder . . ." THUD! "Did the best I . . ." THUD!

An amusing sight. But Luther was not one for spectator sports. He preferred personal involvement.

He forked the two outer fingers of his left hand, placed them in the corners of his mouth, and blew. FWEEEET!

The whistle, more than loud enough to refocus their attention, turned the heads of all four men—even the one being booted—at Luther.

"Mother of God," one of the men—not the kicker—said in what could only be described as an awed voice.

Luther shook his head. "No," he said, "nor am I her son."

"Four Deaths," the lanky man who'd just spoken said.

Luther spread his arms to either side. "Yes, I've been called that. And you are?"

"You don't need to know who we are," said the burly man who'd been taking out his frustration on the unfortunate navigator.

Luther nodded, not so much in agreement as in anticipation. He much preferred resistance to passivity. Though there would be little challenge from the man on the ground—now taking the opportunity to scuttle off to one side like an injured crab.

The fourth man, whose voice had not yet been heard, pointed at the side of the broken balloon where the letters *L* and *T* were visible. "That's who we work for," he said in a slightly shaky voice. "You don't want to . . ."

He ceased his remarks as the grin on Luther's face grew so wide that his sharp canine teeth were fully exposed.

"Guys," Luther said, "no need to worry. I only want to ask a few questions, and then we'll be done."

The burly man's right hand was on the butt of his gun, a full-sized Sig Sauer semiautomatic P226, Luther noted. Chambered for a 9mm Parabellum round, with a twenty-round magazine. An effective sidearm—assuming one had time to draw it.

The fourth man, a sardonic smile on his face, looked at Burly. "You got twenty answers for him. Right, Maxo?"

Maxo, Luther thought. *I've never killed anyone named that before. Mack, Marcus, Mark, Max. But no Maxos. Till now.*

Maxo nodded. Having his hand on his gun was making

him feel in charge. "Yeah," he said. "Sure. Go ahead. Ask."

Luther crossed his arms, then lifted his half-sized right hand to his lips. "Your mission?" he asked, observing all three men taking note of his newly grown appendage. Everyone at Haven knew about the terminal part of his right limb being severed. The sight of a newly grown one had to be disquieting.

The only person not staring at the pale, prehensile, multi-fingered organ of Four Deaths was the unlucky pilot who had been absorbing Maxo's displeasure. He was dragging himself into a narrow crack at the base of a sandstone pillar.

"Wipe out that nest of traitors west of here," Maxo replied. "The one led by the damn Apache girl."

"Ah," Luther said, raising a diminutive index finger. "And did you?"

Maxo's expression changed slightly.

"We would've. But she threw some kinda bomb at us, knocked out our steering. Then the wind blew us out of range."

Enough said, Luther thought.

He might have waited, asking more questions. But his patience was lower than in the past. A result, perhaps, of repeated nights of disturbed rest.

He moved, an incredibly swift step forward. And, as assumed, Maxo had no chance to use his gun.

It was over a bit too soon for Luther to take much pleasure in it. He examined the pockets of the deceased, looked through their packs. From the belt of the late, not at all great Maxo he unclipped a bowie knife. Two-thirds the size of his previous prized blade, it was, nonetheless, a pleasure to once again have such a weapon on his side. Guns and poison darts were always rewarding. Fists and feet employed in hand-to-hand combat were gratifying. But there was nothing like the feel of a fine knife slicing through flesh.

He looked down at the bodies of the three men. Only three. The fourth one had crawled so deeply into that narrow crack in the bedrock that Luther could neither see nor reach him. All he could hear, an ear to the opening too narrow for him to do more than reach in an arm, was the sound of labored breath.

No time to wait for the man to come out. No sense making this more than a minor interruption in Luther's journey to Lozen's valley.

Luther stood, wiped the sand from his knees, and turned his face again toward the west.

CHAPTER TWENTY-SEVEN
Not Even a Spark

Doomed to die. That is what the twelve of us are. There's only one thing that could be said to be the bright side of this mess we are in.

Maybe it's just us.

The Dreamer seems to have heard my thought.

"I believe," he says, "that you are correct to speculate that none other than we few, we happy few, have been infected. An airborne pathogen would have been too capricious, dangerous to friend and foe alike. Plus, if my memory serves me well, this particular strain was being developed to have a short life after its initial exposure—not much longer than the brief, painful span experienced by the unfortunates infected. Time enough, though, to wipe out an entire community such as ours."

He sweeps his hands at the back of the dispensary, where we have a big woodstove, vented out through a pipe leading into a crack in the rocks. That stove is needed at night, even in spring. In the desert, the temperature might drop forty degrees from day to night. Right now, the stove is being used as an incinerator. Rogelio is using a poker to shove the last pieces of the contaminated flying suit into the flames.

"And," the Dreamer says, "that conflagration will make certain that no others will be exposed to any residual toxins."

Somewhere in all those words he just spoke is, I think, the message I want to hear.

"So nobody else out there"—I look toward the latched door—"is going to get this? We're the only ones it's going to kill, right?"

"Direct as always," the Dreamer says. "But to your queries I must reply both yea and nay."

Huh?

"What do you mean?"

The Dreamer raises a hand to silence me and turns to the person who has just come up to stand next to him.

"Lorelei, my dear," the Dreamer says, "I trust that you have it."

The pale, elegant woman, who has proven to be both compassionate and effective as a nurse since shedding her disguise as a cold, emotionless accomplice, is holding a spray bottle.

"What's that?" I ask.

Her answer is to lean over Mohindas, cup one hand behind his head, and then squeeze the bottle. A cloud of mist envelops the dying boy's agonized face. His moaning stops almost immediately. As he lays his head back, his face begins to relax and return to normal, the red blotches fading.

Within a matter of minutes, each of us has been administered the spray, some sort of serum or antidote to the genetically modified microscopic pathogen that infected us.

The Dreamer, the last to be given the treatment, accepts a tissue from Lorelei and delicately dabs it at his nose.

"And thus, my impatient little Lozen," he says, "you now perceive why my answer was bifurcated between the positive and the negative?"

Maybe I will still kick him in the teeth.

It's been a couple of hours since Lorelei's antiviral antidote saved me and a considerable percentage of the people I care most about in the world from a gruesome and painful death. My hands feel hot. They should. After all, I've been rubbing them together trying to build up some heat. I lift them, look at my palms. Then I point my fingers at an innocent, flat boulder nearby and strike my hands together in exactly the same way I did when I shot that ball of lightning at the airship attacking us.

Nothing. Nada. Not even a tiny spark.

Why? I have to be ready. But I now realize—with the info we gained from Mohindas—that I can't just run out with a gun and a knife on my hip hoping to take down Haven before they get here. Tanks? Atomic bombs? Unkillable assassins? I still need to take the fight to them. But first I have to make sure I have every possible weapon at my disposal, now that I know about everything that is going to be thrown at us.

Jeezum! Give a girl a break! I have to be able to do this, use this new weapon I seem to have been given.

But all I've been able to do is make my palms sore.

I feel like screaming. However, I've already done that twice over the last half hour or so that I've been conducting my little exercise in futility. The first time brought Hussein running. Even though I thought I'd found a place no one would see or hear me, I hadn't counted on my loyal partner staying close enough to watch my back.

So I just content myself with gritting my teeth and growling.

I totally need to be able to do this. To shoot that Arrow of Lightning. After Killer of Enemies got the Thunder Bow and Lightning Arrows from the Sun, it seemed as if he never had any trouble using them. Or so the stories say. But maybe they don't always pass down the fact that even heroes may have trouble figuring out how to use their Powers.

Why won't the lightning work for me whenever I want it? Maybe it's the same answer for why my Power seems to come and go. Why sometimes I am able to read the minds of every thinking being around me, and other times all I can hear are the normal sounds that enter any other human ear. Why I have been able on rare occasions to travel into the minds of other people and see through their eyes—like the Jester and Luther while they were engaged in their discussion about terminating me. Why there are times it seems as if everything around me, every rock and tree and place, is telling me its name, and other times, like now, when all I can hear is the wind and the sound of a desert cricket creaking away from the twisted trunk of a juniper.

Maybe it's because my Power only makes itself available when I really, truly need it. I hope that's the case. Because otherwise it means I may be doing worse than bringing a knife to a gunfight. I'll be bringing a rubber knife.

Instead of frustrating myself like this right now, shouldn't I be doing something else? Like maybe celebrating the fact that I am still among the living? Can't I just be happy for a few seconds? Smell the roses?

I wish I could. But that is not me, not the worrywart Lozen I seem to be too much of the time.

I need to start figuring out other strategies. I can't just keep beating myself up mentally about not having realized what the Dreamer did—that Mohindas was the modern equivalent of one of those ancient poison maidens. Though it also bothers me that I did not I foresee that whole attack from the air. When we came back to Valley Where First Light Paints the Cliffs, my only real focus in setting up our defenses was about attacks from the ground. Even after we almost ended up being swarmed by vampire locusts, I still didn't give any new instructions about keeping our eyes not just on the earth but also on the skies.

How could I have been so unforgivably stupid?

And how can people stand to be around me when I am like this?

I must agree that it is not all that easy.

Hally?

At your service. Fortunately, not your funeral service.

The boulder I'd been attempting to use as a target lifts like a trapdoor on invisible hinges, disclosing the gorilla-like sagittal crest of my irksome and sporadically helpful hirsute acquaintance. As he takes another step up the stairs or ladder or whatever the hell else he has under there, his wide face comes into view. Then he yawns, displaying his long, formidable incisors.

It was Uncle Chatto who told me that among the big apes—like some of the gemod ones they encountered in Central Africa—that kind of jaw-dropping behavior does not indicate sleepiness. It's a warning or a threat. *Look how big and sharp my teeth are, sucker!*

"Are you upset with me?" I ask as Hally walks toward me, showing his teeth.

He closes his mouth and shapes it into something that is a closer approximation of a smile.

"Because you were attempting to blow the roof off my house? Why should that trouble me?"

He's baiting me, as usual. But I am in no mood to play his game. Or any other sort of participation sport. I am too busy feeling depressed, unfocused, confused, and, quite frankly, sorry for myself.

My intent is to just keep my mouth shut and walk away while maintaining a dignified silence. But then I start talking and I can't stop.

"What are you worried about anyway? You knew, because you've been spying on me the way you always do, that I couldn't do it. I'm useless, a failure. Why are you interested in me anyway? In fact, why are you interested in any of us? And why didn't you help? Why didn't you tell us we were about to be attacked? We got bombed and poisoned and almost got killed, and where were you?"

Hally has stopped a few feet away and is just looking down at me, his massively muscled arms folded over his chest. I take another step forward, closing the distance between us.

"Why?" I ask again. Then I slug him in the stomach. It's like hitting a granite boulder wearing a fur coat, but I hammer him there again.

"Why? Why? Why? Why?"

He just stands there as I keep saying "why?" and hitting him like he's the world's largest hairy heavy bag.

When I finally stop, my fists are sore, and a strand of my hair has come free from my headband and is hanging down over my eyes. And Hally has not been moved back any farther by my furious onslaught than a deep-rooted cottonwood tree brushed by a butterfly.

He looks down at me, his face infuriatingly calm.

"You know," he says, "that to use a weapon, one must first practice? And be patient with failure?"

He's answering the question I had originally intended to ask him if and when he ever appeared again—namely, why it is that I can't make that lightning arrow shoot from my hands whenever I want it? I think I understand what he is saying. It's been that way with all of my newfound powers. The more I use them, the closer I have come to controlling them. Not completely, but certainly better. Sending other people messages from my mind has become easier for me, especially when the people are those who are dear to me.

I'm flattered. I never knew I meant that much to you.

I try to think of an appropriately sarcastic remark to either say out loud or think back at him. But before I can do so, he asks me a question.

"Shall I tell you a story?"

As if I had any choice other than to listen?

"Go ahead," I sigh.

CHAPTER TWENTY-EIGHT

There Was a World

Mind you," he begins, "this is just a story, nothing more. But, then again, a story is never just a story, is it?"

He raises one of his very hairy eyebrows at me. I don't say anything. I might as well just keep quiet when one of Hally's stories is being spun in response to some question of mine. Like it or not, he is about to give me an answer. Or multiple answers. None of which may actually be true.

"There was a world. And on that world there were beings of great power. Those beings saw another world from their place. They saw that world needed help.

"So a female being from that powerful world decided to descend to that world that was mostly water. She was welcomed by those in that world. Earth rose up from beneath the waters to give her a place to stand. She had carried with her the seeds of all sorts of useful plants, and as she walked the moist soil of that new land, she allowed those seeds to fall into her footprints. Flowers and bushes and trees grew up there.

"That woman gave birth to a daughter, the firstborn, in a shape like yours. Then she returned to her own world, leaving that daughter to work things out for herself. And though there were no male beings, that daughter became pregnant."

Hally pauses, chuckling to himself.

"Why are you laughing?"

"When I told," he says, "or I should say, if I had told that story some centuries ago, some of you human beings were shocked that I said the word *pregnant*. Here I am, a ten-foot-tall hairy being talking about the beginning of life, and the only thing scandalizing my listeners, that word? Pregnant. Gravid? With child? In a family way? Honestly, you people. It's no wonder that we so seldom used to show ourselves to you. But allow me to continue."

As if I could stop him.

"Who was the father? Some say the wind. Then when that woman's time came, not one but two boys were born. One good. One the opposite, and the birth of that opposite baby caused his mother's death. From that point on, those two brothers fought for control of the world and the minds of the humans who came after them. Those in the above world who'd given the help that began it all merely watched and did not interfere.

"The fighting grew fiercer and fiercer as years and centuries passed. Few remembered whether it was the good or the other whose ways they were following. So it went on, until . . ."

Hally raises his eyebrow at me again. It's my cue to ask: "Until what?"

"Until their world was destroyed." Hally pauses again.

"Our world, right?"

"Wrong. Different world. Maybe the one you humans called Mars—after some god of war. If so, apropos."

"That's the story? So you're telling me that it doesn't matter which side you are on if everyone ends up dead?"

"On another world," Hally says, ignoring my questions.

Here we go again.

". . . things had not yet developed. The beings there were formless. So some powerful someone gave them a nudge, and they took human shapes. All went well for a while until, as on that other world, things went wrong. That world was about to be destroyed. Perhaps by fire.

"But this time the people there were given help. They were able to depart from that world and come to a second world, one which was not just all one color, one where they could survive and thrive. However, guess what?"

"They screwed up again?" I actually already know the story that Hally is telling. He's not using the exact words my mom used when she told it, but it's one of the oldest stories of the Navajo and Apache nations, the story of the Four Worlds.

"Some say they had a little help screwing up this time,"

Hally says. "But you are right. And their world was destroyed by a big flood. However, just as before, those beings—humans, animals, insects, all escaped to another world."

I do know this story. The people escaped by climbing up through a big, hollow reed. And I know the one who caused that flood. It was Coyote, who stole the baby of the Water Monster. Then the Water Monster caused that flood. But wasn't it the Third World that got destroyed that way?

While I've been thinking about that, Hally has kept talking.

"At last," he says, "they came to the Fourth World, the Rainbow World where every color could be seen."

"This world," I say. "I know this story."

"Do you now? Are you sure?"

Then Hally does something really weird. He holds out his hands, positions them about four feet apart, and blows. An image appears between his hands. It's a green-and-gray-and-blue ball, floating against a background of bright lights and darkness. It takes me a minute to realize that it's a planet. Our planet? No. The shapes of its landmasses don't look like the continents of this earth—not unless our continents are oblong masses of equal size. I stare at it, fascinated. It's been years since I've seen anything projected in the air this way like the holo-viddys we used to watch.

Then, all of a sudden—BOOM! That planet disintegrates as masses of fiery rock go spinning off in every direction.

"George Lucas, eat your heart out," Hally says. He drops his hands. The image of an exploded planet is gone.

"Voilà," he says. "Now do you understand?"

I don't. And I don't have to say that out loud. Even without being able to read my thoughts the way my enigmatic Abominable Snowman buddy can, anyone could deduce from the look on my face that I was totally bemused.

"Help," Hally says, raising his right hand. "Not help," he says, raising his left. "Same result?"

Maybe I am starting to get it.

"You're saying that it was your people in the past who helped human beings—or maybe other beings like humans? And that the results were always bad? So now you can't help?"

Hally grins. "Close," he says. "Let's just say that things are on a case-by-case basis. Or that I am only allowed to intervene so many times before I have used up my monthly assistance quota. Or that I don't always have to interfere."

"Unless I really need help?"

"Not exactly. Perhaps just until I decide to do something. Or, Little Food, it might be that it's more interesting for me and my kind to see what you are able to do in extremis."

I am starting to get angry again. "Are we just like animals in one of those zoos that people used to own? We just exist for your amusement?"

Hally shakes his head. "You aren't always amusing."

Then he grins again. "And the better zoos did attempt to ensure the survival of endangered species."

I am trying to decide what I can say in response to that when Hally raises his hand. "Salaam aleikum," he says.

"Aleikum as-salaam," Hussein replies.

And no, I did not hear, feel, or sense him coming up behind me. Which makes me even more irritated. I feel like a volcano about to erupt, a feeling which I must be projecting pretty strongly since Hussein makes a sort of half-circle approach that ends up with him a good twenty feet away from me.

"The meeting," he says as I turn to face him.

The meeting. I forgot all about it. I even saw everyone starting to gather before I wandered off to try to use my lightning Power. I pop myself in the forehead with my right palm. While I've been out here trying to blow up rocks and listening to an adipose giant ape engage in philosophical speculation, everyone on the council has been waiting for me to arrive at the meeting that was called at my suggestion.

"Have they been waiting long?" I ask.

I tried not to ask that with too much exasperation in my voice. But I don't think I succeeded.

Hussein takes another two steps away from me before saying, "No more than half an hour."

Hally chuckles. It's a sound as deep as the rumble of rocks. "We shall talk more later," he says. "Remember, follow the Yellow Brick Road. Toodles."

"Wait," I say. But he's gone like a puff of smoke.

No one looks upset at my late arrival. Maybe they're making allowances for me having been attacked by a bat-winged assailant, nearly fallen off a hundred-foot spire, and infected with a lethal pathogen—and all before lunch. It has definitely been one of those days.

But I am calmer now.

The walk back from my less-than-satisfying tête-a-hairy-tête with Hally has given me time to cool off. To remember something Uncle Chatto often said: A life without problems is a life without learning. A lesson I need to recall.

Mom calls the meeting to order. Then she turns to me.

"Lozen," she says, "what are your thoughts?

My first thought is that I would like to be somewhere else. My second thought is that, although I know I have to be here, especially since I called this meeting, I still wish Mom had not called on me to speak first.

But there's no way to avoid it, so I take a deep breath.

"First of all," I say, "I am glad that everyone survived that attack. There were a few mistakes made—and I made some of them myself—but all in all, we did a good job. And if anything like that happens again, we'll do even better. We're a community, and we take care of each other."

People look around at one another, nodding and smiling.

"The next thing I have to do is thank Lorelei and the

Dreamer. If it hadn't been for them, for that medicine, none of us would be standing here now."

Faces are now turning toward the Dreamer and Lorelei.

"Aho!" Tom Yazzie shouts. Others do the same, as well as clapping their hands.

Lorelei turns red, embarrassed but, I am sure, pleased by the attention. To my amazement, the Dreamer also looks as if he's moved by this accolade. He raises one hand and bows.

When the applause has died down, I raise my own hand.

"We've survived," I say. "But this is not the end of it. The Ones aren't going to give up. It's us . . . or them. We have to find ways to stop them before they can do more. All agreed?"

It's not just Tom Yazzie and a few others who say Aho! The agreement is voiced from every throat, including loud whinnying from the Horse People looking in, as always, through their openings in the council house walls.

I hold my hand up a second time. "We're all agreed. Now, before I say anything more, what else do others have to say about what we ought to do now?"

One thing both my dad and Uncle Chatto taught me was that giving people a chance to speak is just as important as any results that come out of a gathering. Our old people learned long ago that the best way to keep a community together is for everyone to listen to each other.

Some, like Tom Yazzie, offer some very useful—and, in his case, surprising—information that will be of help.

Some, like Guy, make specific suggestions about tactics that are better than anything I'd come up with.

Others, like the Dreamer, talk for a long time, basically saying pretty much what I suggested. That we need to strike first against our enemies.

Others, like Rogelio, who follows the Dreamer, simply stand up and say, "I like what the last person said."

Finally, it is my mom's turn to speak. She spends a long time summarizing what she heard from everyone else. She does it so well and with such patience that I wonder why I'd never seen before how well-equipped my mother is to be a real leader.

"Are our minds agreed?" she finally says.

And as one, everyone replies, "Aho."

And here are the things we have decided:

First, as we'd started to do before we were so rudely interrupted by the threat of those inconsiderate, bloodthirsty bugs, Hussein and I are going to leave our valley and attempt to draw Luther Little Wound into attacking us.

Second, while we are out there, I am going to try to use my Power to locate any oncoming threats. I'll be communicating what I know to the two people with whom I've been able to consistently exchange thoughts, my sister and my brother.

Meanwhile, following Guy's tactical advice, two other parties will have left our valley. My sister Ana will be with the first squad, headed by Guy. Their job will be to intercept any armored vehicles being dispatched our way.

My brother Victor will be part of the smaller group, whose job it is to stop the people bearing the nuclear bomb. It's being led by Tom Yazzie, whose engineering background was a little more specialized than we'd realized before he spoke up at the meeting. It seems that his engineering skills were not limited to hogan building. In the pre-Cloud days, he'd earned an advanced degree in nuclear engineering.

I suppose I should also mention that in Guy's futile search for more AT-4s or any other rocket launchers he might find, our former lawman did come up with something else. Something that should be of considerable help against those tanks. More than one something. But more about that later.

CHAPTER TWENTY-NINE

The Great Bird's Prey

The golden eagle, or something like a golden eagle but considerably larger, was circling in an interesting fashion over an arroyo off to Luther's left.

Perfect for the sort of surveillance he needed to do.

Was it close enough? Or, for that matter, would his ability to take over the ocular regions of a lesser creature's brain still work now that he had but one eye? He had not attempted anything like it since his discharge from the surprisingly well-equipped private medical center at Haven. A center, he had been made to understand, that was not for the use of plebs or anyone below the ranks of the highest servants of the two Ones.

Remembering his stay there, he glanced down at the budding appendage at the end of his arm. The new right hand was now nearly normal, aside from the extra fingers. Seven in total, it turned out after the sprouting of a second, smaller thumb opposite the first. Their number and the fact that, whether he willed it or not, those digits were continuously in motion—clenching, unclenching, wriggling—made that hand resemble some sort of octopod more than anything mammalian. It also had, interestingly, more grip strength than his unusually powerful left hand. When he had tested it by picking up a fist-sized piece of sandstone, it had taken no more than a single squeeze to reduce the rock to dust.

Luther rather liked it. It was so much more serviceable than the clawed apparatus he'd discarded. And wouldn't it be a breathtaking sight when, on his eventual return to his current employer, he displayed it? Before taking the Jester's breath with it.

He peered up again at the huge raptor. It was, without a doubt, about to dive down at some prey. Furrowing his brow, he reached out to establish a link.

No. Not quite.

He concentrated harder, and then, as he closed his one intact eye, found himself enjoying binocular vision for the first time since the near-fatal encounter with his little Apache assassin. However, though he could see through the great bird's eyes, he did not have quite enough of a contact to control its movements—and eventually burn out the delicate neural pathways of its brain. All he could do was share what it saw as it folded its wings and stooped, diving so fast that Luther lost his contact.

But he had seen where that dive was aimed and what it was aimed at.

No! said a voice from inside himself.

It was a voice that, though it was his own, he hardly recognized as he began to run as swiftly as he could toward that arroyo.

Perhaps he had never run so fast before. The landscape around him was a blur at the edge of his vision as his feet thudded down on sand, on stone, crushing sagebrush and rabbitbrush, cactus and creosote. He leaped over a fallen tree trunk as he entered the small, deep valley. Carved by a stream that was dry now, it would be flooded when rain fell on the far peaks that rose off to the north in a purple haze.

Halfway between falling and flying, he bounded down the slope. Heedless of any pain, he crashed through the desert cedars and cottonwoods that had found footholds there, driving their roots down deep to the small seeps of moisture that kept their flat needles and tough leaves green.

Blood was oozing down the side of his face from a sharp branch that had scored a line across his cheek as he landed at the base of the hillside. He paid the deep wound no mind. His entire focus was on reaching that place where the eagle's attack had been aimed. Just ahead—there!

Two shapes struggling in a flat area of golden sand between the sheltering roots of a huge cottonwood.

Then the eagle turned its head and saw him.

SCREEEEEE!

The eagle's scream was for him. It was a cry of defiance and possession.

Mine! That was what it was saying. *Mine!*

The giant bird's talons were wrapped around the thrashing body of the furred creature that was refusing to give up its fight. It was kicking, growling as it tried to break free, biting with little effect on one of the claws that held it pinned.

The eagle cocked its head to one side to stare at Luther. It spread its thirty-foot-wide wings to make itself look even larger as it screamed again.

SCREEE!

Go away. I kill you.

Just go away? Another time, Luther might have done just that. There was something admirable about the great bird's power. A supremely self-assured apex predator defending its catch. There was something poetic about that.

Although, on second thought, admirable or not, he probably would have just terminated it. After all, a killer was just what Luther Little Wound had always been.

But even then, in any other circumstance, he would have used a poison dart, or taken out his gun and blown a hole in the bird's self-confident head. He would not have done what he did, which was to draw his newly acquired knife from its sheath and dive at the eagle's chest with a scream even louder than the big bird's scree.

"EEEEE-YAAAAH!!"

The sound of Luther's scream echoed through the arroyo as his shoulder hit the giant golden eagle in its upper chest, knocking it backward off its prey. Luther's legs locked around the bird's lower body, making it unable to claw at him with its deadly talons. As they rolled back, locked together, Luther's head was below the bird's stabbing beak as his right arm reached up for its neck, his left hand raised the knife, stabbed, sawed back and forth . . .

And it was suddenly over. The windpipe and the major arteries of its neck severed, the bird spasmed and then went slack.

Luther pushed the eagle's body off him. He would eventually feel the pain of the wounds on his back where the eagle's beak had slashed through the thick leather of his jacket into his flesh. But not now.

There was only one thing at this moment of which he was aware: the being that had been the target of the eagle. It was lying motionless, head down against the cottonwood roots where it had been thrown when the immense avian released its grasp.

Luther knelt, slid his arms beneath the large animal's heavy head to gently lift it. Its eyes were shut. Its body was limp as a sock filled with sand.

"Sunka?" Luther said, surprised at how hoarse his voice sounded. "Sunka!"

And the big dog opened his eyes . . . and licked Luther's hand.

CHAPTER THIRTY

Images

Another sunrise. I sit at the entrance of our valley, feeling the land speak to me. Everywhere I look, there are places holding our stories in their names.

I think again how this land is not ours, but ours to care for so that the generations that follow us can enjoy its blessing. I think of what my father said so many times.

We do not own this land, but we belong to it.

I'm not alone as I sit here. There are others here with me. Human people. Horse People.

Mom is standing closest to me, her left hand on my shoulder. Ana and Victor are sitting in front of me. Hussein is on my left.

Farther to my right is Guy. He has his right hand on the shoulder of his daughter Luz. And his left hand is holding my mother's right hand.

Even though they are old people—I mean, my mom is

forty years old—they are now . . . romantically involved. It's not just the hand-holding that has led me to that conclusion. I actually caught them kissing when I walked into Guy's armory last night. Surprisingly enough, I was not all that bothered by it. It was actually sort of cute, the way they quickly let go of each other and stepped back like two little kids caught stealing cookies by their mommy.

The Dreamer and Lorelei are standing behind me, flanked on either side by the rest of those who are going to be involved in our triple-thrust into enemy territory. Tom Yazzie, Rogelio, and two dozen others, all armed to the teeth and dressed for combat. Behind them stand the Horse People, Star, Striped Horse, and their other relatives who were all in on our planning and have chosen to join us.

We are posed this way because . . . we are posing. Our images are about to be taken. One of those who recently joined us, drawn like others to our valley of sanctuary, is a large, deceptively jovial man named Eric. I say deceptively jovial because on his well-armed way here, he dispatched a number of gemods using weaponry he had salvaged from an underground bunker stocked decades ago by a now-vanished sect of survivalists.

It was not just on his say-so that we know about his bumping off those beasts. He brought the photographic evidence he'd collected, using the old-fashioned film and cameras and other equipment that he dragged behind him for a hundred miles in a donkey cart—like a smaller version of the Dreamer's weapon-laden cart that hid his books. Another similarity between them is that Eric protects his precious photographic equipment with as much zeal as the Dreamer guards his books. The darkroom where Eric prints his photos by candlelight is located in one of the cooler caverns behind the Dreamer's library.

"Move a bit to the right," Eric says, gesturing to the people on his left. "Good, now you, stripey horse, can you lift your head just a teensy bit?"

As he arranges us, I am thinking about some of the photos my dad had on old postcards that were printed—according to the information on their backs—way back in 2003. Dad kept those nine carefully preserved cards in a wooden cigar box and would bring them out and look at them with Ana and Victor and me every now and then.

"This is who we were," he'd say. "This is who we still are."

Those photos and that cigar box had traveled with him for years, secure in the bottom of his pack whenever he and other men were dropped into one combat zone or another. They disappeared, though, after the men we'd allowed into our camp as friends seeking refuge killed my father and my uncle and took us as prisoners to Haven. But I had looked at the pictures so often that their images are stored in my mind even more securely than in that treasured box. I just have to close my eyes and remember to see them.

They were images of Chiricahua people from the late

nineteenth century, back when Geronimo and Lozen and Victorio and their small bands of fighters had not yet given up their resistance.

Most of those nine photographs were from 1886, according to the information printed on their backs. A photographer named Camillus Sidney Fly took them during the Canyon de los Embudos peace conference in Mexico. One of them shows Geronimo holding a model 1873 Springfield infantry rifle. He's at the far right of the picture with three others: Yanozha, his half-brother Fun, and Geronimo's son Chappo. Chappo, Dad said, was later forced to go to the Carlisle Indian School in far-off Pennsylvania. There he (and most of the other Chiricahuas exiled there) would die from one of the infectious diseases that burned through the student ranks at regular intervals in those government boarding schools.

The photo that is my favorite was taken at Geronimo's own request. There were some Native people back then, or so my father told me, who were leery of cameras. They thought that taking an image of them would also take something from them, weaken them or injure their spirit. But not Geronimo. The crafty old medicine man was always looking for ways to use the things of white people to his own advantage. That is why his dress was always a mix of traditional garb and clothing obtained—one way or another and sometimes with bullet holes in it—from the whites. He also valued the weapons of the White Eyes and their various gadgets. Though I never saw it,

Dad told me there was a photo taken years after his surrender of Geronimo behind the wheel of a big automobile called a Locomobile.

In the case of pictures, Geronimo wanted his image to be remembered on the one hand, and also was aware of the value of publicity on the other. He knew those photos would be printed in newspapers and would show the public—and the U.S. military—that he was unbowed, his fighters still a force to be reckoned with.

In the picture I saw, he is astride a horse and facing the camera. A scarf is wrapped around his head. He's wearing what looks like a suit coat over a waist-length tunic, and he's bare-legged with his moccasined feet firm in the stirrups.

There's a look on his tight-lipped face that is hard for me to describe. It's defiant and determined. But I think there was also sadness there. When that photo was taken, he was nearly sixty years old. He'd seen the deaths of so many people he loved—his first wife and their children, other close relatives and friends. He'd tried more than once to live in peace with the Americans, but he'd been deceived so often that it was hard for him to ever trust any agreements between his people and the government. That was why he ended up taking the path of resistance again and again.

The horse he's riding has a white blaze from its forehead all the way down to the tip of its nose. Its ears pulled back, it looks as ready for battle as its rider. When I look back over my shoulder at Striped Horse standing behind us, I see that same look on her face. Next to Geronimo and his steed, another mounted Chiricahua man holds the reins of a beautiful horse that looks, in the old black-and-white picture, to have been chestnut-colored. That man, who I used to think of as the best-looking Apache man who ever lived, is Naiche, the son of Cochise. Maybe I used to think that about him because my Uncle Chatto looked a lot like him.

In the picture, Naiche's face is shaded by a wide-brimmed hat, and he looks deadly serious. Like his famous father, Naiche himself became a chief. He was one of the very last of our people to finally surrender. Then, like all the other members of our small nation—men, women, children, even the Chiricahuas who served as scouts for the army against their own people—he was put on a train and sent to a prisoner of war camp in an old stone fort by the great water far to the east.

"Everyone," Eric calls, "eyes front."

I turn back to the camera.

"Ready?" Eric says.

He doesn't ask us to smile. I'm glad of that. I want the look on my face to be as determined as the expressions of those people from all those years ago. This may be our last battle, but I hope not. I hope that maybe, just maybe, someday some child of our people in the future will look at the photo of us the way I remember looking at those pictures of Geronimo and his stubborn comrades.

CHAPTER THIRTY-ONE

Nicely Done

Luther sat like that for a long time, the dog's head in his lap, feeling the steady in and out of its breath beneath his left hand. His dog. Even though Sunka was larger— much, much larger than when he'd last seen the animal—there was no doubt about its identity.

It was strange how at ease Luther felt.

You've grown up, he thought.

Not exactly a brilliant observation, the sardonic part of his mind countered. However, that part of his brain which had nearly always been in control before now, somehow, seemed separated from what he was now experiencing.

Luther had never been of two minds before. Was it because of his last almost-death? Or was it because of his reunion with this being from a past that he thought long gone?

He felt confused in a way that was also quite new to him.

He pushed that confusion aside as his right hand stroked Sunka's broad head and the huge dog sighed at his touch.

Sunka was huge, indeed.

How long had it been? Luther counted the decades in his mind. Ten of them. One hundred years since he left that training facility in the Black Hills, his hands and legs shackled. Never to return to that place again. And now here, a thousand miles away from the Paha Sapa, they had come together again.

A century. Long enough for ten normal dogs to have grown old and died. More than long enough.

But what was it that the late, unlamented Sergeant Barker had said? *A special animal, one that might outlive your useless asses.* That was it. A dog that had been genetically modified in various ways, including his expected life span. It meant that, rather than old, Sunka was merely mature.

In the long years since their parting, the canine had grown to his full size—a thousand pounds at least, double the size of a lion. Powerful, judging by the heavy hands of musculature. More than able to hold his own against anything his size or bigger. Including that giant golden eagle.

Had it not been for the fact that Sunka was already weakened by bullet wounds, he would never have been vulnerable to attack from that avian monster. Nor would the immense bird likely have attacked him at all, despite its own size. Though most thought of eagles as hunters of nothing but live game,

Luther knew no eagle would pass up the chance to tear at the tasty flesh of something recently dead. No doubt it had been surprised when the seemingly deceased animal began to put up a fight as soon as it was grasped by the raptor's talons.

Luther looked at the slugs he had dug from the dog's flesh. Sunka had lain there uncomplaining as he did that. There were seven of them, two of them totally flattened when they struck but did not break bone. It seemed that the big dog's body had that in common with Luther's—bones that were only a little less hard and unbreakable than steel. None of the .45s had penetrated farther than the length of one of Luther's little fingers, nowhere near deep enough to damage any vital organs.

However, being shot like that had been enough, from the shock of the impact alone, to seriously weaken and temporarily impair the large dog. Luther ran his hand carefully over the nearest of the wounds he had widened with his knife blade so he could pry out the bullets. The flesh was already knitting itself back together in a way entirely familiar to Luther, since his own healing abilities were much the same.

Who did this to you? Luther thought.

As soon as that question crossed his mind, Sunka raised his head to look over to the right, farther down the arroyo.

You heard my thought?

Sunka's tongue licked the back of Luther's hand.

I'll take that as an affirmative, Luther thought, patting the dog's head—a response that was totally unconscious on

246

Luther's part. What he did notice was how dry the dog's tongue was and the white flecks of foam at the corners of his lips.

Luther lifted Sunka's head with both hands and slid himself out from under as he stood up.

I'll be right back.

He followed the drag marks and footprints in the sand that led farther up the draw.

As soon as he climbed the rise in land that had hidden the narrowest part of the small valley from his view, Luther saw the answer to his question below a rock outcropping that jutted out like the roof of a shed to create an area of shade. Four answers, to be precise.

Their broken rifles thrown to the side, they lay there. One of them was missing a face, the result of large, strong jaws crushing the forepart of his head. Another had his throat torn out. The remaining two dead men appeared to have been grabbed—one by the front of his chest, the other by his back, and then violently shaken until they resembled battered puppets with disjointed limbs.

All four of them wore the white armbands and the embroidered *L. T.* on their shirts that marked them as minions of Lady Time.

Former minions.

Nicely done, Luther thought as he looked around.

The glint of metal caught his eye. There, under a juniper. Inside the open flap of a backpack was what he was looking for. The pack had been thrown free during the brief, violent struggle—a struggle that began only after they fired their guns.

How did Luther know that with such certainty? Know that the giant dog's attack had not been premeditated but done purely in self-defense? No words, no message as such had come to him from Sunka's mind—yet he knew it had been that way. In fact, he saw it in his own mind as clearly as if it was his own memory.

Resting in shade of rock. Peaceful.

Four men come over hill, see me.

Shout, shoot. Shout, shoot. Shoot, shoot, shoot, shoot, shoot.

Pain of bullets striking shoulders, chest, hip.

Growling, leaping.

Screaming, crunching of flesh, taste of blood and bone, tearing of cloth, shaking. Metal and wood hard in mouth. Breaking guns that shot.

Thirst, pain.

Try to reach spring. Smell of water flowing.

Spring many steps away. Too many. Crawling now.

Exhausted, breathing hard, slugs burning beneath skin, burning.

Eyes closing.

Sudden strike of eagle's claws.

Then, HIM.

The one missed so long.

The one whose face is warm, whose body glows golden.

HIMHIMHIMHIMHIM.

Me? Luther thought. *Is that how I look?*

He pulled the canteen of water from the pack and went back over the rise. Sunka had rolled over to his belly now, but looked as if his head resting on his front paws was still too heavy to lift.

Luther knelt. He placed his right hand in front of the dog's muzzle and poured water into the cup of his wide palm. Sunka opened his mouth and began to lap the water with his wide tongue. The feel of that warm, rasping tongue against his hand made Luther feel something that seemed altogether strange. It took him a moment to find the word to describe that feeling.

Contentment.

He poured more water, and the dog drank, raising his head as he felt the strength returning to his body.

"Good boy," Luther said, stroking his head. "Good boy, Sunka. Good boy, partner."

CHAPTER THIRTY-TWO
Two Cedars Waiting

We're passing through an area where red and gold flowers carpet the trailside, their colors throbbing like thousands of hearts.

I've been trying so hard to reach out with my Power that my head feels like a balloon about to burst.

I can hear every creature around us—the tiny blue butterflies flapping their wings among those flowers, the long line of tiny ants scraping up the side of a wide-armed saguaro, the thudding hooves of a herd of javelinas snuffling along the arroyo to our right.

I'm not just seeing the colors of the flowers, the stones glittering with mica and quartz, the bushes and trees—I'm feeling those colors, tasting them, swallowing them.

I can hear Hussein's heartbeat and that of our horse companions, the flow of the blood through their veins.

I'm part of it all, the roots of the plants as they probe slowly through the soil, the steaming lava lifeblood of this planet moving miles below us.

It's too much. I'm swaying, about to fall off Striped Horse's back, fall and keep falling forever. The soil will open up before I hit it, and I will tumble into the deepest darkness.

Hussein and Star are moving closer so he can reach out to steady me, but they're too late. I . . .

STOP.

Hally's soundless voice hits me like the slap of a hand across my face. I jolt upright, aware of nothing more than the usual information gathered by my five senses.

"Lozen," Hussein says, holding one hand out to me, the other hand on his chest. "You are well?"

I can feel the warmth of his concern. It mixes with a similar wave of caring from our two four-legged companions.

"Not quite," I say, patting the neck of Striped Horse to reassure her.

"Rest?" Hussein asks. A good idea.

"Yes. We need to stop for a little."

We both dismount, and after he brushes an invisible bit of dust off his knees, he hands me a canteen of water with a graceful gesture.

I nod my thanks, unscrew the top, savor the coolness of the metal, the sweet flow of water over my lips and tongue as I drink deeply, mentally thanking the spring in our valley from which this welcome water came.

I let out a deep breath as I hand the canteen back to Hussein. We've been riding since just after dawn without stopping, and the sun is in the middle of the sky now. But it was neither thirst nor weariness that nearly unhorsed me.

I survey our surroundings. No sense of danger from any direction. There's an exposed outcrop up the hillside above us where two small cedars are growing. I feel that place calling to me. I point up there with my lips, look back at Hussein, gesture for him to wait. I start walking up the steep, almost invisible trail to Two Cedars Waiting.

As is often the case, what seems close in the clarity of the desert air is farther than one might think. The climb is taking longer than I thought. There's time for something to come to mind, another of the stories my mother told me about a place called High Trail Between Hills.

"Old Man Owl," my mother said, "he was walking along that trail there between the two tall hills when he saw a girl on top of one of those hills. She called to him.

"'Come up here to me,' she said. 'Come here now.'

"That got Old Man Owl all excited. He stepped right off the trail and started to climb up that hill. But when he was no more than halfway to the top, he heard someone else calling to him. It was another girl standing on top of the other hill.

"'Old Man Owl,' she called, 'Come on up here to me.'

"That got Old Man Owl even more excited. He went back down and started to climb that other hill.

"But before he could reach the top, that first girl called, 'I'm still waiting for you. Come on up here.'

"So Old Man Old turned and went back down to start climbing the first hill again. But he never got to the top because the second girl called him yet again.

"It went on that way for a long time. Old Man Owl never reached the top of either of those hills. Finally, he was so worn out that all he could do was limp back home while those two girls laughed about the way they had tricked him."

I laughed, too, when my mother told me that story. But I also learned from it. When you set out to do something, don't allow yourself to get distracted. Keep going along the trail you chose.

It takes me a while to get to my objective. When I finally reach Two Cedars Waiting, I see that they're not small at all. They just seemed that way because they were so high above us. I peer back. Hussein looks smaller than an ant. I can see a very long way in every direction. None of my senses are alerting me to any sort of danger nearby. I hold up my hands, turn in a small circle. My palms remain cool.

The cedar trees are four times my height, almost identical. Their trunks are gnarled and twisted from age and the thrust of the winds that wash over this high place. Two low branches have grown together, twined around each other so it seems as if they are holding hands. They've shaped what looks like a seat.

"Friends," I say to them, "can I rest on your branches?"

Words don't come back to me in response to my question. But I do have a feeling of being welcomed, and so I lower myself onto that woven seat of living wood.

Living, indeed. Trees are living beings. Perhaps all humans know that. But I'm not sure that they know just how alive trees and all the other plants truly are. We could not live without them, and we believe they know that. They communicate with us and with one another, even though people seldom pay attention to their voices, saying that what they are hearing is nothing more than the wind passing through needles and leaves.

Some of our old stories tell how long ago, the trees agreed to allow human beings to use them because there was no other way we could survive. They would allow it as long as we remembered to respect them, ask permission to use them, and always give thanks for their sacrifice.

That is why every tree cut and brought to Valley Where First Light Paints the Cliffs was spoken to, given an offering of pollen before it was cut. That's why inside our hogans and shelters, we feel protected and accepted by the logs themselves.

The two branches woven together give just a little when I sit. I lift my feet off the ground, and they swing back and forth. It's a reassuring feeling—like being a baby again in a cradleboard hung from a branch rocked by the wind.

I breathe in, breathe out. I close my eyes. All the tension and anxiety is leaving me, the anxiety and tension that led me to not just try to use more of my Power—as Hally had suggested—but to try too hard, too much.

Good.

Where are you? I think.

Here. Where else?

The mental voice inside my head is amused. I open my eyes, half-expecting to see my Bigfoot buddy. But no. Nothing but this ledge, the trees, the cliff at my back.

Where, I think, **is here?**

Not there.

Just when I am finally starting to relax, he butts into my brain to play word games. I almost start growling. Then I shake my head. So what if he wants to have his fun? After all, he did just help me again. But I do not need to keep playing his game. Next thing I know, he'll be saying, "Who's on first?" Which he has said before—though I have no idea why. Keep it simple, Lozen.

Thank you for your help, Hally.

Don't mention it.

Then, for once, I wait. I do not get exasperated or ask more questions. Just stay as silent in my mind as I possibly can. Well, not totally silent. Actually, I am counting.

One and one pony, two and one pony . . .

I get to one hundred and twelve before Hally's breathless rumble fills my cerebral cortex again.

No questions?

No.

You are certain?

Yes.

I almost smile as I think that. Keep it simple, and maybe just for once, Hally will be the one who loses his patience.

Excellent. In that case, since I am no longer needed, farewell forever.

Whoa! No, wait.

Got you again! Eh!

Hally's unspoken words arrive with a mental picture of him rolling with laughter and holding his sides.

I'm so glad that I amuse you.

I try to make that reply as sardonic and dignified and self-controlled as possible. But I don't succeed. I can't conceal that I'm laughing, too. I'm entertained by my inability to get the better of him almost as much as my hairy mentor is.

Finally, when our mutual mental mirth subsides, Hally gets serious.

You know, you almost went too far.

Yes.

Luckily, almost does not count.

Then I was on the right track? I ask.

A train track, perhaps, with the Midnight Special rapidly approaching. But, no, it was good that you tried. And you learned.

I hope so.

Ah, hope. That thing with feathers.

Huh?

Ask your lanky librarian friend. Now carry on with your mission. And remember, look where you are going.

Look where I'm going? What does that mean?

I don't intend that as a direct question, but Hally plucks it from my thoughts anyway.

Would it be clearer if I suggested you might look before you leap? Mentally, that is?

Something like a bell goes off in my head. For once, one of his enigmatic remarks makes sense. Maybe I am finally figuring out how to communicate with him without ending up feeling frustrated and wanting to kick him in his overlarge teeth.

One further thing. How shall I put it? Two legs bad, four legs good? No, not that. Orwell was such an optimist. Ah, yes, let me put it this way. Watch out for two legs and four legs!

Then, like a soap bubble bursting, Hally's presence is gone from my mind, once again leaving me feeling bemused and in need of delivering a roundhouse kick to his chops.

CHAPTER THIRTY-THREE
Everything

Look before I leap. Mentally.

That was the advice given me by my Bigfoot brain twister. And not only do I think I understand what I should do, I'm about to test it out.

I'm still sitting on the cradling branches of the two cedars. Somewhere off to the northeast is the group led by Guy. His daughter Luz and my sister Ana are with that group. Their aim is to head off the armored assault of Lady Time's troops that's now coming our way. Steam-powered tanks and all.

I turn my eyes to the southeast. In that direction is the smaller group headed by Tom Yazzie and Rogelio. My brother Victor is with them. Their objective is to neutralize the Jester's soldiers and the tactical nuke they may have.

The Dreamer's with Tom's group, too. It turned out his encyclopedic knowledge includes some basic facts about pre-Cloud weapons of mass destruction. The most chilling of those facts is that if the Silver Cloud hadn't arrived, many of those weapons would no longer have just remained in storage. Our defunct planetary Overlords had planned a nuclear solution to their disagreements. Though they had more power than any other time in human history, it wasn't enough for the rulers of the seven global corps.

That became abundantly clear while listening to the Dreamer's discussion with Tom the night before we left our valley.

"I knew," Tom said at the start of their conversation, "that something big was up. At the site where I was in Vegas, they called everyone in who knew anything about the robo-delivery systems, payloads, continental hard sites to hit, and all."

"Bigger," the Dreamer said, "than one might imagine. In my role as a researcher, I could access data classified above my station. They were planning a truly final solution."

"A hot time in the old town tonight, eh?"

"As hot as the surface of the sun. A conflagration unmatched in human annals, leaving nothing but a parboiled planet in its wake. As effective as an asteroid strike. The Eighth Extinction event. Welcome to the Plain of Meggido."

The hair stood up on the back of my neck as I listened. Every nuclear weapon was to have been loosed in the sequences run by artificial intelligence banks programmed to continue until the last rocket roared free.

Tom was shaking his head. "They would have killed themselves along with every other living thing."

"Every living thing," the Dreamer said, raising his long index finger, "unless one changes the definition of living."

"You mean . . . ," Tom said.

"Indeed," the Dreamer replied. "When one is able to download one's entire intellectual and emotional being and place it in safe storage, it can be transferred to a nonbiological unit intact and alive. If one defines 'intact and alive' as being made entirely of tungsten steel, various other metals, and sufficiently sophisticated circuitry, who needs all that superfluous flesh? Or so they reasoned. Plus it was but one planet. There were always the Mars bases and Luna 12. "

Tom shook his head. "And no one was going to stop it."

"Well, I've not confided this ere now, but a few of us of intermediate rank," the Dreamer added, "were less than enthused. Though we doubted its efficacy, we were on the brink of introducing a worm into the world-net servers, a Trojan horse that just *might* have forestalled the launch date. But then our lustrous atmospheric visitor arrived."

"Damn," Tom said.

Damn, indeed.

I looked at the Dreamer in a way I'd never looked at him before. Just when I thought I knew everything about him . . .

Having—it seems—caught some of what I was thinking, the Dreamer looked at me, spread his hands, and shrugged.

"A moot point at best," he said. "Since we were saved from ourselves by said silvery arriver."

That we were close to total extinction had never entered my mind before. I'd just been thinking of survival on a day-to-day basis. Was this how Hally saw things, a huge canvas stretching over eons, and not just in my tiny terms? It made me feel dizzy. I probably couldn't function if I was always thinking about everything, EVERYTHING in big letters.

EVERYTHING.

I had to stop thinking about that. Uncle Chatto had given me good advice when he said it was always best to live now, because now is all we ever have. When tomorrow comes, after all, it is no longer tomorrow.

Now was where I had to be.

But I did pause for just a moment to send out a mental message.

Hally, I thought, *if you are listening to me right now and you and your people had anything to do with sending that Silver Cloud this way, then thank you!*

Here and now, seated on the tree boughs, I am about to see if Hally's advice works. Assuming it actually was advice and not just him joking around.

I look, picturing my sister Ana in my mind. Then, mentally, I leap.

Ana?

Lozen!

You hear me?

Loud and clear, Big Sis.

It's worked. I'm in contact with her, our mental voices as hearable as any carried through sonic vibrations from a few feet away.

How are things going? I ask.

No problems so far. Got anything for us?

Not yet.

Okay. Should I say "over and out" now, Lozen?

"Bye-bye" is okay.

Bye-bye, talk to you soon.

Yes! I rock back and forth in the cradle of cedar branches, a big smile on my face. It was so easy I can hardly believe it. Can I now have regular conversations mind-to-mind like it's no big deal?

Maybe. My Power's been growing. Perhaps it's reached the point where I can do this on a regular basis. Just look first—as Hally suggested. Then leap.

I try it again.

It only takes a few seconds of concentration before I see, really see, my little brother's serious face. Victor actually turns round and looks over his shoulder.

"Where are you?" he says out loud.

Here, I say. *But not there.*

Victor smiles. I am seeing him and everything around him while I am touching him with my mind.

You sound like Hally, he says. *I thought you were right here next to me.*

I know, I reply. *Isn't it cool? Are things okay?*

Yup, we're moving right along. No gemods, no problemas.

Great. I'll be back in touch when I have anything.

Okay. Adiós, then.

Adiós.

I look downslope to where Hussein is sitting in a shady spot next to Striped Horse and Star.

Is everything good, habibi? His question comes to my mind so easily that I realize we can converse this way all the time—if I want us to. I sense, somehow, that I can keep him from hearing my thoughts if I don't want him to. Like shutting my mouth—only doing it in my head.

He's waiting for my response.

Really good. I was able to contact Victor and Ana. Easily.

You are wonderful.

Can a blush be heard mentally?

I step back from the edge. No need to say bye-bye to Hussein. Matter of fact, I never want to say bye-bye to him. But enough of that before I get mushy.

The intertwined branches seem to be waiting for me.

"Thank you," I say to the cedars as I sit down once more.

I need to think about how I'm going to do what comes next. I can easily picture Lady Time and the Jester. All too easily. There were times when my family and I were still at Haven, back when I was held hostage to the whims of the Ones, that their evil visages haunted my dreams. Back then, being as far as possible from them was my most fervent desire.

Of course, it's way different now. But unless they are accompanying their troops, seeing through their eyes as I did that one time might not be all that helpful.

I also need to cast my mental net for the third prong of the attacks headed our way—Luther Little Wound.

Not that I want to do that. I'm hesitant to touch his mind or any member of that lethal trio.

So far all I have done today is reach out to friendly presences, family members or people who care about me, not someone who wants to kill me. I managed a few days ago—without even meaning to—to project my consciousness into first the Joker and then Four Deaths. But all I did was mental hitchhiking, seeing through their eyes, not communicating.

Can I do that again without their being aware of my presence? Just listen in on their thoughts?

The last time I saw Luther Little Wound in the flesh was the day Tahhr sent the two of them off the edge of that cliff. I did not touch the murderer's mind that day, but I was chilled sufficiently by the words he spoke, by his cold, lethal presence, to believe that mental communication would be more disturbing.

Am I strong enough to do this? Why am I the one who always has to do everything herself?

A story comes to mind. One my mother told me once when I was little and feeling sorry for myself.

One time, Rabbit was being chased by Coyote. Rabbit ran and ran, but Coyote was right behind him. Finally Rabbit came to a hole in the rocks and jumped into it. Its entrance was too small for Coyote, but that hole wasn't very deep.

"I've got you now," Coyote said. "I am going to reach in and pull you out."

Was he going to get Rabbit? But Rabbit got an idea.

"Here comes Coyote's paw," Rabbit said loudly. "I will grab hold of it. Then the rest of you can take your knives and cut his paw off."

"Eh!" Coyote said as he snatched back his paw. "I am too smart for you. You are not going to get me!"

Then Coyote ran away.

I'm not as small and defenseless as Rabbit, who was all by himself but used his wits. Not only that, I'm not alone.

So why are you feeling sorry for yourself again, Lozen? Buck up, girl.

As usual, my mom's stories make sense. Remembering that one reminds me not to feel sorry for myself. Enemies can be defeated by those who keep their wits about them.

There's no point in asking why I have to do what I have to do. It is time to move on to the how.

CHAPTER THIRTY-FOUR

Where Have You Been?

No doubt about it. The big dog had been very hungry. Fortunately, a substantial supply of fresh-killed meat had been handy for Luther to feed him. All that had been needed was a bit of dressing—or rather undressing—and then butchering.

True, it was not the sort of meat Luther himself preferred (under normal circumstances), but it proved more than adequate to sate a large carnivore's appetite. Further, from the gusto Sunka showed in devouring the livers, hearts, and various cuts that Luther provided him, it was a diet that the huge animal was familiar with.

As Sunka gnawed determinedly on a thigh bone, his massive jaws crunching through it to get at the marrow, Luther ran his hands along the dog's broad, muscular back. It was a pleasing sensation, the feel of that warm, thick-furred flesh against his palms, made even more pleasurable by the way Sunka wagged his tail with each stroke.

"Partner," Luther whispered.

How strange that word would have seemed but a day ago. How natural it was now for him to say it, think it, feel it. All the years between now and the time he had last seen the dog, then only a less than half-grown pup, seemed as insignificant as a few grains of sand.

He leaned against the animal's side, allowing his arm to drape around Sunka's neck. Not quite an embrace, but close. A happy growl escaped from Sunka's mouth as his molars began grinding up the thighbone.

"Where have you been?" Luther asked. And as soon as he spoke, the answer came to him. As before, it was not in words or in any other form of communication he had experienced with other beings. It came as a knowing.

He knew of the time when Sunka, still finding shelter among the ancient ranges and ridges of the Paha Sapa, had been hunted by the men from the training center. They had guns and other weapons, drones and infra-scan systems. Yet none of those two-legged hunters were as swift or as clever as they thought themselves to be. Sunka's ability to avoid, to evade, to seem to foresee their attempts, was uncanny. And many of those who sought his termination learned too late what it was to suddenly be not just the hunted, but the downed prey.

Throughout all that time he hunted. But the hunt he was on, with amazing determination, was not for prey. It was for HIM. He came back to the base where they had trained, easily bypassing the security. But he did that only once. His enhanced senses told him that HE was no longer there, nor anywhere nearby. (For by then, Luther was learning the brutally taught ways of the staff, the sword, and the ninja on Hokkaido, the farthest north of that pearl necklace of islands once known as Japan.)

When Sunka left that base, deeply displeased at his failure to reunite with HIM, the one human whose spirit was linked to his own, he had left behind an impressive trail of carnage.

He'd suffered his first bullet wounds then, but none of them—even though he was still far from full-grown—had impaired his ability to attack, to terrify with his ferocity, and then to escape.

He began his long hunt then, one that took him out in ever-increasing circles. He avoided confrontation with humans and their machines whenever possible. But when the possibility of such avoidance did not exist, he never hesitated, striking first with shocking effectiveness, then vanishing like a ghost into the mist.

Years passed, and he reached his adult size, still as evasive as a phantom. By now he was far enough from the place where his life began that few would expect his presence. And always, always, he was looking for that one with whom he had bonded. For HIM.

At times, Sunka came close. But because Luther's own work required both quick insertion and then an equally swift departure—more often than not by air—all that Sunka found were traces of HIS scent, as well as, now and then, the incarnadined evidence of the facility with which his missing master plied his trade as the deadliest of assassins.

Perhaps Sunka might, himself, have been caught. Over the years, his own escapes from peril became more narrow—especially when examining a kill zone and then raising his head to howl in futility because he had arrived too late.

But then the Silver Cloud came, and the sky changed. Not just in its color, the deep blue replaced by a paler translucent sheen. No longer were there humans up there among the clouds, being carried by machines or wearing devices that allowed them flight. Gone were all the drones, the electronic sensors, everything that might have aided in his final capture and demise. So it was that he ranged freer of human peril.

But his existence had not been made easier or less perilous. Prior to that end of the world of electronic machines, Sunka's travels had taken him as far as any feet might walk or run, to the southernmost tip of land in the Americas. He had been drawn there by HIM.

Luther's professional activities had mostly been in that southern continent, loaned by his masters to SouthCorp and based high among the Andes in a place that had once been an Incan merchant city made of stone. The final locale to which Luther had been sent before being recalled north had been to Tierra del Fuego. There he had quite definitively wiped out a particularly stubborn pocket of resistance in a cloaked stronghold dug beneath a desolate place named Puerto Harberton.

It was there that Sunka's senses had led him. There, by the cold Estrecho de Le Maire he found himself again too late. He had followed HIS scent to Ushuaia Airport. Again, too late, though only by a day. But the day he arrived there, peering at the runways from the concealment of a patch of small bushes, that day was the longest—or the shortest—in human memory.

It was there at Ushuaia that Sunka had watched the heavens change, the lights go out forever, planes fall like broken birds from the sky. He raised his head to howl, howl longer and harder than ever before, as if sensing how long and hard his endless journey had now become.

But the big dog had not given up. It was from that southernmost point of the former nation of Argentina that he began his own long trek back north where his enhanced senses told him he might find HIM.

It was a journey that had taken years, not merely because of the great distance but because of what Sunka began to encounter with ever-greater frequency—monstrous, genetically modified creatures set free now from the control of humans. Avoiding, escaping—or, when flight or evasion failed, defeating—such terrible adversaries had caused innumerable delays, often because his body needed time to heal from wounds that would have killed any canine without his amazing recuperative ability.

But now, at last, they were together. His life was once again complete.

As he sat there, Luther experienced all of that. He was not hearing it or being told in any easily describable fashion, but absorbing, feeling Sunka's long, impossibly determined quest. Luther shook his head, then reached up with his new right hand to run it back through his long black hair.

"Partner," he said again.

As Sunka turned his head to lick Luther's arm, the burly assassin tightened his grip around the dog's body into what even he might have admitted was an embrace.

CHAPTER THIRTY-FIVE

Reaching Out

I am alone on this rocky hilltop an hour's ride from our valley. I'm facing the sunrise direction again, my hands held up in front of me. My mind is calm, my insides are cool. I'm in that state my Dine ancestors described with a word meaning beauty and balance and more than that.

Hozho. Not hochxo, when I was suffering from enemy sickness, and all around and within me seemed out of balance. Hozho, a state in which all is in order and you're in right relation with nature, with creation, and growth and order and the beings of this world that are good and positive.

Conflict is about to occur. But there are times when conflict is right. The Hero Twins on their long journey to the Sun were tested every step of the way. I've had to fight, too, and my aim, like theirs, has been to protect life, to try to do what I can to restore balance. I'm nowhere near as important or powerful as they were. I am only one small human being. My battles are not going to change the whole world for generations to come. But I'll do whatever I can in my little corner to make things better.

At first I thought it was just me against the monsters. I've learned since then there are others who'll stand beside me. And it is not just humans who are part of this struggle. It's also our new allies, the Horse People—who seem in some ways to be better than humans. We have a lot to learn from them.

And then there are my friends and my family and Hussein, who, as I turn my head briefly to look down his way, is standing and facing east with me, lending me his support.

His quiet voice touches my mind then, bolstering my certainty.

As I shall always attempt to do.

Haven. I picture it in my mind. Small at first, as if seen from a hilltop the way I saw it that day after dispatching the porcupine cat. I draw its image closer, like making the image in a telescope bigger by twisting the barrel. But not precisely like that, because it's not enclosed in a small circle, but seen as widely as if through the eyes of a hawk sweeping down.

It looks much as it has in the past. High walls topped with razor wire, truck tires kept burning to discourage intruders (with the added benefit of poisoning the nearby air for any of those unfortunate enough to be within fifty yards), towers manned by armed guards, though twice as many rifle-toters as there used to be. I should feel flattered. That doubling of the guard is almost certainly the result of my successful foray over the walls several months ago when I launched grenades into the barracks and rescued my family and Hussein. There's another small addition, I note as my disembodied gaze brings me closer. On each corner of the huge, grim-walled prison, there are machine gun nests.

I blink once, and like the old fast-forward arrows on viddy-vus, my vision sweeps past gates, inner courtyards, and into what was once the education wing of the prison.

Not that it was either a place of minimal education or a correctional facility anytime during my lifetime. All the earth's prisons were abandoned before I was born. What need had inhumanly enhanced planetary Overlords for prisons when they were committed to the noble pursuit of reducing "surplus population"?

This place that became Haven was abandoned until the Silver Cloud arrived. Only then did semisecure places such as this become desirable again. The need for walls to protect them from the appetites of rampaging gemods led the Ones to retreat here with their little armies and captive proles to serve their needs.

Who first? The female ticking time bomb or her woodpecker-crested cohort? Even the thought of Lady Time sends a chill down my back. So, since running into fires has always been my forte, that is where I project myself first.

There's no *poof* or any other sort of mystical special effect. Suddenly I am just there. I'm in Lady Time's white room of a thousand timepieces. The lighting is so bright from countless candles burning here that the shadows seem to have run away.

I do not see the One who dwells here, but there's no doubt about it being her chambers. All around me is the maddening cacophony of more clocks than I can count. Timepieces of every shape and size cover all walls. Her insane lust for them resulted in search parties being sent far and wide to bring back every such clock that could be found—no matter the risk. These archaic spring-wound timekeepers were retrieved at the cost of human lives.

Though I was not (obviously, right?) killed obtaining it, that black Swiss cuckoo clock at the top on the farthest right led to a dozen stitches in my right forearm. In all fairness, the critter that inflicted that claw wound—a beast part bear, part wild boar, and entirely voracious—fared worse. Its meat tasted quite good.

It is close to one P.M., and all the synchronized hour hands are poised to—CLICK—strike.

BONG

DING

CLANG

DONG

PING

And so on, but only once. I'm thankful that it was not noon when my phantom self got here. Even outside my body, I'm still able to feel deafened.

BING.

One clock strikes a second late, as happened when I was here before. It's the sort of lack of timing that drives the already nutty Time Mistress even more bonkers.

Poor Walter, I think, remembering the nervous little workman in charge of her timepieces. When last this happened, he suffered her displeasure. If he has any teeth left to lose, he's about to have another dental appointment.

But I hear no angry scream, no hissing voice, as cool and sibilant as a spitting cobra's, ordering punishment for an imperfect servant.

I'd thought that at any minute she'd uncoil her tall, perfect frame from one of the white sofas facing the clock walls, step out from behind the elegant ivory floor-to-ceiling drapes at the back of the room. I was wrong. She's not here.

Which poses the question as to where exactly she might be. Or where would she be if she was planning an assault?

The most logical answer is a location I've yet to see personally—one I used to hope I'd never see, one of her underground workrooms where activities occur that might stain her snow-white carpets.

I picture her in my mind, her elegance and menace, as she looked a few days ago through Luther's eyes.

And there she is. Or, rather, here. My insubstantial self is now in a large garagelike chamber poorly lit by hissing hurricane lanterns. She is standing there, imperiously towering over and giving orders to a squad of men whose numbers I can't yet count in the gloom. The shadows of large vehicles loom in the semidarkness to either side.

"Open!" she commands. The light of day streams in as two hangar-style doors are swung wide. It illuminates the seven large trucklike vehicles with treads rather than wheels. All of them have armor fastened to the fronts and sides with slit windows for the drivers to look through.

Much of each machine is taken up by a boiler and a wood-burning furnace. The steam-powered tanks I'd hoped had not been built. After Mohindas told us about them, the Dreamer disclosed what he knew about Lady Time's tanks.

"Ah, yes," he said. "My dear compatriot's armored steam vehicles. Alas, all those attempted while I was at Haven blew up quite spectacularly—with such an accompanying loss of life that further attempts to harness steam power would have deterred anyone but an insane megalomaniac."

Speaking of which, Lady Time is giving her final orders.

"Failure issssss not acceptable thisss time." Her high-pitched sibilant voice is close to a shriek as she makes herself heard over the sound of the steam engines. "No prissssonerss. Go straight to their cursed valley. Kill them all. Jusssst bring back headssss."

Well, that's clear enough.

The seven engines of death rumble out of the underground

garage. Each is mounted not only with with 120mm smoothbore tank guns, but also flamethrowers with large gasoline tanks and long nozzles. The garage entrance was beyond the wall. They've come out on the flatland west of Haven, heading for Highway 10 toward our valley.

I have all the intel I need for now. But I can't help but pause to look at the bloodthirsty witch herself in her clock-faced mask and her robes as pale as the flesh of a corpse drained of blood.

My mom always told me to look for the good in everyone. In the future, even an enemy may turn out to be a friend. But I can't imagine this figure of menace ever being anything other than a foe. She's everything that made the super sapiens rulers of our planet so heedless of anything other than their desires.

Her back is partially toward me as I study her. Suddenly she turns, moving even more swiftly than her former peer, the pantherlike Diablita Loca, moved in the battle with me that resulted in Diablita's end. But her turn is partially hampered by the fact that one of her feet is bandaged, and that bandage catches on the rough pavement.

She halfway stumbles and would have fallen had it not been for her inhuman grace, a grace only partially thrown off by the amputation of a toe—a result of the wager with the Jester, which she lost when we thwarted her plan to bomb our valley.

"Who," she hisses, "who isss here? Who issssss lissstening?"

"No one, Mistress," a small voice replies from the shadows. It's the little man known as Walter, her clock-keeper, engineer, and personal valet. His voice sounds choked. As he steps into view, he's nodding nervously. His cheeks are swollen as if from an infection. Or from having teeth pulled out.

THWACK!

The serpent-swift slap of her open palm across Walter's face is like a gunshot. He goes reeling back to drop down on one knee.

"I wasss not asssking you," she says, her voice inhumanly calm, more chilling than when she was shrieking.

"Sorry," Walter whispers, arms over his face. "So sorry."

If more than my consciousness were present at this moment, I might be making a leap for Lady Time's throat. But there is nothing I can do in my present state.

Though Lady Time may have sensed my disembodied intrusion in some way, she is not looking at me, not seeing me.

"Where?" she snarls. "Where are you?" She is stalking now toward the back of the garage cave, heading most likely for the hidden stairs that will lead back to her glacial lair.

Maybe there is something I can do.

I draw closer to little Walter, imagine my lips shaping sound from the molecules of atmosphere around him.

Be patient, I make the air whisper. ***Help is coming.***

He looks up. He sees no one. But he's heard me. I know he has because of what he says in a voice so small that it would seem tiny coming from a mouse.

"Thank you," he whispers.

CHAPTER THIRTY-SIX
An Unfamiliar Feeling

Sunka," Luther said, gesturing toward the ground with his open left hand. "Down."

The big dog dropped to his belly. His eyes, locked on Luther's, looked pleased at being able to do as he was asked. But it was more than pleasure, wasn't it?

Luther found himself remembering the words someone said about eyes looking into yours that way. Was it his mother when he was very small? You feel it go into your heart.

Luther slung his rifle over one shoulder, his pack over the other. He swung one leg over the animal's broad back, grasping the heavy fur of its neck with his multifingered right hand as he settled himself in place.

"Up," he said, pulling on the dog's ruff held firmly in his hand.

The dog stood up, not in a leap, but in a careful fashion as if trying not to dislodge Luther from his perch.

Luther leaned forward, holding on with both hands. His feet could not touch the ground on either side, but when he drew them in, they rested comfortably above Sunka's massive ribs. The shape of the dog's back was that of a natural saddle.

Again, that unfamiliar feeling came in his chest.

Time to try something else.

Walk forward, Luther thought.

And Sunka walked. One step, another, another.

Stop.

Right front foot still raised, the big dog halted.

Luther laughed out loud, surprising himself with the sound. He grasped the fur of the huge animal's neck tightly.

Now run, he thought. *Run.*

The wind whipped back Luther's long black hair as Sunka ran, carrying them across the land with a speed that Luther had never known before. He had ridden machines that took him faster than this, but it was different, so different, to feel the heat of the big dog's body beneath him, the movement of Sunka's heavy muscled limbs, the easy in and out of the animal's breathing that was in perfect rhythm with his own breath. They left the arroyo behind them. Ahead of them, the land pushed up hills that they reached with easy strides, crested one after another. They leaped over great boulders, dove down steep slopes, feet never uncertain, speed never slowing as they began to follow a river that snaked its way through thick-leaved cottonwoods.

To the left, he thought, then, *to the right*. And with each thought Sunka responded as swiftly as if his limbs were connected to Luther's own body. And now Luther was no longer just a passenger, not being carried. The two of them were one being, and they were running together.

Something big reared up its head between two large boulders at the water's edge fifty yards ahead of them. It was a golden-haired, four-legged gemod creature with a long elephantine trunk. At least twelve feet tall at the shoulder, somewhat larger than the second similar creature belly-deep in the water just in front of it, its short hair slicked with the cooling river waters. A third, much smaller one that was surely the pair's calf was playing in the water next to its mother, splashing the water with its trunk.

The first giant gemod raised its trunk, long ivory teeth thrust out ahead of a mouth that was bigger and filled with sharper canines and incisors than those of the woolly mammoth whose DNA must have been been part of the mix that created it. In a split second they'd be upon the creature. It gave a trumpeting cry as it tried to turn toward them, protect itself, its mate, and their little one.

TUUURRUUNNHHH!

But it was hampered by the big rocks to either side. There was a mix of defiance and fear in its red eyes—orbs that that might soon be darkened by death.

An easy target. Three easy targets, to be precise.

Another time and Luther would have considered the best way to kill these creatures and then, having made a choice, followed through to the fatal conclusion.

But that would have meant pausing, taking the rifle from his shoulder, aiming and firing three or four shots. All that would have required no more than a few heartbeats, a simple exchange for the cutting of their breath. Yet Luther found that he was not ready yet to stop this headlong running. This feeling of near flight far outweighed the pleasure of taking a few more lives.

Up, he thought.

With one great leap after another, Sunka's feet took them to the top of the first of those great boulders, high above the creature's head to the second huge rock, then down the other side, leaving the gemod mammoth behind, bugling its defiance—with perhaps a note of relief in its trumpeting.

Where were they running? What direction were they taking? What goal did they have in mind? None of those questions were in Luther's mind. He was lost in the pure bliss of it. No moment but this moment. No time but this time. They ran and kept running.

Together.

CHAPTER THIRTY-SEVEN

More to Do

A third of my task is done. Well, actually less than that. I've located Lady Time and her forces and know what they have and that they are headed straight for our valley on Route 10. What I need to do to complete this part of my mission is pass on that information.

I look down toward Hussein, who is standing now with one arm on Star's back, his cheek pressed against the big gemod horse's neck. The sight of him doing that makes me want to go down there and hug him. But not yet. I have to keep my focus on what needs to be done, not what I want to do.

I raise my right hand in a thumbs-up gesture, knowing his hawk-keen eyesight will pick up that sign. He raises his hand to send the same message back to me.

I face the northeast, close my eyes, lift my hands, and feel the warmth filling them.

Ana?

Lozen?

It was even easier this time, almost as simple as turning my head to speak to someone next to me, though I can only communicate this way with one person at a time.

Is Guy there?

Yes.

Okay, repeat to him everything I'm sending to you.

A-okay, Big Sis.

I fill them in on what I've seen, Ana saying out loud the info I'm passing on to her. By the time we're done with our conversation, I'm reasonably sure that they know everything they need. But now I have a question.

Can you ask Guy where he plans to set things up?

You bet.

There's a moment's pause, and then Ana's voice returns inside my mind. As she describes the spot, I have to smile. Perfect. Just the place I would have chosen. The hills squeezing the line of sight better from above, the bend in the road that will make each armored tank invisible to the ones following—all qualities needed for a good ambush.

Even better, it's a place that Hussein and I can reach before Lady Time's armored column does—if that's where we can be of the most use, a decision depending on what I find out next after I end my confab with Ana.

Tell Guy that's great. I'll be in contact again to let you know if we'll be joining you.

We can handle this, Lozen.

I appreciate that note of pride and self-confidence in my sister's voice, even if I am worried she *won't* be able to handle it without us. I don't let her know that. One of the best things a big sister can do is not act like one all the time.

I know you can, Ana.

Catch you later, Big Sis. Over?

Over and out.

I lower my hands, take a deep breath. Doing this doesn't tire me as much as it used to, but I'm going to need nourishment before we hit the road. Did I pack that jerky?

No, but I did, habibi.

I open my eyes and look downslope. Hussein has the packet with the venison jerky in one hand. A bowl of fresh-picked berries is in his other hand. There's a broad smile on his handsome face.

How did I get so lucky?

But more to do first.

I face forward, directly east, hold out my hands, close my eyes, and picture the second nasty character I need to contact with my Power. Four Deaths, the one who will be hunting me. The one I plan to decoy in with my presence.

But when I do that, I get a surprise. He's not directly in front of me, not heading straight my way. Why?

I reach further, using my Power to sweep the land like people in the pre-Cloud days used a searchlight to illuminate the darkness. Still nothing between me and Haven.

This is weird. I know Luther Little Wound has powers of his own. He's used them in the past to control animals and birds—like those red lizard monsters he used against us. Has he found some way to cloak his mind so that I can't locate it? That would be so bad I don't want to think about it.

I don't give up, though. I try reaching farther than I have ever tried to reach before with my Power. It's giving me a headache, but I can't stop now. I probe past Haven, beyond the former prison. And I catch a faint mental glimpse of his presence, a blurry image of his smiling face and none of his surroundings. He's moving fast, faster than a man should be able to run, heading away from me. I touch his mind ever so briefly, and what I feel surprises me.

Instead of that cold lethality that I have come to associate with everything about him, I get this feeling that I can only call, if you can believe it, contentment. And, even stranger, companionship. Warm, furry, familiar . . .

What the . . . ?

But before I can feel or see more, he's out of range.

I have no idea what's going on. I guess I should be grateful. For whatever reason—whether he's on some kind of drug or he's gone crazy, he is not a threat, at least not right now.

Time to consider the third of our enemies, one who is certainly certifiably insane. The Jester.

I turn toward the southeast. Take three.

I take one breath, then another, and my presence has been projected into Haven once again. I've accomplished it more than twice as fast this time. I guess such mental exercises as my confusing attempt to find Four Deaths have developed enough psychic muscle to make me better at this stuff.

I'm in front of the green door emblazoned with a yellow smiley face, crooked smile and fangs leering at me. Then I am inside. But what has drawn me here is not the actual presence of the Jester himself, it seems. It's my memory of being here and not the semihuman being who haunts this abode.

His big lounging chair is empty. No sign of him anywhere, including behind the green curtains where I've never looked before. And now that I've looked there, I wish I hadn't. Everything that I used to imagine the Dreamer had concealed in his chambers is actually here. Where the Dreamer kept hidden shelves of books, the Jester has things—most of them stained reddish-brown—that I'd rather not describe.

So where is he? And how is it that I've managed to see a part of the green-haired demon's private quarters that I never laid eyes upon previously?

I think I know how. I'm following where the Jester went, seeing what his eyes saw. Just as a dog can follow a scent, my disembodied self is sensing a trail left by the one I'm seeking.

It's not his scent—my olfactory sense doesn't seem to be part of the equation when I'm projecting myself this way. What I'm registering might be called a psychic odor. It's undeniably the Jester's. I see it as a wavery green line of mist. Although my nose is not picking it up, it has a truly awful mental odor.

Phew! I am going to need a hot bath after this!

But at least it makes it easier to follow him. I come to a concealed door and pass through it as easily as light through a pane of glass. Metal stairs lead down that might echo under my steps if I was presently accompanied by physical feet. Another door, one that looks to be made of stone. Of course I don't open it. Just continue forward, and I'm on the other side in the main yard of the former prison. That door I wisped my consciousness through is in a shadowed corner of one of Haven's walls. A hidden way to take people—probably at night—up to the grinning madman's lair. If I had my body with me now, there'd be goose bumps on my arms at the thought of what he did to them when they got there. It explains why in the past, now and then, proles would vanish and no one would know how or where they'd gone.

I mentally clench my fists, wishing they were punching his sardonic face.

Follow the trail, Lozen. Don't get distracted.

It leads to the door of the Armory. As usual, there are two guards outside. One wears a white armband, one wears a green one. They don't see me, even though they are looking right in my direction. The heavy door is locked. No problema. Whoosh. I am inside what used to be my friend Guy's domain.

No hurricane lanterns lit. Certainly no candles. An open flame in a room full of explosives is not a great idea. But enough light comes in from the four high, tightly barred windows for me to see. Perceiving light like this may mean that my projected consciousness would be as blind in total darkness as a physical self.

Interesting. But this is not the time to speculate.

I look around. The walls are lined with guns as always, and there are boxes and belts of ammunition, but no human presence.

There's something new, though: a very large, heavy table in the middle of the room. Atop it are wooden crates, all open. There's evidence in the form of various tools that something was put together here. I drift to the far end of that work table. There's a box bigger than any of the others, made of thick metal. The design on it looks like a planet with rings around it. The lid's off, and packing materials obscure the words written in red on it.

I can read the first word and enough of the second to know that whatever was in that lead box bodes ill.

DANGER NUCLE . . . .

Damn it.

I leave the Armory, following the Jester's disgusting trail. Out through the front gate of the former prison.

There are tracks in the soft earth between the gate and the other, smaller highway that leads away from Haven to the southwest. They tell me a lot.

First is that the Jester is accompanied by a lot fewer men than Lady Time's armored brigade following Route 10. A dozen, by my best count, registered their tracks in the soil, plus the Jester, whose feet are bigger.

The second is that the white-gowned witch hasn't shared her new steam-powered tech with her crazy cohort. No sign of any of the deep tank treads her mechanized minions left when they departed Haven.

Third, which is surprising, is that although they do have some sort of wheeled vehicle with them—one with wide-spaced, heavy tires that have left a deep imprint—they're not pulling it themselves. Some sort of animal's doing it for them.

Its three-toed hoof prints register sizable claws. From the way they sank into the ground, it's a big four-legged beast. The other visible evidence of it being here consists of several large piles of poop. If I were able to move anything in this state, I could poke at those piles and deduce how long ago the animal passed through here.

Until I encountered Tahhr and our Horse People allies, I always thought about gemods the way everyone else did— fierce creatures that can never be tamed. Interesting that the Jester's people have this gemod ally.

The tracks end when they reach the paved roadway, but I

can still follow. The Jester's vile green spoor is still visible to me. I trail it west, past Casa Grande. At the next intersection thirteen miles south, it turns onto Highway 8.

His going this way is not good for us. He may avoid both forces we sent out to intercept our enemies.

I pause there. The uncared-for highway is cracked by sun and weather. Where the road has broken down to gravel, the tread marks of the wheeled vehicle and the animal pulling it can be seen. But there's no sight of the Jester's party. All I can see is the road diminishing and disappearing into the distance, the mountain peaks of the Maricopas.

Though taste and smell and touch are lost when I travel this way, I can still hear things.

So I listen. All I can hear is the faint whisper of the wind in the mesquite and a single cricket chirping.

Damn it again. The Jester is much further along on his deadly mission than is Lady Time.

But how far? I have to know.

I leap forward so fast that for a moment I feel dizzy. My eyesight and hearing are blurred, almost as if I was underwater. I have not done as Hally told me to do—looking before leaping.

AWWWWRUUUNHHH!

That brings me back to focus. That awful sound just came from the creature bearing down on me. Just before it passes through me—harmlessly—I see that it's some blend of an enormous camel and an equally large carnivore. Its muscles ripple as it strides along—a formidable foe to face free and in the flesh.

A heavy leather-and-metal muzzle is wired over its huge, long-nosed mouth—from which large canine teeth protrude. Its limbs are constricted by straps around its body to pin it in place between the shafts of the vehicle it's pulling. It's protesting, but not stopping because sharp metal prods are being thrust into its backside by the men running along to either side. Those prods are not the only thing that is keeping the gemod camelion going. A broad-shouldered man with a whip is cracking it across the big beast's shoulder. I'm guessing he's the poor animal's head trainer or, more accurately, chief tormenter. From the wave of resentment I feel as the huge gemod turns one tortured eye toward that man, I'm pretty certain my guess is accurate.

The animal's direction is being controlled by a metal bit between its teeth. The bit's sharp edges have cut just enough into the beast's tough lips to cause a trickle of blood from the edges of its mouth. It's causing so much pain to the animal that I can feel it from within its tortured brain. All the gemod can think about is moving forward to try to escape.

The reins lead back to the one I'm seeking. He grips those reins languidly in his left hand. A large sun umbrella is being held by a lackey over his head to shield him from the heat of the hazy sun. He's not running, like the sweating men prodding the camelion, but perched on the wheeled vehicle.

The vehicle itself was shaped out of the back end of one of those old-fashioned trucks they called tractor somethings, the ones that were abandoned after the advent of mag-levs made wheels a thing of the past, until the past caught up with the present.

Seeing the Joker without being able to do anything to wipe that evil grin off the visible part of his face is bad enough. But what's worse is seeing what is mounted on that trailer bed just behind him. I'm not sure exactly what it is, but I know its purpose. And there's not just one of them. There are three!

Triple damn.

The convoy is moving fast—too fast. I try to count the number of men in the Jester's crew. Three runners. And on the trailer with the Jester there's a bunch of others. Big men, heavily armed. Probably all red-eyed and hyped up from being on Chain, the super-amph drug that the Ones feed their mercenaries. There's a dozen of them, maybe more. I can't tell exactly how many, since they are under a canvas canopy to keep out of the heat of the sun.

As I watch, the prodders peel off, hand their metal spears to two more men who've slid out from under the canopy to take their place, and jump on the truck.

Running in relays like that, they'll be able to keep going without rest. They'll be in range of Valley Where First Light Paints the Cliffs all too soon. Is there enough time for Tom Yazzie and his crew to intercept them?

I turn my disembodied eyes to the landscape around them.

Quadruple damn!

They're closer to our valley than I feared.

No need to linger here any longer.

Back in my body, I descend the slope from the cliff faster than most ordinary folks would dare, leaping from rock to rock, not even bothering to zigzag to keep on the trail. I'm probably going even faster than someone with my abilities should attempt, but there's no time to waste.

Hussein is already on Star's back with everything packed and ready to go. He and the two Horse People are watching as I leap down, my feet barely grazing the tops of the last three boulders. All three of them are worried that I might break a leg—or my neck—before I get to them. But I do not have time to worry about my own safety. I just have to get us moving.

"Where to?" Hussein says as I hit the ground, raising a cloud of dust that I leave behind as I bounce up and vault onto Striped Horse's back.

"Tom's crew," I say. "We're close enough to join them in half an hour if we ride fast. My idea is that . . ."

I tell him and our four-legged allies what I've seen and what I plan to do as we head off at full gallop to the southeast.

CHAPTER THIRTY-EIGHT

Two Miles

Davy Crockett," Tom Yazzie says, scratching his chin. It took a little longer than I thought to reach him. He's had time to think about the message I sent to him by way of my little brother Victor, who looks as grim as I am feeling right now. Maybe having time to cogitate about it is why Tom does not look as upset as I feel. Or maybe it is just how Tom is by nature. I have yet to see him look perturbed about anything. I mean, if he was on fire, he would probably just calmly ask where the nearest water was.

"Davy Crockett," Tom says again. "King of the Wild Frontier."

A supercilious smile crosses the Dreamer's lips, and he nods. "Ah, indeed. That device. The one named for none other than that renowned Indian fighter, member of Congress, and sainted defender of American expansion until his demise at the mission of the trees of the genus *Populus*."

I'm pleased to see that Tom Yazzie at first looks as clueless as I am about what the hell the Dreamer is talking about. Then he snaps his fingers.

"Wait, I got it. Aspen trees. The Alamo, right?"

"Full points." The Dreamer grins.

I shake my head. "English, please. Or some other language I can understand."

Tom and the Dreamer exchange meaningful glances and then turn to me.

"First of all," Tom says, "you done good, Lozen. What you saw and described to us is a simple, rocket-propelled short-range nuclear device. The military men that tested it called it the M-29 Davy Crockett."

"Said cognomen having derived from . . ."

I hold up my hand. That, and the glare I direct his way, stops the Dreamer in mid-sentence.

"How short range?"

"Two miles."

"What can it do?"

"Aside from blowing things up real good?" Tom says. "But no, I ought to get serious about this. Assuming that it still works—seeing as how these things were manufactured over a century and a half ago—each one carries a payload equal to about twenty or thirty tons of explosive. Within five hundred feet, everybody's dead pronto. Within a quarter mile, everybody gets a fatal dose of radiation. If one lands in our valley, then that is all she wrote. We've all just bought the farm. Plus, even if we evacuate ahead of time, the radioactivity will make it impossible for anyone to ever live there again."

A range of two miles. When I used my Power to see them, they were only about twenty from our valley and moving at about ten miles per hour.

The fact that they left so much sooner than I expected and headed farther south to approach us means that Tom and his crew have overshot them. As did Hussein and I. We're now forty miles from our valley. I should have reached out sooner to try to find out the Jester's plan.

Even with the help of our Horse People, there's no way we can reach them before they are close enough to fire one of those awful weapons. They have too much of a head start on us.

Lovely. Everyone there is doomed as doomed can be, and there's nothing I can do about it.

Really? How dramatic.

Hally?

You rang?

No, I . . . never mind. Do you know what's happening? Can you help us?

Was it not said that the Lord helps those who help them-selves?

Maybe. Whatever. Just tell me what you mean for once.

I swear I get the feeling of a broad, toothy smile being projected into my mind. And then I hear Hally's voice singing in my head again.

You go back, Lozen, / And do it again.

What? No answer. I say it out loud. "What?"

Everyone turns to look at me, several of them rather confused.

But not Victor or Hussein. They've been here before and recognize the look on my face.

"Hally?" they ask at the same time.

I nod. Words are failing me at the moment.

Hussein nods back at me. "And did the djinn speak in riddles again?"

More accurately, the lyrics of ancient pop songs. But what Hussein just asked turns a light on in my dim brain. Devious as my hairy, big-footed friend may be, he has always been helpful. Even when he speaks in riddles. And riddles always have an answer.

Go back. Back where? Back in my bodiless state to the Jester's caravan.

Do it again. Do what? I can't touch anything physically, certainly cannot—even assuming I learned how to do it at will—send a fireball from my hands to melt down those three nukes. But I can reach out with my mind. And suddenly I know who—or rather what—I need to reach.

To stop the wheels turning round.

I look at Hussein, and I can tell he's been hearing—as he often does when I subconsciously want to share my thoughts—that interior conversation I've been having with myself.

"Go," he says.

I turn around, start to raise my hands, and I am already there. The Jester is looking even more pleased than he did before, and there's good reason for that. He's at least a mile closer than he was when I last looked in, and the beast yoked to his four-wheeled trailer is running faster than it was before, its huge splayed feet kicking up the reddish-gray sand.

Time to give it a try. I reach out for the gemod camelion's brain, feeling once again the pain and resentment flowing washing through it like a flooded stream.

Perfect. Step two, a simple suggestion, not voiced in words but in an image of the camelion itself.

Head turning to the right.

The camelion's head moves in that direction, prompting the Jester to pull hard on the reins to keep his captive beast going straight.

Pain from the razor-sharp bit cuts into its mouth.

I'm sorry about that, but I need to make sure this is working before trying anything extreme.

I send the tortured gemod a mental image of its head turning to the left.

As before, it responds instantly, prompting another brutal pull on its reins by the Jester.

"You there," he calls to the man running on the camelion's left, "use your prod."

The man does so immediately, jabbing the sharp pike into the gemod's right flank.

AWWWWWRRUUUNNNNHHH!

Its bellow is accompanied by a very graphic mental image of what it would do to the prodder if it were not strapped into place as it is. That resentment, that anger, is what I now intend to harness—or rather unharness. I am not intending to tell it what I wish it to do. Instead, I am going to strongly suggest to it what it already wants to do.

I've noted the way that the camelion has been fastened in with those heavy metal-and-leather straps across its back and chest. But, perhaps because they either didn't want to impede its ability to run or just considered the beast too stupid to require any further restraints, there are no straps around or behind its long legs. Legs, I believe, that are just long enough.

Just two more images need to be sent.

Numero Uno: the camelion coming to a dead halt.

And it stops, stands without moving despite the prods, the crack of the whip, the snapping of the reins, and the accompanying curses of the Jester and his stooges.

Image Numero Dos: the camelion digging its front feet into the sand and kicking backward as hard as it can.

It is an incredibly powerful kick, delivered with every ounce of resentment, anger, and frustration the gemod has been feeling mile after tormented mile. It is, indeed, long enough to reach the trailer behind it, and it's even more effective than I'd hoped. Those long, hugely muscled legs deliver a blow to the front of the trailer that doesn't merely drive it backward, ripping the reins from the Jester's hands. That kick is powerful enough to break the traces, lift the front, and flip the entire trailer over on top of the Jester, his umbrella, his henchmen, and those three tactical nukes. Not only that, the trailer breaks in half between its two sets of wheels.

The gemod camelion shakes its head, and the sharp, bloody bit goes spinning from its mouth to knock down the broad-shouldered whip-wielding trainer. Whatever accidental damage is done to the man by that razor-sharp metal is moot, because one of the camelion's well-aimed front feet flattens him a split second later.

I'm no longer in contact with its mind, but am watching this unfold from a point well above the carnage the unfettered animal is wreaking on its former tormentors. The two men with pikes are rapidly transformed from masters to midday snacks as the creature, whose head is four times as big as that of a normal lion, grabs and swallows first one and then the other nearly whole—aside from a few stray limbs.

Seeing nothing moving, and proving to have a more calculating brain than even I imagined, it wheels and takes off at a ponderous but rapid gallop toward the mountains to the north. It is headed away from Haven, its former place of confinement. Thankfully, it is also heading away from our valley. I watch until it is nothing more than a distant speck.

With not a word of thanks to yours truly.

Then I hear a groan from the direction of the overturned trailer. Survivors after all.

The first of them to crawl out, more or less uninjured, is none other than the Jester. The fact that he is thrusting in front of him not his umbrella but a very large rifle with an attached grenade launcher is proof that the camelion was wise to make its exit a rapid one.

He is followed by ten more men, most of them still with their weapons. One of them is dragging an eleventh man who is—unless one's skull being crushed is not a mortal impediment—deceased.

"Leave him," the Jester snarls. Then he giggles. "And dig out my lovely weapons."

CHAPTER THIRTY-NINE
Doing Too Much

I open my eyes and look at the people who've gathered closest to me: Hussein—who has one arm protectively around my shoulder—the Dreamer, Tom Yazzie, and my brother Victor.

"You're smiling," Victor says. "What happened?"

"Enough to buy us some time," I say.

By the time I've finished filling them in, everyone else is smiling, too.

"I wish I could have seen that," Victor says.

"Ah, indeed," the Dreamer agrees. "One might say that you truly upset my former colleague's applecart—to borrow an old colloquialism."

"Rotten apples." Tom chuckles.

"How do you like them apples?" the Dreamer replies.

"If all your apples are bad, can one bad apple still spoil the bunch?"

I am starting to get a headache. It's not just from this cliché fest the two of them are engaging in. I may have delayed the Jester, but he didn't seem to have been hurt much, and he still has at least one usable weapon. I try to hold up my hand to ask them to stop and get serious. Then I realize that my hand is heavier than usual. It seems to weigh a ton.

"Lozen," a concerned voice says. Hussein's? I turn to look at him. All I see is a dark hole. And I fall into it.

"Her pulse has finally stopped racing," someone says.

Her voice is soft, and even though she hardly ever says anything, I know right away who it is, whose lap my head is resting in, whose long, slender hand is holding my wrist. Lorelei.

But I can't see her or anything else. Have I gone blind?

How about opening your eyes, dummy? my inner voice says.

Oh.

I do just that. A circle of staring faces all looking down at me. Hussein stroking my head, Tom Yazzie holding his chin with one hand, my brother Victor with both hands clenched, the Dreamer with his one eyebrow raised quizzically. Behind them the heads of the Horse People: Star; Striped Horse; Tom's four-legged partner Yellow Wind; Hard Rain, my brother Victor's mount; and Black Cloud, who—to everyone's surprise—chose the Dreamer as his rider. Even the horses look worried.

Despite the fact that I just blacked out and that mortal

danger is heading toward our place of refuge, seeing all of them like that almost makes me laugh. Almost.

"Give yourself a moment to recover," Lorelei says.

No time for that. I start to get up.

"Too much, habibi," Hussein says, trying to keep me from standing. "Rest. You've done too much. You need to drink some water, eat something, get your strength back."

I push against him a little harder than I mean to, and it sends him staggering back twenty feet.

"It appears," the Dreamer says, quickly stepping back, "that a sizable modicum of said strength has already returned."

I look over at Hussein. My push not only propelled him backward, it knocked him off his feet. The dirt he's brushing off his clothing now is far from imaginary. I start to apologize. The smile he beams at me tells me that's not necessary.

"Are you okay, Sis?"

"Fine, Vic." I smile at my brother as I say that, but I am not completely fine yet. That headache I was feeling before I fainted is still there. My mouth is dry. My ears feel as if they have cotton in them. I've probably been doing too much. More than probably. Try to take a step right now, and I'm going to end up on my ass.

Someone hands me a cup of water. The Dreamer, with a look on his face that someone might mistake for caring. I drink from the cup, feeling some of the dryness in my mouth being washed away, even if I can't taste the water.

Something warm has just been placed in my hand. It's a piece of flatbread. Lorelei just put it there.

"Eat now!" she says. "You need your strength."

Her voice is so firm and gentle that it sounds just like something my mom would say.

Lorelei is holding something else. "Tom brought this with him," she says. "We just heated it up. Here."

She places a bowl in my other hand. Rabbit stew, my nose tells me. And I begin to realize just how famished I am.

"Go ahead," she says again. "Eat."

I do just that. By the time I've finished, I've gulped down four pieces of bread and two more bowls of the best stew I've ever tasted. I'm starting to feel like myself.

"Here." Victor hands me a canteen, its lid hanging on a chain clinking like a silver bell against the shiny metal surface. I lift it to my lips. This time I can taste sweet water, the living spring from which it was dipped, the minerals washed from the old stones through which it flowed.

Somewhere nearby a cactus wren is singing, and a warm desert breeze is bringing me the scents of sage and cedar, creosote and chamisa.

"How long was I out?" I look up at the silvered sun. One hand farther over the sky since last I saw it. No more than an hour.

Tom sees the look on my face. "No worries," he says. "Gave us all time to rest a bit. Now, you feel up to it, we ride hard and get ahead of them, them on foot and us having our horse friends. There's this place I got in mind. We can get there by dark. An old camp of mine where we'll be safe for the night. There's firewood and a good spring. Right between our valley and the Jester's bunch. Settle in for the night, get up before dawn, and get ready to entertain visitors, eh. Good idea, innit?"

It's a decent plan. Tom knows the place he's described. Our little band and what's left of the Jester's forces—are both going to have to pause for the night. Far too many hungry things prowling the shadows, to make any further travel foolhardy.

Should I make any additional mental forays just to make sure? See where the Jester's decimated crew is now? Check out Lady Time's forces with their steam tanks and cannons? And then there's Four Deaths to consider.

No. I can't keep trying to do more. My inner voice is telling me that I shouldn't push myself any more today. I'll need to be at full strength tomorrow.

But there is one thing I do need to do. Check in with Ana.

I walk away from our little group. No one tries to follow.

I don't go far, just to a boulder with a flat top shaded by a sandstone overhang. I run one hand over its smooth surface, my father's words coming back to me.

Rocks are the bones of Earth. Just as alive as the animals and the plants. Alive as your own bones. Without them, there would be no firmness to the world.

I take a pinch of pollen from my pouch. "Thank you," I

say. Then I ease myself down onto the boulder, feeling its cool surface rising up to accept me.

I lift my hands. Right away, Ana's voice reaches me.

Lozen, are you okay?

I'm fine, I think back to her. *Just overdid it a little.*

My sister's own Powers seem to have grown. She sensed my being totally out of it a short time ago. That's good in one way. But maybe not so good in another. I do not want her having access to what's in my head all the time—especially when I am alone with Hussein.

What's that about Hussein?

Oops. Need to have a sisterly talk. But not right now.

Nothing, I think, hoping she can't read any mental inflection in my unvoiced response. *He's fine, we're all fine.* I let a little intentional chuckle come into what I'm sending. *I can't say the same for the Jester and his jolly band.*

As I relate how I've impeded our green-tressed adversary's progress, I can for sure hear her chuckling, too.

That is so great, Big Sis, she says.

So what's up at your end? I reply.

It's all gone as smooth as slipping on butter, she says. Then she laughs. *At least that's how Luz puts it. But we've done just as Guy said we would. We found that spot where US 10 narrows and goes over a hill. And we are all set up in the big boulders above that place. From what you told us, those steam tanks should get here tomorrow by mid-morning.*

Great, I reply. *That's great. I'll check in before then and give you guys an update. But I'm sure you can handle it.*

Uh-huh. But you know what Uncle Chatto always said. You need to always expect the unexpected.

I wonder if my baby sister realizes just how much she sounds like me when she says things like that?

Okay, I say. *Be safe tomorrow.*

You, too, Big Sis. Over?

Over and out.

CHAPTER FORTY

Both of Them

Something warm and wet was being wiped across Luther's face. It was not an unpleasant sensation. It brought something else to mind, an experience from so long ago that he was surprised he remembered it now after it having been buried so long. Someone was singing.

"Hee ya, oh ya hey he!"

It was his mother, washing his face with a soft, warm cloth. She was humming. An old song in that language he'd also assumed till now was nowhere in his recollection. It was the last time he'd heard her voice, the final time she had touched him before both his parents were . . .

Luther came fully awake. He tried to sit up, but could not. A heavy weight was on his chest, not crushing him but holding him firmly in place as that wet warmth was carefully washed over his face again. And again.

Sunka, Luther thought. ***Off.***

The huge dog obediently lifted his front paw from Luther's body. But he also ran his big tongue across Luther's face one final time before leaning back from him.

His eyes were still shut, sticky from the big animal's tongue. Luther wiped them with the back of his hand before opening them.

Both of them.

For the first time since that blast from the little Apache assassin's walking stick shotgun, Luther found himself seeing the world with binocular vision. He reached up to feel his unscarred face, closing first one eye and then another until Sunka's big head came down to bump against his chest and belly.

"Good boy," Luther said, running both hands back across his dog's—no, his partner's—wolfish skull. "Good, good boy."

Luther stood and looked around. At first it seemed they had passed the night quietly, undisturbed in this shallow cave partway up a cliff face in this valley of red, wind-carved stones that loomed around like giant beings. Then he smelled something. Something other than the dog's increasingly familiar, pleasant smell.

It came from over there, something partially concealed by one of Sunka's paws. As soon as Luther turned his attention there, toward whatever it was, the huge dog tried to slide it back out of sight—like a small child hiding something forbidden from a parent.

"Sunka," Luther said, "what have you got?"

Almost sheepishly, Sunka pushed forward what he had earlier been chewing as he lay across the mouth of their shelter. *Here. Want some?* was the big dog's meaning.

It was a seven-foot-long, thick-muscled leg that appeared to have belonged to an exceptionally large green-banded lizard. From the distended nature of his gigantic canine's belly, it was clear to Luther where the rest of the reptile had gone.

Seeking either shelter or food, perhaps scenting their presence, it had ventured into their cave and met a swift and unusually silent demise. Luther had not been wakened—which was a surprise to him. For years he had always kept himself at least half awake at night. But now, with Sunka guarding him, he'd allowed himself to sleep that soundly.

Amazingly, the fact that he had so totally let his guard down, so completely trusted another being with his life, did not disturb him. Instead, it brought a smile to his lips even broader than the one that had found its way there with the realization that he was no longer one-eyed, that a world of depth he thought he would never know again had returned to him.

More than that, it was as if a part of himself that had long been missing had finally been returned.

When had he last felt this way? It came to him immediately. The last time he'd had that feeling of completeness had been during the last days of training with Sunka.

Who am I?

The no-longer-solitary killer ran his left hand back through his thick black hair as he stared down at his right hand. A right hand with not five, but seven fingers. A hand that he was observing with not one, but two eyes.

Who?

As he thought that question, an answer came to him from the big dog. It washed through his mind, a wave as warm as the caress of the animal's tongue had been across his face.

HIM.

And then, as he patted Sunka's side, Luther laughed out loud . . . and began to think.

Luther read books. It was not something he was proud about, nor did it bring him shame. Something about holding one of those rare, banned, often burned artifacts appealed to him. It had been so for him even before the coming of the Cloud. Reading from a page as opposed to a screen was rather a different experience, and among the objects in his pack was usually at least one volume of some sort or another.

Further, even when compared with the immersiveness of plug-ons and sense-nodes, much less viddys, he found the pictures he made in his own mind while reading more imaginative and satisfying. Further, one could much more easily put down a book and pick up a weapon than detaching oneself from a digi-device, should one suddenly find oneself under attack.

Although he did enjoy stories with some sort of warfare in them, he read all sort of books. Biographies of supposedly important people, histories (which usually struck him as rather biased according to the time and place from which their authors came), romances, books filled with pictures that told their stories as well as the words, collections of legends and myths, all sorts of books. The only ones he found of little note were the how-to ones, how to build something (made obsolete by either progress or the ensuing lack of power caused by the Silver Cloud), do something, gain friends or influence, better one's self physically, spiritually, blah, blah, blah. Those he either tossed or used, page by page, for fire-starting.

Among the books he'd found in ruined buildings, in metal boxes in basements, shoved into hiding places between the joists in broken walls, were some that purported to tell about the various indigenous nations of the continent before the Freedom from Religion edicts banned all forms of not only worship but all other "overt tribal behavior" as counter to the interests of the corporate states. A few of those volumes were interesting, if not inspiring. Especially those that told of warriors made bulletproof by medicine. Luther felt a bit of identification with them, some of who came from his own buried tribal past. Yet Luther also found the romanticism and nostalgia about those old ways rather cloying. Especially so in those books that were not written by Indians themselves.

It was, as he sat in the cave with his hands on his dog's warm side, feeling the beating of its huge heart and feeling a strange sort of change coming over him, that he began to remember some of the stories he'd found in books he had read.

Those stories were about people who had, like him, found themselves transformed by some great experience. A vision, perhaps. Often it was some sort of religious thing. Like what's his name, Saul, was it? On the road to Damascus. Or like that Roman emperor, Constantine, who saw a cross in the sky and changed his religion? Conversion? Was that what he was feeling?

Luther shook his head. *Ken*, he thought. That was the Japanese word that Kobiyashi used as he attempted to teach his resistant pupil about Zen.

"*Ken* means seeing. Add to *sho*. Sho meaning essence, meaning nature. It becomes *kensho*. Way of seeing the essence of things. First step toward Buddhahood."

Each sentence, of course, had been punctuated with a blow of Kobiyashi's stick across Luther's back.

Luther knew who Buddha was. He had first been Prince Siddhartha. Luther had, among the books he'd read, somewhat enjoyed the one about Buddha, a spoiled, wealthy young man who had never seen old age or death until he ventured from the walled compound where his overprotective parents had kept him.

Then the young prince saw the world through new eyes and embarked on the long quest that led him to satori—true comprehension, true understanding.

A quest? Not a bad idea. Luther enjoyed travel. But what kind of quest?

Luther shook his head a second time.

Boring, he thought. *Who wants to just end up squatting interminably under some tree?* His days of sitting cross-legged and pretending to meditate had ended when he thrust his blade through his former master's throat.

Yet he felt he was getting closer to grasping what it was he wanted.

Grasping. That word brought a pleasant image to his mind: the fingers of both his hands homicidally wrapped around a certain throat. It made him realize just what his awakening was. Not to be someone or something else, but to be his own man, a man more fully himself . . . an expert in the art of killing.

Even more, rather than being a weapon employed by others, he would serve no further masters.

A crunching sound from behind him turned his attention to his left just in time to see the last macerated piece of the lizard's arm disappearing down Sunka's maw.

"But I am not alone," Luther said, once again patting the big dog's shoulder. In response, the huge animal dropped to its belly and began to enthusiastically wag its tail.

"Good boy," Luther said. "Good boy, partner."

He walked over to the mouth of the cave and looked in the opposite direction of the morning light. That was where the two of them would be heading.

To take a certain person's head.

CHAPTER FORTY-ONE
The Unexpected

'm once again facing the dawn, searching. And as I do so, I begin for the first time in several days to sense the presence of Luther Little Wound. Still too far for me to make that mental leap to be psychically in his presence, but nearer than before and, I believe, heading this way.

I can also sense something else which confuses me. It's as if his aura—or whatever it is that I hook into when I make this sort of contact—has become twice as big. I've mentioned how the Jester's trail is like a green, wavery line that has a bad mental smell. In a similar way, Diablita Loca's presence always had an oily inkiness about it, while Lady Time's can best be described as smoky white, as killingly frigid as the coldest ice.

In the past, Luther's has been red, sharp with the iron smell of blood. But now, now it's browner, not less strong, but with a weird warmth to it.

Are you as confused as I am about this? I am just going to

stop thinking about it. The one good thing about that contact with Four Deaths was finding out that he is still too far away—somewhere to the east of Haven. He won't be able to attack us before we take care of our immediate problems.

We traveled yesterday until it was nearly dark. Just as Tom promised, he led us to his camp. It was actually quite a bit more than I'd expected. So much more that I asked Tom why he'd left it to join us in our valley instead of staying here.

"More'n one reason," he replied. "Safety in numbers was part of it." Then he grinned. "But I think it was mostly because my family got so tired hearing my jokes that I needed a new audience."

Rather than the rough shelter or small hogan we'd expected to find, what Tom and his family had constructed here was an actual house, but one so well concealed—built as it was into a rocky hillside with a roof that was covered with earth and vegetation—that we never would have found it without Tom's guidance.

"Made the walls of layers of truck tires filled up with rammed earth," Tom said as he moved about the three interior rooms lighting propane lanterns. "Piled rocks round them, then more dirt. Good enough place for a few folks to hole up."

Good enough, indeed. Bullets wouldn't pierce its outer walls. Even a rocket shot at it would hardly dent its surface. The interior walls were made of rough-cut planks, the ceiling partially crisscrossed timbers and partially the outcrop from the cliff. The floor was the natural stone of a wide ledge, a little uneven, but smooth underfoot. There were cots stacked inside and a chest full of blankets. A small storage room was stocked with dried food, flour, sugar, coffee, and military-style jerricans filled with water from that nearby spring. The fireplace—stacks of wood next to it—vented back up through a narrow crack in the rocks and the cliff behind us.

All of that, as well as an old-fashioned composting toilet, meant that we could spend the night in relative comfort with no need to venture outside. The whole place felt warm and welcoming. If we had been there for any other reason than to stop a madman from murdering everyone I knew, I would have loved my stay.

Tom's hidden house was even large enough for our five four-legged friends to have spent the night inside with us. But Striped Horse, who had assumed the role of leader of their herd, stayed put when I stepped aside to make room for them to enter.

The image of a sheltered meadow with fresh grass not far from here, a place they'd scented, was sent to my mind. They had no concerns about anything being able to trouble them. It would do so at its own peril.

"Ah, all snug as the bug in the proverbial rug," the Dreamer said as Tom closed the door against the swift-falling darkness. That big, steel-banded door with the double bars across it ensured that none of us had to worry about any hungry night critter making its way in.

"No problemas," Tom said, moving over to the fireplace, where he soon had a stew cooking in a black iron pot. "And tomorrow, when your green-haired joker shows up, we're going to get the last laugh, eh?"

Everything about Tom Yazzie was like that. Making a joke and not worrying about tomorrow. He was so certain we'd be able to intercept and stop the Jester. As a result, he slept like a baby—on his back, his big belly shaking like a hill in an earthquake as he snored.

As for me, I spent more than half the night sitting up and looking into the fire, hardly sleeping at all.

And now it's morning.

Putting my thoughts of Luther Little Wound behind me, I turn slightly to the south. The burning in my palms tells me just how close our would-be attackers are. They're close enough that I should be able to see them with my own eyes if I just climb a little higher on this ridge.

"Come on," I say to Hussein, who's standing closest to me. He nods, then signals to the others to stay put in the places where they've concealed themselves on either side of the road.

The two of us climb up another hundred feet to the top, where I've noticed some handy bunches of sagebrush growing.

If you want to be seen by the enemy, Uncle Chatto used

to say, just stick your head over the top of a hill like one of those metal ducks in the shooting galleries in old viddys.

But if you just stay behind and peer through the brush already standing on top of that hill, you will be more or less invisible.

There aren't all that many leaves on the pale branches of that sagebrush, but there're plenty enough for camouflage. As I look through it, I can see that my Power had been right on. On the road below us, no more than a mile away and rapidly approaching, are our enemies. I lift the binoculars to my eyes.

What I see is upsetting, but not just because they are so much closer than expected, going at a rate that'll bring them in range of our ambush within no more than ten minutes.

Instead, there's a bunch of other reasons for my concern.

Numero uno, apart from being a little scuffed and only half of the original vehicle, that trailer looks to be in good shape. It makes me realize the four-wheeled trailer didn't just break in half by accident. It had been made of two parts fastened together.

Numero dos, there's only one of those lethal little nuclear devices on that trailer.

Numero tres is that the large, strong men wearing green armbands and pulling it at a fast trot appear to be in better health than I'd expected. Having been injected for years with all those chemicals that made them bulge with muscles is probably part of why they were not more seriously injured when the camelion broke free. Plus being on Chain makes those hooked on it not just shorter-lived than most people, but also more resistant to pain.

There're only six of them, though. Four are pulling while two others are sitting on the trailer to either side of their bomb in its launch cradle, guarding it. What happened to the remaining four or five? Could some creature have attacked and lessened their numbers during the night?

Numero cuatro, which is the most disturbing thing of all, is that the Jester is not among them. There's no place to hide on the flatbed of the trailer. So where is he?

I pass the binoculars back to Hussein. As soon as he looks through them, a low whistle escapes through his teeth, followed by a few words I do not literally understand. But I am pretty sure they are curses. He's seen exactly what I saw and drawn the same disturbing conclusion that more may be going on than we expected.

He lowers the binoculars, and his eyes meet mine.

Not good, he's thinking.

No.

I close my eyes, trying to concentrate better, think about what is happening.

I'd originally thought I understood what our enemies planned. Whether working together or by coincidence, they had set in motion a three-pronged attack on me and our valley. Lady Time's forces coming from the northeast, the Jester's from the southeast, and Luther Little Wound coming in head-on.

That original plan—if plan it was—has already gone other than I expected with the unexplained actions of Four Deaths, who headed off in a different direction.

And now this?

What do I know about my enemies other than they want me dead? They're devious, even in their dealings with each other. They're also crazy, especially the Jester, who has always been the nuttiest one of them all. Devious and crazy.

What Ana said when we last made contact, and she reminded me of Uncle Chatto's words, comes back to me.

Expect the unexpected.

"You can find him?"

I open my eyes to look first at Hussein, whose question has brought me back to this moment, and then at the road where the men pulling the trailer are still approaching but have come only a little nearer. All that thinking took me no more than a few heartbeats.

"Yes," I say. "I can."

I look down the hill to the choke point on the road where Tom set things up. The logs we pulled across the road with the help of Star and Striped Horse will force them to stop. They'll be told to surrender, and if they don't, they'll be exposed to the cross fire from five or six points above them on either side of the road. That's where Tom, Victor, the Dreamer, and Lorelei have been placed within the shelter of the rocks.

They've all taken their places and are visible from up here.

The fifth point, directly below our hill, is where Hussein and I were going to be stationed. But now he'll be down there by himself.

Hussein reaches out, takes my right hand in both of his.

"You will succeed, habibi," he says. Then he turns and begins running down the hill, as agile and sure-footed as an antelope.

I raise my hand so the others can see my signal at the same time as I make contact with Victor.

They're almost here. Be ready.

Born ready, he thinks back to me.

But am I? I turn back toward the east to search with my mind for our green-haired enemy.

CHAPTER FORTY-TWO

Eyes, Eyes

One time, they say, Coyote was out hunting for rabbits. He sniffed around and found their scent and followed it. Before long, he came to a place where the rabbits had gathered together. He sneaked up very quietly and could have grabbed them. He was feeling very proud of himself for being so clever.

But those rabbits acted as if they didn't even notice Coyote. They were busy playing a game. It was a game Coyote had never seen before. They were taking their eyes out of their heads and tossing them up into the air.

"Eyes, eyes, fly around," they sang. And their eyes flew through the air above them.

"Eyes, eyes, come back now," they sang. And their eyes flew back down into their sockets.

Coyote was fascinated. He forgot that he had been hunting those rabbits to eat them.

"Can I play that game, too?" he asked.

"Go ahead," the rabbits said. "Just take your eyes out and throw them up and sing, 'Eyes, eyes, fly around.' "

So Coyote took out his eyes. He tossed them up into the air.

"Eyes, eyes, fly around," he sang. And his two eyes flew through the air above him.

"Eyes, eyes, fly away," the rabbits all sang. Then Coyote's eyes flew off, and those rabbits ran away, leaving Coyote blind.

"Eyes, eyes, come back to me," Coyote sang, but his eyes did not return.

Coyote was blind like that for quite a while. He wandered around and wandered around until he came to a pine tree and took some of the pitch from that tree to make new eyes. That is why Coyote's eyes are as yellow as pine pitch to this day.

Why do I find myself remembering that story my mom told me when I was little just when I am about to send my own eyes out looking for the Jester? Maybe it's because like so many Coyote stories, it's a reminder that sometimes when you try to trick others, you can be tricked yourself. That sometimes when it seems as if something is easy, it is harder than you think.

I look out onto the road crossing the plain. That trailer being pulled by the men is getting closer. I don't have a lot of time. But I can feel that I need to know something as soon as possible.

329

I close my eyes, try to send my vision out to that place where the camelion broke free. And just like Coyote did, I send my eyes flying there. What I see there is troublesome. There's no sign of any wreckage from the broken trailer, though what's left of the bodies of several men is being fought over by vultures. And the two remaining Davy Crocketts, those lethal little nuclear devices, are also gone. There's just wheel tracks in the golden sand—two sets of them. One set is leading west—made by those men I've just seen. But the other deeply rutted trail, strangely enough, heads back eastward. Toward Haven. And along with those east-leading tracks there's the psychic residue, that sickly green smoky spoor, left by the Jester. Like the second set of wagon tracks, it leads east. For some reason he's also turned back toward the former place of imprisonment that was never my home.

Why? Has he given up? Does he have some other plan?

Those are questions I'll have to wait to answer. Just knowing that the green-haired maniac is not among our immediate attackers is enough for now.

But that's all I have time for.

I open my physical eyes and see that the trailer bearing that deadly missile is out of sight now, making the turn around the hill between me and them. Any second now, they'll come into view again as they enter the choke point of Tom's carefully designed ambush.

No one, not even Hussein, is looking up at me. They're all

totally concentrating on what is about to happen down there. Part of me wishes I could be down there with them, helping them. But part of me doesn't, the part that no longer wants to kill another human being, because if those men do not surrender, then stopping them may mean bringing them to a bloody and terminal halt.

There they are. They have rounded the bend and seen the logs across the road. The men pulling the cart are letting go of the lines they were holding and shifting their guns off their shoulders.

"Put down your weapons!" Tom Yazzie's shouted command reaches me a second or two after it reached them and produced the opposite result.

BAPBAPBAPBAPBAPBAPBAP

I see the spurting bursts of flame from the barrels of the big men's submachine guns before the stuttering, echoing sounds of the gunshots reach me. Dust and chips of stone are being blown off the big sandstone boulders to either side of the road. But Tom and Victor and Hussein and the Dreamer and Lorelei are well sheltered behind their rock fortifications. None of them are being hit, and no one is standing up to shoot back like some stupid cowboy in an old viddy.

Hussein is lying on his belly, aiming through a low opening at the bottom of the massive stone that's protecting him. He fires once. A broken-nosed blond man wearing a green armband spins backward and falls to his side before I hear the crack of

Hussein's rifle. Now my brother and the others are firing, and the sound of rifle fire is popping like strings of firecrackers as the large, bulky men who were pulling the trailer are trying to load new clips into their automatic weapons.

The two men on the back of the trailer, shielded by its sides, are also trying to do something. They are fiddling with the apparatus that cradles the nuke. That's when Tom Yazzie does stand up so he can see over the trailer's sides, his rifle on his shoulder. He seems oblivious to any danger as he takes careful aim. He fires one shot, and the man on the right drops to his knees, his arms loose as a puppet whose strings have been cut. A second shot, and the other man tumbles off the back of the trailer.

That second shot of Tom's is the last one fired. All six of the men wearing the green armbands of the Jester's stooges are down.

I make my way down the hill slowly. I can see that no one I love was hurt. But I'm in no hurry to get close to the bodies of those men who fell. Evil and twisted as they may have become after years in thrall to their insane master, they were living human beings only a few breaths ago.

However, when I get there, it's not as bad as I thought. It turns out that one of the reasons those minions of the Jester looked so bulky was that they were wearing body armor. The shots that brought them down were the ones that struck them in their limbs. None of them escaped injury from the well-aimed shots that Tom and the others rained down on them. But they're all still alive, even if most of them are going to find it hard to walk for a long time. Plus two or three of them would be bleeding to death right now if not for Lorelei's efficient first aid.

As soon as each of them is adequately treated, they're turned over to Tom. He's taking particular pleasure in it.

"Duct tape," Tom says with a chuckle as he pulls off their green armbands and then straps their ankles and wrists together, with help from my brother Victor. "This season's perfect fashion accessory for every prisoner."

Hussein, who's keeping his rifle leveled at our captives, looks at me and raises one amused eyebrow. I nod back at him, just plain relieved that our ambush actually succeeded without anyone dying.

We'll load the wounded men onto the trailer and then, with the willing help of our Horse People, use it to bring them to our valley. Maybe some of them are not really bad people but just doing what they had to do. Maybe some—once they've gone through withdrawal from the drugs the Jester fed them—will turn out to be willing to change their allegiance. Or maybe not, in which case after they're well enough to get around, we'll take them a long way away from the valley and then set them free to live or die on their own.

Time to check on Guy's party. I close my eyes, thinking of Ana.

Right here, Big Sis.

Her unspoken voice sounds cheerful, and that's great.

How did it go? Is it over on your end?

You should have seen it, she replies. *It was over as soon as Guy fired his first shots from that big gun. They went right through the armor of their first tank, and the whole thing blew up.*

She's talking about the weapon that was Guy's ace in the hole. It was a Predator motor gun, a .60-caliber beast that fired armor-piercing rounds made of depleted uranium.

What happened then?

They all just gave up. Lots of little injuries from that explosion, but none of them killed. Though we are going to need some help from Lorelei taking care of their wounds when she gets back. Anyhow, it was awesome. How did it go there?

Good, I reply. *I'm so proud of you, Ana.*

Thanks, Big Sis. Over?

Over and out.

I open my eyes and look at Hussein, who's waiting expectantly.

"It's over," I say. "None of our people got hurt."

He smiles at me and gives me a thumbs-up. It seems as if nothing can go wrong today.

"One also wonders," a deep, sardonic voice drolls from over my head, "what was espied during your most recent non-physical foray from yon hilltop."

The Dreamer, of course.

In the midst of all this, though, I've almost forgotten what I saw when I tried to figure out where the Jester had gone. And now I remember something Uncle Chatto told me. "Genghis Khan," he said, "was a man whose Mongol armies conquered most of the known world more than nine centuries ago. One of his favorite sayings was that there was no good in anything until it is finished."

We've had victories, but it is not finished. These were just two battles won out of who knows how many more my people and I still have to fight.

"Yes, habibi," Hussein says. "Did you find out what we need to know?"

As the Dreamer waits expectantly, looking down his long nose at me, while Hussein stands patiently by my side, brushing that usual bit of imaginary dust off his chest, I'm not sure what to say. What did I find out?

I shake my head. "I'm not sure," I admit. "From what I saw, it looked as if he took the back half of that trailer—and those two other missiles—and headed back toward Haven. Why would he do that?"

"Alas," the Dreamer says, his voice totally serious for a change. "One fears that he might know."

CHAPTER FORTY-THREE
His Strategy

O ne dreamed last night," he says. " 'Twas a nocturnal visitation one devoutly hoped to be no more than a phantasm from some bit of poorly digested food, as Dickens's sainted Scrooge would have it. But now I think not."

As usual, when the Dreamer makes one of his enigmatic remarks, I feel like kicking him in the teeth. But I can see that whatever he just said is serious to him. He simply can't stop talking like an out-of-control dictionary. So I just grit my teeth and ask him.

"What do you mean?"

The Dreamer lifts his steepled hands to press his long index fingers against his lips. "Who," he says, "does our virescent-tressed adversary despise the most?" ·

"Me?"

"Au contraire, my little assassin. You rate no higher than a three on his top-ten to-be-hit list. But then again, how would you know, never having been one of the Ones and thus not privy to the subtle internecine warfare among us at all times?"

"You mean . . ."

The Dreamer nods. "Indeed, full marks. Our albescent lady herself. Though feigning a full-on attack against those of us ensconced in our vale of refuge, seemingly working in tandem with the similar foray assayed by her armored column, the Jester's stratagem was doubly pronged."

"Then what you saw in your dream was . . ."

"Indeed. A weapon of mass destruction loosed upon the unsuspecting inhabitants of my former walled abode, producing a wasteland wherein no bird sings."

"But why would he destroy his own place and kill every person in Haven just to get at Lady Time? It's crazy."

The Dreamer nods. "And of whom are we speaking but a lunatic? More than once the Jester has stated that the sound of her constantly clacking timepieces fills him with unquenchable rage. He would go to any length to still them forever. One suspects he has some lair set up for himself far from the planned conflagration."

The hair on the back of my neck is standing up. All those people, most of them innocent, slaughtered? Just to get one person and stop her damn clocks? I don't want to think about it, but I have to.

I turn toward Hussein, whose normally calm face looks as shocked and stricken as I feel right now.

What can I do?

"What you always do," the Dreamer says, hearing that desperate thought of mine. "Whatever is necessary."

I look at him and Hussein, who both nod. I turn to Tom and Victor, who've joined us now that our six prisoners have been trussed up and stacked on the trailer. They trust me.

But do I trust myself?

Hally? You there?

No answer. But thinking of him brings back his advice.

Look before you leap.

Okay, Lozen. Stop stalling and get started.

"I'm going to take another look," I say.

I close my eyes and find myself back where I was only moments ago, the place where the two roads diverged in the yellow sand. For whatever reason, it's always easy for me to send my far-seeing to places I've seen before. Not far past the place where the trails separated is an abandoned building—an empty mag-lev garage back from the road, its doors gaping wide.

There's the Jester's smoky green trail, like a slime track left by an enormous snail. It's as easy to follow as the flow of a river, though much less pleasant. If I had my body with me, I'd be holding my nose as my sight flies along. Faster than an arrow shot by a bow, faster than a speeding bullet. Trees, hills—everything below blurs together because of how quickly my disembodied self is traveling. So fast that I am wondering how the Jester could have gotten so far this quickly.

There's a distant cloud of dust on the road ahead of me. Another few seconds and my vision is hovering above that dust cloud, and I have my answer. Even without my physical body I get a sick feeling in my stomach because of what I see.

I see the back two-thirds of that trailer. I see the two fully intact little nuclear rockets firmly mounted in their launching cradles. I see the other four men of the Jester's squad sitting on the trailer next to those deadly devices. And worst of all, I see what's now being used to pull that trailer along at a steady rate.

It's a machine similar to the clockwork cycle that Luther Little Wound abandoned—the one that Guy has been working to restore. This one is twice as big and in perfect working order, even though it looks to have been much more crudely made, lacking the craftsmanship of something from Walter's workshop. This rough three-wheeled mechanical beast, its hour come round at last, is being straddled by the Jester.

It's just as the Dreamer thought. The Jester's been planning this all along. The clockwork cycle must have been secretly constructed and just as secretly sneaked out of Haven to be concealed somewhere along the way—probably in that abandoned garage with the open door.

How fast is he going? Fast enough that he'll be in range of Haven before we can physically catch up with him. And I can't slow him down the way I did before. No way to mentally confuse a clockwork motorcycle.

I try to touch the minds of the four men riding the trailer. Their brains are like mush from the drugs they've ingested in the last few days. They are just this side of being zombies, focused on only two things: doing the Jester's bidding and getting their next dose of Chain.

And who might that be, a–knocking on my mental door?

That psychically sent question jolts me. The Jester is aware of my extrasensory presence. I shouldn't be surprised. All of the Ones have shown the nascent ability to hear and send thoughts. None, though, have done so as well and as often as the Dreamer. I'm certain none of them have anything aiding them the way my Power helps me.

But I am not about to reply.

No need to reply. Who else would it but you, my meddling Apache assassin? Come in, my dear. I have so much that I'll soon show you. Such lovely, satisfying devastation. A miniature little Armageddon destroying everyone within those walls—including a few for whom you have some sympathy. And you can witness it all. They all are doomed. Doomed!

Even when he is only doing it with his mind, he can't stop talking. But while he's delivering that monologue, I notice his cycle is slowing down. It's nothing of my doing, though. His machine just needs to be wound up again.

He purses his lips in irritation, turns to look back over his shoulder.

"Krager! Rislen! Make haste!"

Two men slide off the trailer. Their motions are mechanical as the device they wind using a long metal bar. The spring's stiff. It takes all their effort, muscles straining, sweat beading on their foreheads. Turn by turn, turn by turn.

I have no idea how long it will take to rewind the mechanism, but I am sure it won't be long enough. I recognize the place he's reached thus far on his insane journey. He'll be within range of Haven by the end of the day.

I open my eyes yet again.

And this time the first things I see are two large brown eyes. Striped Horse is leaning her head over Hussein's shoulder.

The message she sends tells me she's already aware of what we must do.

Ride fast.

CHAPTER FORTY-FOUR

Like the Wind

Running like the wind. I know it's a cliché, but I can't think of a better way to describe the swift way we are moving across the land. Like the wind. Like a whirlwind. Like three whirlwinds. Moving so fast we might seem like mirages to anyone who should chance to see us.

According to Navajo traditions, the Sun was the one who originally owned all the horses and kept them in the other world. Then a hero known as Turquoise Boy, who somehow knew that the people needed horses, went looking for them. He found his way to the heavenly corral where those horses were kept. It was not easy to find that place. Their huge sky pasture had a guardian, who had been formed from a mirage and was known as Mirage Man.

But Turquoise Boy saw that place. He saw Mirage Man, who allowed him to look beyond the gates. To the east he saw white horses; to the south were turquoise horses. To the west were yellow horses, and to the north were spotted horses.

"Here they are," Mirage Man said, "those which in time to come shall live with the people."

And so it came to be.

And so it is again today. As we ride, Striped Horse's powerful, long strides eating up the miles, I think of that story, a story shared with my dad by his Navajo grandmother. Striped Horse's color is almost green, with shades of blue-gray. So perhaps she might be called a turquoise horse, like Sun's blue horse, a horse that runs all day without pausing. Not only that, the one who rode that horse after it was given by the Sun was the older of the Hero Twins who were named Killer of Enemies and Child of Water.

As I feel Striped Horse's muscles rippling against my bare legs, I think of the songs we used to sing to praise and thank our horses back then and find one coming to my lips.

> My turquoise horse dances,
> Lightning flashes from her as she runs.
> She stands on the top rim of the rainbow.
> Her bridle is a sunbeam,
> Her saddle is white cloud,
> Her hooves are white coral.
> My horse is on my side.
> With her I shall always win.

We are not moving as swiftly as I did in my vision traveling state, but Striped Horse and I are going faster than any normal horse might run. And so are our companions.

Next to us, his flanks almost touching those of his mate as he gallops along, is Star with Hussein on his back.

And to our left is the last person I would have expected to have by our side only a few short seasons ago. There, on the back of Black Cloud, his long limbs making the big horse look like a pony, is none other than the Dreamer.

It was clear that not everyone could go with us to intercept the Jester. We had six wounded prisoners to consider. It just made sense to have at least two people accompanying them, in addition to Lorelei, whose services as a nurse were still needed by our captives and would be needed by those men of Lady Time's taken in Guy's efficient ambush.

At first, my idea had been that we'd bring either Tom or Victor with us. But it was the Dreamer who was chosen—or chose himself.

"One needs," he explained, "to be present when just deserts are meted out to my odious erstwhile peer. And what chef is better suited than myself to help prepare that dish which is best served cold? Indeed, it is more than time for one to return, as it were, to the scene of the crime now that, as the sainted Sherlock said, the game's afoot."

Then, seeing the puzzled expression that almost always

comes to my face after one of his obscure monologues, he spoke the one word I never thought I would hear from his lips.

"Please?"

In fact, the Dreamer probably is the one best suited to assist us. No one knows more about the deviousness of the Ones than a person who managed for so long to pass himself off as being just as cold-hearted and merciless as that trio of monsters. I think again of how long everyone assumed that a torture chamber was hidden behind the ominous curtains in his rooms, when in fact it was shelf after shelf of books. In fact, on recollection, many innocents disappeared into the lairs of the other three evil Overlords of Haven, never to be seen alive again. True, people were also vanished by the Dreamer. But, knowing that his three cohorts would kill them if he didn't, those few he disappeared were actually provisioned, armed, and then allowed to secretly leave and take their chances outside the walls. Most who were escorted to his chambers would, after a subtly threatening interview, emerge shaken and thanking their lucky stars they had somehow survived their encounter with the demon—who has turned out to be more of a librarian than a barbarian.

If things were not so serious, our current mission so crucial, I'd be smiling right now at the thought of how things have changed. How could I ever have dreamed just a year ago that it would be like this, that I'd no longer be a lone Killer of

Enemies? How could I ever have dreamed that I'd be riding into battle on a gemod horse that may be smarter than me, accompanied by a former dreaded foe and with—okay, now I am really going to get corny—my true love by my side?

The angle of approach we're taking should get us ahead of our enemy. We're not following the road, as he has to with his wheeled vehicle and trailer. We're going cross-country, pounding through canyons, cresting hills, leaping old fences, and crossing abandoned fields, splashing through streams. If there's anything lethal, anything dangerous that would seek to catch and eat us, it's out of luck. We're running too swiftly— nothing can react fast enough to catch or stop us. It's amazing how fast and agile Striped Horse and all our gemod horse partners are.

It makes me take back what I was thinking before. It's not that we're running like the wind, it's as if we *are* the wind.

Time has no meaning now as we whip across the land. I don't know if minutes are passing or hours. I lean forward as I ride, pressing my face against Striped Horse's neck. I'm no longer a passenger, but a part of her, our breaths one, our minds perfectly melded together. I feel as if we could run like this forever.

On and on we go. On and on. On and on and on.

Then we're climbing, and Striped Horse is slowing her pace. I find myself feeling as if I'm waking from the sort of dream you didn't want to end. I sit up straight on her back and look around as, for the first time since we began our headlong run, I feel a sense of time having passed. The silvered sun has moved the distance of six hands across the sky.

We're on my favorite hilltop by a standing stone, not far from where I killed that porcupine cat. We are exactly where I began to tell you my story more than a year ago. We're also close to the place where my mind was first contacted by the huge, apelike being I've come to know as Hally—and still do not understand enough about.

I can see the familiar shape of my former prison home of Haven five miles away, its double row of walls like a giant concrete tire. It's intact, its walls unbreached, its buildings still standing and not annihilated by a nuclear blast.

We've gotten here in time.

Hussein and Star have come up on my right. Black Cloud and the Dreamer are just below us to my left. I can feel what is foremost in all their minds, all five of my companions. It is a straightforward question that can be expressed in two simple words.

What now?

I hold up my left hand.

Wait.

Then I hold up both my hands, using my Power to find my enemies before we rush in to danger.

The first is the closest and easiest to locate. It's Lady Time. I'm viewing her as if through a cloudy, cracked mirror, the incessant sounds of ticking clocks all around. My white-gowned enemy is inside Haven, in her own inner sanctum. She's pacing, favoring one foot and muttering under her breath. What I can see of her face below the white clock mask is red with rage.

Suddenly she turns toward the person who is watching her, the one whose sight I'm borrowing. My perspective shifts to her one eye, and I see the cowering shape of her much-abused clockmaker and chief engineer, Walter, whose eyeglass lenses are smeared and broken.

"Where isss my ssspecial clockwork bird?" she's hissing at Walter. "You ssssaid it would fly back to me with newsss."

It seems that no word has gotten back to her about the progress of her armored attack on our valley but that some sort of mechanical flying device was supposed to be bringing her a message. It's a good bet that whatever her clockwork bird was, that metal-bodied pigeon or hawk or whatever, was knocked out of order by the explosion of the boiler on the lead tank.

Poor Walter. But there's nothing I can do right now. It's clear that she is totally ignorant of both the Jester's treachery and our nearby presence. No need to spend more time in her poisonous company.

I open my eyes for a moment, look over at Hussein.

"She's there . . . and unaware?" he asks.

I nod, turn on Striped Horse's back to face southwest, then close my eyes again.

I do not have to reach far. The psychic leap to reach him is almost as swift as it was for me to pass over Haven's walls to Lady Time's lair. It means that in terms of actual physical distance he's not far, probably less than a dozen miles behind us and approaching swiftly. Then, as I see through his eyes, a bent and rusted road sign turns the probability into certainty.

SOUTHWESTERN PENITENTIARY

10 MILES

Returned to observe my little holocaust?

Just as before, he's sensed my disembodied presence. There's a fork in the road just ahead of us. Both roads lead to Haven, though the left turn swings first through a little junction where the ruined walls of a group of storage buildings stand. The Jester pauses just before the junction, holds a long-fingered, graceful hand in front of his face, and gestures to his left.

"Men," he calls. "To me!"

From out of the most intact of those buildings, a second, smaller trailer than the one he's been using emerges. It's being pulled by yet another roughly constructed clockwork cycle driven by a lanky, red-bearded man wearing one of the Jester's green armbands. I recognize him from the no-holds-barred fights that the Ones would stage at Haven for their sadistic amusement. His name is Monroe, and he's the most merciless and worst of the Jester's mercenaries. He's killed at least three men in the ring with just his fists. With him are three other men on the trailer, who leap down as soon as it is close enough. All of them are wearing body armor.

It only takes a moment of further shared vision through the crimson-locked madman's insane eye to realize what's happening. The new arrivals are shifting one of the small nuclear rockets onto that second trailer.

The attack on Haven is going to come not from one direction, but two.

CHAPTER FORTY-FIVE

A Mad Dash

'm so upset by what I am seeing that I involuntarily lose contact, opening my eyes in shock.

As I do so, there's a psychic tug at me, as if my Power is trying to direct my vision somewhere else. Impending danger, I know. But whatever it is has to wait. I cannot waste time or energy thinking of anything else other than what I've just witnessed. And I have to do something.

Hally, I could really, really use your help now.

No answer.

I have to act right now, even though I have one of the worst headaches I have ever experienced. But I'm not alone.

Both the Dreamer and Hussein are looking at me in a concerned way. I may have let the pain I'm feeling from that headache—which is making my head feel like an overinflated balloon—bleed through whatever part of my consciousness communicates mentally with them.

Not good.

And my human companions are not the only ones worried about me. Striped Horse has turned her head to look over her shoulder at me with one eye, and both Star and Black Cloud are concentrating their full attention my way.

Double not good, Lozen. Get it together.

I take a deep breath and sit up straight on my four-legged ally's back.

"Listen," I say.

And then, saying it and thinking it at the same time to all five of them, I tell what I've seen and explain the simple—and I hope not simpleminded—plan I've come up with. The Jester has divided his forces, and now there are missiles being moved within range from two locations. We have to split up to try to stop them both.

Hussein is the first to object.

"You should not go alone, habibi," he says.

"I'm not alone," I reply, trying to sound more self-assured that I feel. "Striped Horse is with me. No time for discussion. We have to go now."

Hussein knows me well enough to say nothing further. He just drops the index finger of his right hand, the ancient gesture signifying agreement that my ancestors used—part of the sign language he's been absorbing from me almost without my noticing it. It makes me want to hug him.

"One wishes you luck, Lozen," the Dreamer says. The unaccustomed sincerity in his voice makes me feel even more unsure about what I'm doing.

I don't answer him. If I try to say anything, my voice will probably come out all choked up. Not the way a self-confident Killer of Enemies should sound at all. I lean forward, tighten my legs around Striped Horse, grasp her mane tightly in my hands. She rears, turns, and leaps, carrying us downslope to the left as fast as a diving falcon. Out of the corner of my eye I catch the briefest glimpse of Hussein and Star, followed by Black Cloud and the Dreamer disappearing over the opposite side of the steep hill.

Though I did not see which direction the Jester took where those roads diverged, I'm guessing he chose the one that would take him within range the fastest—the one to the left. If so, we are going to intercept him just short of that missile's effective range.

We leap a gully, pound across a rocky ledge where Striped Horse's hooves sound like a volley of rifle shots, dodge between two huge saguaros. I don't know how fast we're going, but it's much faster than any normal horse has ever run.

There's no doubt that Striped Horse knows what I'm thinking, has the same mental picture in her mind as I have in mine of where we're going and what way we need to go to get there as quickly as possible.

Which is why when the gemod creature that's been conceal-ing itself under a layer of sand rises from the desert in front of us, we do not turn aside. It looks like a red-horned, thirty-foot-long version of the desert rattlesnake called a sidewinder. Its black eyes fixed on us, its head is reared back to strike.

But that strike never comes. The reason is either one of two things. Numero Uno is that I have just blasted a hole in its right eye with two quick shots—BAM-BAM!—from my .357 Desert Eagle. Numero Dos is that Striped Horse has just ex-ecuted an aerial move that entailed leaping high and striking sideways with both hind legs in an immensely powerful kick that crushed the left side of said now-deceased serpent's skull.

I hold tight with my right hand and lean into Striped Horse's neck as her feet hit the ground again. I almost lose my seat on her back, but manage to hold on. After all, if my ancestors could stand on a galloping horse's back and fire a bow, I should be able to do this. Even so, sensing me almost losing my balance, Striped Horse adjusted as she landed, slowed a bit, and strayed a few yards off course.

It's caused a delay that can be measured in seconds, but seconds are as crucial as hours right now.

Faster, I think to Striped Horse, and once again we are outracing the wind.

But not my headache. It hasn't lessened since we started our mad dash to avert the deaths of the hundreds of people within the former penitentiary's protective walls that will be of no use at all if that missile is fired. Once again, even though it feels as if my cranium is being stretched to the point of almost bursting, I focus every bit of mental energy I can muster on our goal.

We burst up out of the sandy soil onto the road that leads to Haven. I look to my right, the direction they should be approaching from. No! There's nothing there.

But to my left, closer to the old prison, is a cloud of dust being kicked up from the dry, deteriorated surface of the road by the passing of a motorcycle and trailer.

Crap! Double crap!

"GO!" I scream to Striped Horse, who is already spinning toward the direction of that death-bearing dust cloud. "GO!"

We're faster. We're catching up, not more than a hundred yards away. But the two things I see as we get closer make me want to scream.

Numero Uno is that the Jester is not astride that three-wheeler. It's Monroe, the lanky red-haired murderer. The Jester took the longer left-hand way after all.

Numero Dos is that they are too close to their intended target, much too close. So close that they are slowing down to a stop, and the men on the trailer are pointing the missile to land within Haven's walls.

But we're not slowing down. We're closing in, close enough for me to start attempting to reason with them by way of several ounces of lubricated lead alloy.

BAM-BAM!

It's more luck than skill that those two shots strike home, center mass. The man who's just stood up to the right of the launch cradle tumbles off the trailer.

BAM-BAM!

This time I've aimed better, and it looks as if both slugs catch the man to the left in his thickly padded chest, knocking him backward.

My Desert Eagle holds ten shots, one in the chamber plus nine. I used two bullets on the snake, which means I have four left and no time to reload.

BAM-BAM!

And this time it's bad luck more than skill that results in both slugs bouncing harmlessly off the missile cradle, behind which the third man has now ducked.

Then someone hits me in the left shoulder with a club. Or that is what it feels like as it knocks me off Striped Horse's back. I've been hit by one of the slugs being fired our way by Monroe, who's pulled a gun of his own and is crouching behind the three-wheeler, using it as a combination shield and rest.

Striped Horse has also stumbled, fallen to her front knees. Hit, it seems, by that same volley of shots.

That's what I see as I plummet toward the broken pavement. But I manage to twist in midair, duck my head, and roll over my intact shoulder. Somehow I manage to hold onto my gun and come up to my feet.

I'm just in time to see the spurt of fire from the back of the nuclear missile as it bursts up from its cradle into flight.

CHAPTER FORTY-SIX
Stop Thinking

The missile arcing up in front of seems to have been perfectly aimed at its target. It's going to land inside Haven, killing everyone inside. The mushroom cloud will loom over it like an evil genie as the explosion blasts out the walls, dropping fallout on everything within a mile. The radiation from it will linger, making the place a dead zone for years. I'm frozen, helpless.

I've failed, and that thought hurts even more than the headache, which now feels as if someone is driving a spike into the center of my forehead.

Yet as I'm thinking that, I feel something touching my mind. It's Hally.

Stop thinking. Act!

And as soon as that message comes, everything changes. My paralysis vanishes. I point my right hand at the rocket, pull back my left arm as if drawing the string of an invisible bow.

Then I shoot my left hand forward so that it strikes my right palm with a slap that sounds as loud as thunder.

Just as before, but with a hundred times the force, a bolt of something like condensed lightning shoots forth from my hands. Its speed is so much greater than that of the missile that it strikes the rocket before it reaches the top of its arc.

WHOMP!

The missile doesn't explode. It just vanishes, totally obliterated, reduced into harmless molecules that dance in the sunlight and then disperse.

I've done it. I've stopped it. Not only that, there's no nuclear dust raining down on Haven. The nuke is just gone!

I have also gotten rid of that headache, which must have been that Arrow of Lightning building in me, that weapon I needed to do what I just did.

Oh, and one other little minor detail. I am as limp as a wrung-out dishrag. I can't even raise my arms. Which normally would not have been that much of a problem. Except that right now, I have two guns being pointed at me by Monroe and the guy from the trailer who fired the missile I just destroyed.

They're only thirty feet away. No way they can miss at that distance. Just bang-bang, and bye-bye, Lozen.

However, one must be conscious in order to make a gun go bang-bang. There's just enough time for a little smile to come to my lips before . . .

THUD-THUD

Striped Horse's hooves strike the two men so hard from behind that they are not just knocked out, they are lifted off their feet to land in the cradling arms of a clump of cholla cactus.

Some of my strength is starting to return. I pick up the firearms they dropped, eject and pocket the magazines whose bullets will fit my own weapon—then toss the guns into a deep crack in the rocks by the road. I suppose I should try to tie up the first two men I shot, who still seem to be knocked out— either by the impact of my heavy slugs hitting their bulletproof vests or by hitting their heads when they fell off the trailer. But I'm still too weak for that. All I can manage is to toss their weapons and then walk shakily over to Striped Horse.

Are you all right?

It takes an effort to send that simple question to her. But it's worth it as I feel her self-confident assent, combined with equal concern for my own well-being.

I feel along her side. Her wounds are minor. The two bullets that struck her in her flank failed to penetrate any farther than an inch into her tough hide. I pry the flattened slugs out with my fingers.

"We're both okay," I say out loud, still feeling too mentally drained out for more mind messaging. "But now we have to check on our friends."

I use a boulder as a stepping stone to get up onto her back. My knees are trembling as I do so, but though I am weary, I can't stop to rest.

Fortunately, Striped Horse hasn't been weakened. As I cling to her mane, she leaps forward, once again outracing the wind. We cut up and across the saguaro-filled hill that rises to the south of Haven between the two roads.

If I had the strength, I'd be reaching out to contact Hussein. But I haven't recovered enough yet. What I probably need right now is to drink something, eat something. But we separated in such a hurry that I left all the canteens and food with Hussein.

We round a bend, Striped Horse's speed making the landscape blur around me. I can see the road half a mile ahead, and my heart leaps up because I can also see Hussein. He's crouching on top of the trailer next to the unlaunched second missile. Three of the Jester's men are on their bellies next to him. Hussein is just finishing securing their hands and feet. There's no need to tie up the fourth man, who lies in a pool of blood beside the trailer.

Star, who seems as uninjured as my Bedu partner, is standing by the trailer. He nudges Hussein with his nose, and Hussein turns to see us. A broad grin crosses his handsome face as he raises his right arm and waves it back and forth, signaling that all is well.

But is it?

The three-wheeled cycle is no longer connected to the trailer. In fact, it is nowhere in sight. Nor is the Jester. Nor, for that matter, are the Dreamer and Black Cloud.

CHAPTER FORTY-SEVEN
Time Out

Lady Time was not pleased. She paced back and forth in her white-curtained chamber, limping slightly, hissing under her breath.

"Isss it time? Iss it? Isss it?"

No answer came, not even the uncoordinated clacking and ticking of her beloved clocks. The last of them had been removed an hour ago and stowed on one of the vehicles in the sub-basement workroom three floors below.

"Walter? WALTER!"

No answer to that, either. Just the echo of her own voice off the walls where only the outlines of missing timepieces remained, etched in dust.

Her feet brushed against a metal pry bar used to lever free the largest of the clocks. With serpentine grace, she bent, plucked it up, and hurled it spinning across the room.

"WALTERRRR!" she shrieked.

As before, no reply. Not even a terrified whisper.

"He will pay for thissss," she snarled as she pressed the hidden stud that swung open the door concealed in the back wall. "Teeth? No. It will be fingernailssss thissss time."

Her hissing continued as she made her way down, cursing as always the lack of a mag-lift or even something as primitive as an elevator. The loss of electricity had brought so many inconveniences into her life. As she rounded each corner of the convoluted stairway, she noted with pleasure that the charges had finally been placed here—just as they earlier had been everywhere else in the tunnels beneath the entire walled complex. It had been the toil of months, but the efforts had been worth it. At her signal, her most loyal retainers would light the long fuses that would give her just enough time to get far enough away to be unaffected by the total devastation, but close enough to have a superb view.

An extra amount of explosives had been placed below the Jester's quarters. She so hoped he might return in time to be caught in the blast. If not, at least she'd have the satisfaction of imagining the shock on his face when he returned to see she'd made the most definitive move in their contest of wills.

Everything she cared about had been removed and carefully packed. The invitation from the Overlords of the underground facility two hundred miles to the northwest assured her there'd be room for all her things. Her expertise and innovative workmen made her a most welcome guest.

She had little doubt of her worth or that she would be appreciated by her hosts . . . at least until the opportunity came for her to eliminate them and put herself in their place.

A final turn, thirteen more steps, and she was at the door that led into a second underground garage, the one where her steam-powered carriers were waiting.

She reached for the door, and it swung forward in front of her as none other than Walter opened it from the other side.

"Ma'am," he said, bowing low, gesturing like a courtier.

It was rather pleasing to see. Perhaps she would only remove his remaining teeth and leave his fingernails for later. However, she was not pleased at the smile he was trying to hide as he nodded up and down like a drinking bird.

Smiles, unless her own, always irked her. She slipped her right hand inside her gown, feeling the hilts of the long-bladed, razor-sharp knives sheathed there.

Two toes for that.

She glided past the little man, who stepped back to avoid being pushed aside. Did she hear a chuckle as she passed?

Three toes—no, four. Or perhaps . . .

Her musing about the appropriate punishment suddenly came to a halt as a figure stepped out of the shadows.

"You?" she said. "What do you want?"

CHAPTER FORTY-EIGHT
Do Shut Up

Thehey went thataway," Hussein says with a grin.

It's a line from one of those western movies they used to allow us to watch on our handscreens. Corny, but it still brings a smile to my face. I guess anything would make me smile right now. We have actually averted the immolation of hundreds of people.

I slide off Striped Horse's back to climb onto the trailer. It takes me two tries. I am still wobbly limbed, and Hussein has to pull me up. Then I wrap both arms around him and squeeze.

"Oof!" Hussein groans. "Leave me one unbroken rib."

He's only partially joking. I guess more of my strength has come back to my arms than my legs.

I fill him in on what happened—my Arrow of Lightning blowing up that bomb in mid-flight.

"But now I am about as weak as a kitten," I say.

Hussein rubs his side and takes a deep breath. "More boa

constrictor than kitten." He beams that beautiful smile at me again. "I am so proud of you, Lozen. Here was less dramatic. It was like one of the old cowboy viddys. The bad guys were just turning the trailer into position when we came over the rise, our guns a-blazing. His men falling, the Jester headed for the hills with the Dreamer hot on his heels as a posse."

Hussein really has gotten into the mood of one of those ancient melodramas my dad always called oaters.

"Why didn't you go with him?" I ask.

"Good reasons, habibi. I had to wait for you, secure our prisoners here to prevent them from escaping. And"—Hussein reaches into his pocket to pull out a handful of metal and plastic objects—"make sure that bird of death"—he nods at the bomb, which now has several parts missing—"would not again be able to fly."

I want to hug him again. This time I probably would at least crack a rib. So I just nod and give his arm a squeeze—more my usual way of expressing appreciation.

"So now?" he says, pointing his chin in the direction that the Jester disappeared, pursued by the Dreamer.

"Now we follow."

It's not hard to pick up the trail left by the Jester. Even if we didn't have the visible evidence of his tire tracks—and the deep imprints of Black Cloud's hooves—enough of my Power has returned to me now for me to register the green-haired madman's psychic slime trail. And to wish I didn't. The green cloud left by his demented mind is disquieting.

At first he headed out into the desert, but then his vehicle's tracks, and the hoof marks that overlay them, veered back toward Haven. Perhaps the Dreamer was gaining on him and he decided it was better to seek sanctuary in the very place he'd tried to nuke into oblivion.

His plan has not succeeded. When we crest the one remaining hill blocking our view of Haven, a mile away, we see that the Jester's attempt has failed. Black Cloud and the Dreamer have managed to get ahead. They're standing sideways between him and the front gate. As we come up from behind, he's boxed in. To the right is a jumble of jagged rocks that would be too much for his machine. To his left is another steep hill that even a mountain goat might strain to climb.

The only sensible thing for him now would be to surrender.

Sensible, though, is not in his vocabulary.

"TRAITOR," he screams, as he leans to one side of the vehicle's saddle to pull out a long-barreled machine pistol. Pointing it at the Dreamer, he pushes the lever that engages the gears of his clockwork three-wheeler. Then, as the machine surges forward, he pulls the trigger.

POP!POP!POP!POP!POP!POP!

Shell casings fly off to the side as he fires a volley of tracer bullets that leave streaks in the air behind them.

None hit their target. The Dreamer has just done something

I never expected, even though it's the sort of thing my own ancestors were known for. As soon as that gun was leveled at him, he swung off to one side, gripping Black Cloud with his legs and one hand wrapped in his gemod steed's mane. He's dropped so far down that it's as if he's disappeared. The bullets fly harmlessly over Black Cloud's back.

Then, quickly as he vanished from sight, his head and one arm appear in front of Black Cloud's neck. That arm is holding a rifle, which the Dreamer fires a single time.

BLAM!

The Jester falls off his three-wheeler, which continues forward without him, veers off the roadway, and tips over.

The Dreamer slides to the ground, still holding his rifle. He walks toward the Jester, who has pushed himself up with his right hand.

The Dreamer's single shot tore off the green-haired lunatic's mask. Even from fifty yards away, I can see how disfigured the Jester's countenance is from the implants burned out by the first surge of the Silver Cloud's electricity-killing energy. His eye socket is a ragged black crater. His right forehead and cheek are covered with livid scars twisting like snakes around ridges of exposed, blackened bone. Blood dribbles down the Jester's cheek from the bullet that struck the formerly unmarked left side of his face.

This is the point when, in some stories, the two adversaries engage in banter. For example, the wounded villain on the ground taunts the hero, feigns weakness, lures him closer.

The Jester holds up his left hand, pointing it at the Dreamer.

"You can't kill me," he says—a clear start to just such a climactic dialogue.

But being a librarian means the Dreamer's read enough stories to feel no need for another such final verbal confrontation. "Oh, do shut up," the Dreamer says. BLAM!

A shot to the forehead is a lot more emphatic than an exclamation point to end a conversation.

I slide carefully off Striped Horse's back, still feeling a bit of shakiness in my knees. Hussein, who's already dismounted from Star, grasps my arm with one hand to steady me.

"Habibi," he says, "please?"

He's holding out a canteen of water, its top already unscrewed. I take it from him, feeling, hearing, almost already tasting the water as it sloshes inside the half-empty container.

"Thank you," I say to him. Then, before it touches my dry lips, I speak those words again, to the water itself. "Thank you."

It washes over my teeth and my tongue, a gift from the living earth beneath my feet, from the stones that held and guided it up to the spring where it flowed. Before that it was in the clouds we've always recognized as living beings who bless us with the gift of the rain. I drink this water, deeply grateful for the healing it brings me, the strength returning to my being. I am fully alive.

Unlike the one lying there before us on the ground. I've

heard it said that people may seem smaller in death than in life. That they look pitiful. But it's not that way right now. Aside from the fact that his mask was torn away and there's a hole in the exact center of his forehead, the Jester appears unchanged and undeserving of sympathy.

"Horatio," the Dreamer intones, "I knew him."

I don't bother to inquire as to who the hell Horatio is. But I do have to ask one thing.

"You knew him?" I point with my chin toward Haven. "You mean before all this?"

The Dreamer nods. "One was," he says, "rather a disappointment to one's parents. Despite all the proper DNA selection and de-selection, I turned out to be lacking in worldly ambition. Drawn, as it were, to the accumulation of knowledge rather than power. Quite unlike my late genetic twin here, whose feet were set firmly on the path of dominance."

I look down at the Jester's dead face, then up at the Dreamer's countenance. All four Ones who ruled Haven were similar in appearance—long-limbed, athletic, and graceful. I'd put that down to genetic engineering, rather than any sibling connection. But now, unmasked, I can see their faces are much the same—aside from the greater distortion and scarring caused by the melting down of the Jester's more advanced electronic upgrades.

"He really was your brother?"

The Dreamer smiles sadly, then shakes his head. "Not

exactly. We shared ancestry, a near-identical mix of DNA, and—I was told—the same rack of test tubes and adjacent meta-wombs. At most, cousins."

He nudges the body with one foot. "Past tense."

Then he sighs.

"Malice was his forte, even before"—he gestures at the silvery sky—"the arrival of our extraterrestrial visitation drove him into overt insanity. He alone knew of my past and my pacifistic propensities, tolerated my presence because it amused him to have so many opportunities for petty cruelties. Such as, it pains me to recall, the time he looted several thousand volumes from a long-deserted library, had them carted here, and then set ablaze in a huge bonfire just outside the walls while I watched in helpless anguish."

He nudges the Jester's body again with the toe of his boot, a little harder this time.

"One does wish that he might come back life—so that one might kill him again."

Perhaps the Dreamer is not quite as pacifistic as he claims.

As for me, I am finding it a little hard to believe that another of my original four mortal enemies is truly no longer a threat. First the Dreamer turned out to be a friend—though a frequently frustrating one. Then I was able to kill Diablita Loca—just barely before she could kill me. And now the Jester has been removed from the picture.

My head's almost spinning as I think of the journey I've

been on since I started sharing this story with you. I can't count how many monsters along the way have tried to take my life and ended up defunct. But what is strangest about it is not the enemies I've killed or even the sickness that infected me from my taking their lives. What has been surprising is how many allies and friends I've found along the way.

At first I thought it was just me, alone against the world, trying to protect my mom and my brother and sister. All three have turned out to be quite competent at protecting themselves, thank you. Then, out of nowhere, there was Hally who went from joking about eating me (assuming that was a joke) to being my helpful and frequently frustrating mentor and occasional rescuer. Then there is (and I hope there always will be) Hussein. The Dreamer and Lorelei, Guy and his daughter, the gentle gemod monster Tahhrr who sacrificed his life for me, Rose and her Lakotas and Striped Horse and the other Horse People, and then a whole frigging valley full of good folks working together.

Whoa-up, Lozen.

All that's great, but this is not yet the place for me to count my blessings. There're still plenty of curses left in the world. Gemod critters roaming the country, power-hungry former Overlords ruling their own little kingdoms like we had here at Haven. We have, at the very least, years of work still ahead of us before we might actually bring balance back to this wounded land.

Plus, right here and right now, lurking somewhere inside Haven like a spider in a silken web, there's Lady Time. We have yet to clean her clock.

CHAPTER FORTY-NINE
The Front Gate

We are almost at the front gate of Haven. And I am wondering two things.

Numero Uno: How are we going to get inside?

Numero Dos: What am I doing?

Most of the four hundred or so people in Haven are proles—men, women, and children who have been little more than slaves. Most, if not all of them, knew me as the Killer of Enemies.

Also from what little Mohindas told me, since my family and I escaped last year, I've become sort of a hero to them. Not that I actually deserve to be seen that way. Mohindas added that the ordinary people trapped in the old penitentiary even whispered—when their guards couldn't hear them—that Lozen would come back someday and free them all. Which is sort of cool, aside from the fact that anyone overheard whispering like that was drastically punished by the sadistic guards . . . who would definitely not be glad to see me, unless they had me in their gun sights.

Those mercenary forces of mean-spirited guards and Chain-addicted berserkers controlled by the Overlords never numbered than two hundred men in total. Then the events of the past months drastically reduced their numbers. After Diablita Loca's attempt to kill me ended in her demise and the deaths of most of her men, the few troops left that had been hers were absorbed by the forces of the Jester and Lady Time. And now the Jester has been defeated, along with the troops who accompanied him on his mission to wipe out both our valley and Haven itself. Since his plan was to wipe Haven off the map, it's unlikely that any of his green-banded mercenaries were left behind. It's also true that a large percentage of Lady Time's forces were just captured by Guy in that ambush earlier today. But not all of them. Since Lady Time did not accompany that armored foray, she must still be here inside the walls with some of her bodyguards.

I'm just guessing now, but I'm pretty sure there can't be more than a dozen of those mercenaries left, since so many—including the doubled patrols on the walls—were sent off with Lady Time's tanks. But a dozen heavily armed men guarding the walls and watching over the gate are still a force to be reckoned with. They may not be all that impressed at the sight of only three mounted riders approaching the gate and demanding entrance.

I wish I wasn't so worn out from using that lightning blast to neutralize the nuke. I can't even reach out with my mind to see what's going on now behind the walls, much less use my Power to blow open the main gate with an Arrow of Lightning.

However, something—call it intuition, if you like—is telling me that doing just what we are doing now, riding straight up to the gate, is the right thing. And for some reason, my five companions—Hussein, the Dreamer, Black Cloud, Star, and Striped Horse—are just fine with my decision.

Here's hoping they were right to trust me.

The gate is only a hundred feet away now, and thus far no one has shot at us. Whoopee!

I hold up my right hand, and we all halt. Some of my Power seems to be returning because I hear the minds of my companions as we do so.

A good sign, Hussein is thinking, while in something other than words comes a feeling of reassurance and trust from Striped Horse and my two other four-legged allies.

Abandon hope, all ye who enter here, is what the Dreamer is thinking. Thanks a lot.

"Hello, the gate!" I call out.

No answer. Not even someone asking me for the daily password. And no sign of life in the nearest guard tower.

But there are people on the other side of that gate. Lots of them. I can sense them, even though they are all keeping quiet.

Friends?

Enemies?

Just one way to find out.

"HELLO!" I shout, cupping my mouth with my hands.

A hand is thrust out of the guard tower, followed by the top of someone's head. It's someone much smaller than the average guard, who is hopping up and down to be seen.

"Is that you?" a hesitant voice calls down.

"It is most assuredly not Godot," the Dreamer replies in a sardonic voice.

I glare over at him, and he shuts his mouth before making any further comments that no one but him can understand.

"Wait!" the voice replies. "Let me just . . ."

My hearing is now returning to normal—by which I mean four times as good as a normal human being's. I know this because I now hear the faint sound of wood scraping against stone from up there.

I'm guessing whoever is in the tower is dragging something over to stand on.

Sure enough, a second later the entire head of a small man is thrust up to peer down at us.

"It is you! Lozen!" he shouts. "I am so glad to see you!"

"Hello, Walter," I reply. "What's going on?"

Walter, the much-abused keeper of the pale madwoman's

timepieces, points down behind him. "They're just trying to find the right key. I'm going down to help."

He disappears from sight again as Hussein, the Dreamer, and I exchange glances.

One and one pony, two and one pony, three and one pony—and the big gate begins to swing open, pushed by Walter and half a dozen others. Most of them are holding weapons, but they're not pointing them at us. Many others are behind them. They're talking now, welcoming us.

"You came back."

"It's Lozen."

"Lozen is back."

All around us men and women and children are smiling, reaching their hands up to gently touch ours—even the long hands of the Dreamer, who appears both pleased and a bit bemused by this outpouring of emotion—as we ride inside.

Hussein leans over to me.

"It is good, habibi."

"Yes," I reply, "It is good."

It is all a bit overwhelming, being welcomed this way. I recognize many faces, some of people whose names I know, others who are familiar from having seen them in passing. Among them is an older man with glasses whose face looks much like someone I recently met.

"Do you have a son named Mohindas?" I ask.

"Yes," he replies.

And when I tell him that his son is alive and well, he wraps his arms around me, his head on my shoulder as he sobs his gratitude.

When I manage to disengage myself from him, there are others who come up to thank me, to take my hand, or just look at me with so much gratitude in their eyes that it embarrasses me.

Despite the warmth of my welcome, I am still keeping an eye out for trouble. But nowhere do I see anyone wearing a white armband. And there are no men with the surly, angry faces I always associated with the drug-addicted mercenaries of the Ones.

The main gate has been closed again, and most of the twenty or so people who were awkwardly holding weapons they are clearly not yet familiar with have gone up to the walls and towers to keep watch. There are still such dangers outside as the Bloodless and gemod monsters. However, there may be less likelihood of any such dangers approaching the former prison right now, since our three Horse People chose to go back outside rather than be shut within walls. There's nothing dangerous that the three of them together cannot outfight, outthink, or outrun.

But what about dangers inside Haven?

"Lady Time?" I ask Walter. "Her men? Where?"

Walter smiles, displaying a number of gaps in his grin where teeth were removed.

"Not to worry, not to worry," he says. "Come along."

Two of the armed men come with us as self-appointed escorts. Hussein recognizes one of them, a wiry young man with blond hair.

"Donald," Hussein says as they grasp each other's forearm. "How glad I am to see you."

"We missed your music, my friend," Donald replies.

We do not go to Lady Time's chambers in the heart of Haven. Instead, Walter leads us down through a series of hidden entrances and twisting stairs. I take note, as we follow, of the very conspicuous bloodstains inside two of the larger entrances as well as one enormous paw print.

What the hell? I think.

Donald sees me looking at that track in the pool of recently dried blood and smiles.

"Yup," he says. "It was a big one."

A final door and then we step inside a cavernous space lit by hissing gaslights. It looks as if it is only partly human-made. Haven, it seems, was built over the top of a cave. A big door—which I assume must lead outside from the light streaming through it—is partially open at the far end of the cave.

Double what the hell?

"He asked us not to tell you," Walter says, turning to

peer up at me through the cracked lenses of his glasses. "Just show you."

"Show me what?"

Walter points to his right. "Her, first of all."

I turn to look, and my right hand drops involuntarily to my holstered .357. There, standing fifty feet away with her back to me, is the tall figure of Lady Time, her flowing robes reaching the floor. She's strangely still, not moving at all.

I draw my gun, walk slowly over to her, flanked by Hussein and the Dreamer and followed closely by little Walter. There's still no movement from our ivory-clad enemy. We circle, keeping a careful distance, then step in front of her.

Hussein draws in a quick breath at what he sees, and my own eyes widen at the sight.

Only the Dreamer seems unmoved. "One must admit," he says, "that you never looked better. Et tu in Arcadia."

If those final four words he spoke refer to the fact that the last of our three crazy enemies is deceased, then he is absolutely right. Unless it is possible for someone to remain among the living after being decapitated.

What we are looking at is some sort of dummy arrayed in her long robes, a dummy whose artificial cranium has been replaced by the actual head of Lady Time.

Crap!

All of a sudden, I think I know who did this.

How could I have forgotten him?

CHAPTER FIFTY

A Message For You

A giggle from behind me reminds me that Walter is standing next to us.

"She was going to cut off my toes," he says. "But now she doesn't have a leg to stand on."

I take a closer look at the little engineer. But there doesn't appear to be that much craziness in his eyes. It seems to be more the blend of relief and shock that one might expect from what just happened here. And when I reach in his mind—just a little—that's what I find there, as well as the blurred residual images of the extreme violence he recently witnessed.

"Did Four Deaths do this?"

Walter nods his head vigorously.

"And Lady Time's men?"

Another series of nods to the affirmative. "Every, every one of them. Even after she stabbed him."

"But not you."

I know that's obvious, but Walter understands that I do not mean the what, but the why. Why did Luther Little Wound, the seemingly unkillable killer, spare him?

"His dog," Walter says, as if that explains everything. Which it does not. I look over at Hussein, who just shrugs.

I don't look to the Dreamer for an answer. Anything he says will probably just confuse me more. But he makes a comment anyway. "Cave canem," he says.

What? Though Walter's mention of a dog did explain one thing—that big animal footprint we saw.

"Four Deaths has a dog now?"

Walter goes into his nonstop head-bobbing mode again— so hard I'm almost afraid he's going to end up decapitated like his late mistress. I grasp him by the shoulder.

"Explain," I say.

Walter takes a deep breath. "When I went outside, his dog was there. I always liked dogs. I petted it, and it gave me a kiss. That was when he came up to me and said he was not going to kill me. Just the others. So I let him in."

He's said those words faster than I've ever heard anyone say anything. It's as if—probably the case—he was never allowed by his mistress to say more than a few words before being told to shut up. Now that he is finally free to talk, he doesn't know how to stop before he runs out of breath.

Walter looks as if that burst of speech took everything out

of him, like the air rushing out of a balloon. But he's not done yet.

"I have a message, a message for you," he says.

"For me?" I say, reaching up to put my palm gently on the side of his head before he can start nodding it again.

"Yes. He said he would be waiting for you, just you alone." Walter gestures at the open door. "Out there."

I look at the open door. Is Luther lying in wait, ready to shoot as soon as I step outside? He was going to kill me the last time we met. Why should it be different now?

I reach out with my mind and make contact right away. What that contact conveys surprises me.

"Okay," I say.

Hussein looks troubled. "Habibi," he says, "are you sure?"

I kiss him on the cheek. "It's all right."

Still, all right or not, as I slip quickly through the door I am keeping low. Plus I have my reloaded .357 in one hand and the big knife that once belonged to Four Deaths in the other.

"Over here," a voice calls to me.

It's a voice like no other, easy to remember because it's so beautiful. It's as pleasant to hear as the things he's done are awful.

Luther Little Wound is sitting in the shade of a tree, legs stretched out in front of him. Next to him is either a gigantic wolf or the biggest dog that ever walked the earth. It's larger than our horse friends. Luther's right hand rests on the dog's wide head, stroking it. As he does so, a contented growl—like the first rumblings of an earthquake—comes from deep in the big animal's chest.

His right hand?

Didn't I cut that hand off? Not only that, it has extra digits.

Luther lifts that hand and wiggles its fingers at me.

"Yes," he says. "I have been dealt another hand in this game of life. And"—he gestures at his fully intact face—"you may notice that I am no longer keeping an eye out for you."

All I need is one more person in my life using me as their straight man. Maybe I should just shoot him right now.

"I would rather you didn't," he says, hearing my thought. "Should you try, Sunka here might eat you like our late White Lady. Her head was all that remained—as you just saw."

He winks at me with the eye that also apparently regrew back—transplant tech no longer being available.

How? I think.

"The answer," he says, again reading my mind, "is likely in my genetic enhancement. I believe there's a bit of some regenerative creature such as a salamander in me."

I stop when I'm eighty feet away. Far enough for me to shoot both him and his overgrown mutt before they reach me. Fido first.

"What do you want?" I ask.

"Short term or long term?" he replies.

"Both."

"Fair enough. Long term, to be left alone. We go our way to pursue our own destiny—which should not interfere with yours. I no longer have the desire to harm you or yours."

Which was what I had sensed when my mind first touched his before I walked outside to meet him.

"So you're no longer going to be a killer?"

Four Deaths actually chuckles, a warm, melodious chuckle that is nonetheless a bit chilling to hear.

"Waste a lifetime of training? I'm not ready to retire to some cave, like Mushashi, and devote myself to painting. Plus my partner here"—he pats the big dog—"still needs to eat. No, I intend to give up being a hired killer. My life will be that of a ronin, a man with no master. Those whose existences I intend to end—I do have quite a list—none of them are innocents."

I can live with that, I think to him. *Okay.*

"But what about short term?"

"Ah," Luther Little Wound says, "I see you have my favorite knife. You must be on better terms than me with the furry character who took it. I'd like it back—not as a gift, but in trade."

"Trade?"

"Indeed," he says, "two for one."

He runs his hand back through his thick black hair. Then, grimacing in pain, he pushes himself up to his knees. It takes him a bit of effort. When he turns his back to me, I see why. Two long knives are deeply embedded between his shoulder blades.

"A parting gift from our dear departed demon damsel," he says. "But sheathed where I can't quite reach them."

I'm holding those two knives in my hand as I watch Luther Little Wound, riding on the back of his giant dog as if it were a horse, disappear over the far range of hills to the north.

If you'd told me yesterday I'd be doing something like this, I probably would have told you that you were crazy. Even now you may be wondering if it makes any sense at all to believe someone who was our deadly enemy could actually be—if not a friend or ally—then no longer a danger to us.

But then again, you do not have three things that I've got.

Reason Numero Uno is the memories of my father and his stories, such as this one that I remember him telling me. It's not one of our old Chiricahua stories, but a traditional Indian tale that came from way far off. It's a story my dad heard when he was a young man from an Iroquois person whose nation was up there in the northeast. That person, a young man named Tommy Carrier, had decided to travel to our part of the world. Dad was a little fuzzy about how and why he had ended up among our Apache people. Dad just said that this guy Tommy had gotten some kind of message from his dreams and decided he needed to do what he did . . . go visit all the Indians he could find and tell them about the vision he'd been given.

He saw that the world as it was would end. The job of people close to the earth would be to bring it all back together again. This was years before the Silver Cloud settled in. In addition to sharing that vision, and telling people what to do to be ready for the coming time of turmoil, Tommy told them about someone called the Peacemaker, who lived long ago.

Back then, all the tribes were fighting. But that Peacemaker came and convinced the people they needed to live in peace. He didn't just go to the good people. He went to the bad people, too. His closest ally was a man who'd been crazy and even a cannibal before the Peacemaker changed his mind.

"That guy Tommy," Dad told me, "he said human beings, real human beings, can change their minds. They can go from having a twisted mind to a mind that's straight."

So that story of my dad's is one reason for believing Luther has changed. Maybe not exactly into a person of peace, but someone who's not going to kill people of peace.

Reason Numero Dos is what I saw when my Power allowed me to look into the mind of Four Deaths. Not only were no thoughts there of doing me harm, there was something else there, too. Instead of the cold logic of killing that I'd felt there before, there was something else. Caring. And being cared for in return. What he loved—love being a better word to describe it, now that I think of it—was that enormous wolf dog. And it loved him in return.

"Love makes us human." That's what my mom says.

If that's true—and I guess it is—then despite having some amphibian DNA, Little Wound's thoughts are now those of a real human being.

Reason Numero Tres why I'm calmly watching Luther disappear into the nearby hills without foreboding is the one who just made me jump nearly out of my skin when he rested one huge, hairy hand on my right shoulder.

"You have done well, Little Food," Hally rumbles.

Great. Now that all the fighting, nuclear-bomb-neutralizing and former-enemy-assisting, is over he finally appears.

He steps out from behind my back and stands there, beaming down at me with one huge, hairy eyebrow raised.

I almost say thanks for nothing. But that would be wrong. In his own indirect way my giant ape-man ally has been helping me. So I just settle for growling a little.

You are most welcome, Lozen, Hally thinks to me.

A lot of good it does me to hold my tongue when he can look into my mind like it's an open window. So I just sigh and ask him the question on the top of the sill.

"What next?"

"Everything," he replies.

Why do I even bother?

"Because you care." Hally grins, showing his impressive canine teeth.

Okay, I asked for that. Heavy mental sigh. Try again.

"What do you mean by everything?"

"Ah," Hally says, raising his hands as if to embrace the sky. "I foresee a future in which, after long years of strife, you stand smiling, your struggle for a peaceful world complete, surrounded by seven loving children and their spouses and numerous grandchildren, as you accept the thanks and accolades of a newly formed nation."

"Hally, are you making that all up to mess with my mind?"

"In a word"—Hally chuckles—"yes." Then his voice gets serious. "What's next is up to you. You and your people. Maybe this time you'll all find a better path."

Maybe we will. I'm already thinking about how the people in Haven are going to need help getting used to making their own decisions. We can help them set up a community council like we have in our valley. Guy can teach people how to use the weapons in the armory to hunt and defend themselves against gemod monsters. When Rose and her Lakotas get back, we can make plans to liberate other communities. And then . . .

Wait a minute. Has my Bigfoot buddy just used my being lost in thought to pull another one of his vanishing acts?

I look over my shoulder. To my surprise he's still there, grinning down at me, his arms crossed over his massive chest.

"Yes?" he says. "You were about to ask?"

"What about you, Hally? Are you going to stick around this time?"

A sad look comes over his face. "No," he says. "I shall walk off into the sunset, never to be seen again. My work here is done. This world is yours now, not mine, and you humans must do as best as you can without me." He lifts his right hand to his cheek as if to wipe away a tear.

"Oh," I say. I'm actually starting to feel a little choked up.

He drops his hand as that toothy smile returns. "Or maybe not." He grins and touches his long index finger to his lips. "But I do have one important question for you, Lozen."

What can I do but play along? "What?"

Hally squints over my shoulder, a concerned look on his massive face. "What do you plan to do about that nasty thing creeping up behind you?"

I spin around, reaching for the butt of my .357. Nothing there. It's the oldest trick in the book, the one the first Cro-Magnon man played on a hapless Neanderthal. Maybe when Hally was watching them both and laughing.

I turn back around. Hally has vanished into thin air. The only trace is a patch of sagebrush trembling as if rooted on top of a hidden trapdoor that just closed.

Will I see him again?

Will things actually work out? Or was he just joking?

I don't know.

All I can say for now is this as far as my story goes.